THE
WORLD'S
ONE HUNDRED
BEST SHORT STORIES

❦

VOLUME ONE
ADVENTURE

THE
WORLD'S
ONE HUNDRED
BEST SHORT STORIES

[IN TEN VOLUMES]

GRANT OVERTON
EDITOR - IN - CHIEF

VOLUME ONE
ADVENTURE

FUNK & WAGNALLS COMPANY
NEW YORK AND LONDON

CONTENTS

INTRODUCTION

At the outset you will want to know:

What is a short story?

What—or why—are the "best" short stories?

The answer to the first question is implied in a moment at the end of Booth Tarkington's "The Boy Penrod," when Penrod exclaims:

"Well, hasn't this been a day!"

All the days that "stand out," all our memorable experiences, are stories. A story is only a form of enjoying experience, a means of living more widely or more richly than our own particular lives afford.

The experience may be laughable or tragic, pathetic or thrilling. Its nature does not matter but it must be real to us. In other words, we must feel that what happens to some one in the story might possibly happen to ourselves—*is*, in some sense, happening to us as we read.

"Short" story is only a handy way of classifying length. Roughly, any story of 15,000 words or less is a short story. That is, provided it actually is a story, an experience that stands out, and provided it is real as we read it, and afterward.

In saying this I fully realize that dozens of rules have been made as to what constitutes a short story. But for every such rule I have seen a story that breaks it. For the master of story-telling there are no rules.

Well, in this collection, we are dealing only with the masters.

The "best" short stories? What can they be, in

a work of this character, except those which are most
real to the greatest number of readers?

This was the test which I sought to apply in choosing
for this collection. Experience as an editor in buying
stories for a magazine of several million readers had
perhaps given me some sense of what makes a story
real to numbers of people. But in nearly every case
there was plenty of unmistakable evidence of the
story's rank.

Every reader will recollect one or more famous
authors of short stories not represented in this collection. Why were they not included? Because, when
it came to the final narrowing-down process, the close
matching of one story against another, the consideration that every kind of story must have its place, no
one story of theirs survived the winnowing process.

The classification of the stories in ten volumes calls
for some explanation. Naturally the Hundred Best
Stories are not exactly ten stories of exactly ten
varieties. But the convenience of such a classification
more than offsets the difficulty of three or four stories
which fit a little awkwardly into their pigeon-holes.

If the reader find himself perplexed, I would remind
him that one object in assigning the stories under these
ten heads has been to stimulate the imagination.

It is easy to grasp Mary Roberts Rinehart's "The
Trumpet Sounds" as a human drama; but the real
significance and beauty of this story lies in the redeem-
ing courage of more than one character. Naturally a
good story, and every great story, has more than one
salient quality. Thus Joseph Conrad's "Youth" is a
man's story, an adventure story, and a romantic story
all in one. But the intensity of the romantic feeling
dominates everything else.

The classifications themselves hardly need discussion. Adventure, Romance, Mystery, Love, Drama and the rest are simple, definite and inclusive in meaning to everybody. But I should perhaps say that by Ghosts I have not meant stories in which a sheeted figure makes the blood run cold. The Ghosts of this collection are, as well, unreal and fantastic people and experiences; or it may be that the particular ghost is only a haunting idea.

All previous collecting of this scope, so far as I know, have included a much heavier proportion of older stories. This has been partly due, no doubt, to difficulty in arranging for the use of recent ones. But it has also been due to a feeling that time has put its stamp of approval on the work of these writers of the past. The editor has perhaps felt that in using such classical, or semi-classical, material he could not go wrong.

With this attitude I find myself in entire disagreement. The only result, as I see it, has been to produce collections highly tedious and largely unreadable.

The percentage of fiction which can hold its place with succeeding generations is, I believe, much smaller than critics suppose. Every generation has a right to insist that its own enjoyment of experience is in one respect the best enjoyment, because the most complete.

I feel that no apology is necessary for the fact that over half these tales are by living writers. In the nature of things, these are advanced as The World's 100 Best Short Stories at the time of presentation, 1927. They cannot be The World's 100 Best in 2027 any more than a collection made in 1827 could prove satisfactory now. Nor would the inclusion of more nineteenth century work do anything, I am convinced, to enhance the value of this collection throughout the twentieth century.

A word about what is included: Almost exactly half of the authors represented are Americans; of the remaining half, some twenty are English; fifteen, French; seven, Russian; the remainder, other Europeans. This numerical representation, tho not deliberately arrived at, impresses me as being fairly representative of the ratio of excellence of the various countries in the short story—always remembering that we mean a short story for English-speaking readers.

Our stories range in place from the snowy woods of Ben Ames Williams' "Solitude" to the mid-Pacific of John Russell's "The Fourth Man." In period the reader may pass from the acute modernity of Dana Burnet's "Mr. Onion" to the marvelous revival of Cleopatra's Egypt staged by Stephen French Whitman in "That Famous Love Affair." On the side of human personality—the most absorbing, the only enduring, interest of literature—the reader is privileged to turn from Stevenson's portrait of François Villon, poet and low fellow, to Chester T. Crowell's disturbing revelation of a woman's psychology in "Ruth." The mood may be anything from the laughter evoked by P. G. Wodehouse's boneheaded Earl to the ache of sympathy and the compassionate love which F. Britten Austin exacts with "A Mother Sits by the Fire."

There is, after all, only one test of a story—the test of what it makes you feel. I need not point out that this test is double, and that while it measures the story it also at the same time measures us who read.

GRANT OVERTON.

Santa Fe, September, 1927.

THE
WORLD'S
ONE HUNDRED
BEST SHORT STORIES

VOLUME ONE
ADVENTURE

THE WORLD'S 100 BEST SHORT STORIES

THE TWO-GUN MAN

By Stewart Edward White

Chapter I

THE CATTLE-RUSTLERS

Buck Johnson was American born, but with a black beard and a dignity of manner that had earned him the title of Señor. He had drifted into southeastern Arizona in the days of Cochise and Victorio and Geronimo. He had persisted, and so in time had come to control the water—and hence the grazing—of nearly all the Soda Springs Valley. His troubles were many, and his difficulties great. There were the ordinary problems of lean and dry years. There were also the extraordinary problems of devastating Apaches; rivals for early and ill-defined range rights—and cattle-rustlers.

Señor Buck Johnson was a man of capacity, courage, directness of method, and perseverance. Especially the latter. Therefore he had survived to see the Apaches subdued, the range rights adjusted, his cattle increased to thousands, grazing the area of a principality. Now, all the energy and fire of his frontiersman's nature he

(From "Arizona Nights," by Stewart Edward White; copyright 1907, by Doubleday Page & Co.)

had turned to wiping out the third uncertainty of an uncertain business. He found it a task of some magnitude.

For Señor Buck Johnson lived just north of that terra incognita filled with the mystery of a double chance of death from man or the flaming desert known as the Mexican border. There, by natural gravitation, gathered all the desperate characters of three States and two republics. He who rode into it took good care that no one should ride behind him, lived warily, slept light, and breathed deep when once he had again sighted the familiar peaks of Cochise's Stronghold. No one professed knowledge of those who dwelt therein. They moved, mysterious as the desert illusions that compassed them about. As you rode, the ranges of mountains visibly changed form, the monstrous, snaky, sea-like growths of the cactus clutched at your stirrup, mock lakes sparkled and dissolved in the middle distance, the sun beat hot and merciless, the powdered dry alkali beat hotly and mercilessly back—and strange, grim men, swarthy, bearded, heavily armed, with red-rimmed unshifting eyes, rode silently out of the mists of illusion to look on you steadily, and then to ride silently back into the desert haze. They might be only the herders of the gaunt cattle, or again they might belong to the Lost Legion that peopled the country. All you could know was that of the men who entered in, but few returned.

Directly north of this unknown land you encountered parallel fences running across the country. They enclosed nothing, but offered a check to the cattle drifting toward the clutch of the renegades, and an obstacle to swift, dashing forays.

Of cattle-rustling there are various forms. The

boldest consists quite simply of running off a bunch of stock, hustling it over the Mexican line, and there selling it to some of the big Sonora ranch owners. Generally this sort means war. Also are there subtler means, grading in skill from the rebranding through a wet blanket, through the crafty refashioning of a brand to the various methods of separating the cow from her unbranded calf. In the course of his task Señor Buck Johnson would have to do with them all, but at present he existed in a state of warfare, fighting an enemy who stole as the Indians used to steal.

Already he had fought two pitched battles, and had won them both. His cattle increased, and he became rich. Nevertheless he knew that constantly his resources were being drained. Time and again he and his new Texas foreman, Jed Parker, had followed the trail of a stampeded bunch of twenty or thirty, followed them on down through the Soda Springs Valley to the cut drift fences, there to abandon them. For, as yet, an armed force would be needed to penetrate the borderland. Once he and his men had experienced the glory of a night pursuit. Then, at the drift fences, he had fought one of his battles. But it was impossible adequately to patrol all parts of a range bigger than some Eastern States.

Buck Johnson did his best, but it was like stopping with sands the innumerable little leaks of a dam. Did his riders watch toward the Chiricahuas, then a score of beef steers disappeared from Grant's Pass forty miles away. Pursuit here meant leaving cattle unguarded there. It was useless, and the Señor soon perceived that sooner or later he must strike in offence.

For this purpose he began slowly to strengthen the forces of his riders. Men were coming in from Texas.

They were good men, addicted to the grass-rope, the double cinch, and the ox-bow stirrup. Señor Johnson wanted men who could shoot, and he got them.

"Jed," said Señor Johnson to his foreman, "the next son of a gun that rustles any of our cows is sure loading himself full of trouble. We'll hit his trail and will stay with it, and we'll reach his cattle-rustling conscience with a rope."

So it came about that a little army crossed the drift fences and entered the border country. Two days later it came out, and mighty pleased to be able to do so. The rope had not been used.

The reason for the defeat was quite simple. The thief had run his cattle through the lava beds where the trail at once became difficult to follow. This delayed the pursuing party; they ran out of water, and, as there was among them not one man well enough acquainted with the country to know where to find more, they had to return.

"No use, Buck," said Jed. "We'd any of us come in on a gun play, but we can't buck the desert. We'll have to get someone who knows the country."

"That's all right—but where?" queried Johnson.

"There's Pereza," suggested Parker. "It's the only town down near that country."

"Might get someone there," agreed the Señor.

Next day he rode away in search of a guide. The third evening he was back again, much discouraged.

"The country's no good," he explained. "The regular inhabitants 're a set of Mexican bums and old soaks. The cowmen's all from north and don't know nothing more than we do. I found lots who claimed to know that country, but when I told 'em what I wanted they shied like a colt. I couldn't hire 'em, for no money, to go down in that country. They ain't got the nerve. I took two days to her, too, and rode out to a ranch where they said a man lived who knew all about it down there. Nary riffle. Man looked all right, but his tail went down like the rest when I told him what we wanted. Seemed plumb scairt to death. Says he lives too close to the gang. Says they'd wipe him out sure if he done it. Seemed plumb *scairt*." Buck Johnson grinned. "I told him so and he got hosstyle right off. Didn't seem no ways scairt of me. I don't know what's the matter with that outfit down there. They're plumb terrorised."

That night a bunch of steers was stolen from the very corrals of the home ranch. The home ranch was far north, near Fort Sherman itself, and so had always been considered immune from attack. Consequently these steers were very fine ones.

For the first time Buck Johnson lost his head and his dignity. He ordered the horses.

"I'm going to follow that ―― ―― into Sonora," he shouted to Jed Parker. "This thing's got to stop!"

"You can't make her, Buck," objected the foreman. "You'll get held up by the desert, and, if that don't finish you, they'll tangle you up in all those little mountains down there, and ambush you, and massacre you. You know it damn well."

"I don't give a ――," exploded Señor Johnson, "if they do. No man can slap my face and not get a run for it."

Jed Parker communed with himself.

"Señor," said he, at last, "it's no good; you can't do it. You got to have a guide. You wait three days and I'll get you one."

"You can't do it," insisted the Señor. "I tried every man in the district."

"Will you wait three days?" repeated the foreman.

Johnson pulled loose his latigo. His first anger had cooled.

"All right," he agreed, "and you can say for me that I'll pay five thousand dollars in gold and give all the men and horses he needs to the man who has the nerve to get back that bunch of cattle, and bring in the man who rustled them. I'll sure make this a test case."

So Jed Parker set out to discover his man with nerve.

Chapter II

THE MAN WITH NERVE

At about ten o'clock of the Fourth of July a rider topped the summit of the last swell of land, and loped his animal down into the single street of Pereza. The buildings on either side were flat-roofed and coated with plaster. Over the sidewalks extended wooden awnings, beneath which opened very wide doors into the coolness of saloons. Each of these places ran a bar, and also games of roulette, faro, craps, and stud poker. Even this early in the morning every game was patronized.

The day was already hot with the dry, breathless, but exhilarating, heat of the desert. A throng of men idling at the edge of the sidewalks, jostling up and down their center, or eddying into the places of amusement, acknowledged the power of summer by loosening their collars, carrying their coats on their arms. They were as yet busily engaged in recognizing acquaintances

Later they would drink freely and gamble, and perhaps fight. Toward all but those whom they recognized they preserved an attitude of potential suspicion, for here were gathered the "bad men" of the border countries. A certain jealousy or touchy egotism lest the other man be considered quicker on the trigger, bolder, more aggressive than himself, kept each strung to tension. An occasional shot attracted little notice. Men in the cowcountries shoot as casually as we strike matches, and some subtle instinct told them that the reports were harmless.

As the rider entered the one street, however, a more definite cause of excitement drew the loose population toward the center of the road. Immediately their mass blotted out what had interested them. Curiosity attracted the saunterers; then in turn the frequenters of the bars and gambling games. In a very few moments the barkeepers, gamblers, and look-out men, held aloof only by the necessities of their calling, alone of all the population of Pereza were not included in the newly-formed ring.

The stranger pushed his horse resolutely to the outer edge of the crowd where, from his point of vantage, he could easily overlook their heads. He was a quiet-appearing young fellow, rather neatly dressed in the border costume, rode a "center fire," or single-cinch, saddle, and wore no chaps. He was what is known as a "two-gun man": that is to say, he wore a heavy Colt's revolver on either hip. The fact that the lower ends of his holsters were tied down, in order to facilitate the easy withdrawal of the revolvers, seemed to indicate that he expected to use them. He had furthermore a quiet grey eye, with the glint of steel that bore out the inference of the tied holsters.

The newcomer dropped his reins on his pony's neck, eased himself to an attitude of attention, and looked down gravely on what was taking place.

He saw over the heads of the bystanders a tall, muscular, wild-eyed man, hatless, his hair rumpled into staring confusion, his right sleeve rolled to his shoulder, a wicked-looking nine-inch knife in his hand, and a red bandana handkerchief hanging by one corner from his teeth.

"What's biting the locoed stranger?" the young man inquired of his neighbor.

The other frowned at him darkly.

"Dare's anyone to take the other end of that handkerchief in his teeth, and fight it out without letting go."

"Nice joyful proposition," commented the young man.

He settled himself to closer attention. The wild-eyed man was talking rapidly. What he said cannot be printed here. Mainly was it derogatory of the southern countries. Shortly it became boastful of the northern, and then of the man who uttered it. He swaggered up and down, becoming always the more insolent as his challenge remained untaken.

"Why don't you take him up?" inquired the young man, after a moment.

"Not me!" negatived the other vigorously. "I'll go yore little old gunfight to a finish, but I don't want any cold steel in mine. Ugh! it gives me the shivers. It's a reg'lar Mexican trick! With a gun it's down and out, but this knife work is too slow and searchin'."

The newcomer said nothing, but fixed his eye again on the raging man with the knife.

"Don't you reckon he's bluffing?" he inquired.

"Not any!" denied the other with emphasis. "He's jest drunk enough to be crazy mad."

The newcomer shrugged his shoulders and cast his glance searchingly over the fringe of the crowd. It rested on a Mexican.

"Hi, Tony! come here," he called.

The Mexican approached, flashing his white teeth.

"Here," said the stranger, "lend me your knife a minute."

The Mexican, anticipating sport of his own peculiar kind, obeyed with alacrity.

"You fellows make me tired," observed the stranger, dismounting. "He's got the whole townful of you bluffed to a standstill. Damn if I don't try his little game."

He hung his coat on his saddle, shouldered his way through the press, which parted for him readily, and picked up the other corner of the handkerchief.

"Now, you mangy son of a gun," said he.

Chapter III

THE AGREEMENT

Jed Parker straightened his back, rolled up the bandana handkerchief, and thrust it into his pocket, hit flat with his hand the tousled mass of his hair, and thrust the long hunting knife into its sheath.

"You're the man I want," said he.

Instantly the two-gun man had jerked loose his weapons and was covering the foreman.

"*Am* I!" he snarled.

"Not jest that way," explained Parker. "My gun is

on my hoss, and you can have this old toad-sticker if you want it. I been looking for you and took this way of finding you. Now, let's go talk."

The stranger looked him in the eye for nearly a half minute without lowering his revolvers.

"I go you," said he briefly, at last.

But the crowd, missing the purport, and in fact the very occurrence of this colloquy, did not understand. It thought the bluff had been called, and naturally, finding harmless what had intimidated it, gave way to an exasperated impulse to get even.

"You — — — bluffer!" shouted a voice, "don't you think you can run any such ranikaboo here!"

Jed Parker turned humorously to his companion.

"Do we get that talk!" he inquired gently.

For answer the two-gun man turned and walked steadily in the direction of the man who had shouted. The latter's hand strayed uncertainly toward his own weapon, but the movement paused when the stranger's clear, steel eye rested on it.

"This gentleman," pointed out the two-gun man softly, "is an old friend of mine. Don't you get to calling of him names."

His eye swept the bystanders calmly.

"Come on, Jack," said he, addressing Parker.

On the outskirts he encountered the Mexican from whom he had borrowed the knife.

"Here, Tony," said he with a slight laugh, "here's a *peso*. You'll find your knife back there where I had to drop her."

He entered a saloon, nodded to the proprietor, and led the way through it to a box-like room containing a board table and two chairs.

"Make good," he commanded briefly.

"I'm looking for a man with nerve," explained Parker, with equal succinctness. "You're the man."

"Well?"

"Do you know the country south of here?"

The stranger's eyes narrowed.

"Proceed," said he.

"I'm foreman of the Lazy Y of Soda Springs Valley range," explained Parker. "I'm looking for a man with sand enough and *sabe* of the country enough to lead a posse after cattle rustlers into the border country."

"I live in this country," admitted the stranger.

"So do plenty of others, but their eyes stick out like two raw oysters when you mention the border country. Will you tackle it?"

"What's the proposition?"

"Come and see the old man. He'll put it to you."

They mounted their horses and rode the rest of the day. The desert compassed them about, marvellously changing shape and colour, and every character, with all the noiselessness of phantasmagoria. At evening the desert stars shone steady and unwinking, like the flames of candles. By moonrise they came to the home ranch.

The buildings and corrals lay dark and silent against the moonlight that made of the plain a sea of mist. The two men unsaddled their horses and turned them loose in the wire-fenced "pasture," the necessary noises of their movements sounding sharp and clear against the velvet hush of the night. After a moment they walked stiffly past the sheds and cook shanty, past the men's bunk houses, and the tall windmill silhouetted against the sky, to the main building of the home ranch under its great cottonwoods. There a light still burned, for this was the third day, and Buck Johnson awaited his foreman.

Jed Parker pushed in without ceremony.

"Here's your man, Buck," said he.

The stranger had stepped inside and carefully closed the door behind him. The lamplight threw into relief the bold, free lines of his face, the details of his costume powdered thick with alkali, the shiny butts of the two guns in their open holsters tied at the bottom. Equally it defined the resolute countenance of Buck Johnson turned up in inquiry. The two men examined each other—and liked each other at once.

"How are you," greeted the cattleman.

"Good-evening," responded the stranger.

"Sit down," invited Buck Johnson.

The stranger perched gingerly on the edge of a chair, with an appearance less of embarrassment than of habitual alertness.

"You'll take the job?" inquired the Señor.

"I haven't heard what it is," replied the stranger.

"Parker here——?"

"Said you'd explain."

"Very well," said Buck Johnson. He paused a moment, collecting his thoughts. "There's too much cattle-rustling here. I'm going to stop it. I've got good men here ready to take the job, but no one who knows the country south. Three days ago I had a bunch of cattle stolen right here from the home-ranch corrals, and by one man, at that. It wasn't much of a bunch—about twenty head—but I'm going to make a starter right here, and now. I'm going to get that bunch back, and the man who stole them, if I have to go to hell to do it. And I'm going to do the same with every case of rustling that comes up from now on. I 'on't care if it's only one cow, I'm going to get it back —every trip. Now, I want to know if you'll lead a posse down into the south country and bring out that last bunch, and the man who rustled them?"

"I don't know——" hesitated the stranger.

"I offer you five thousand dollars in gold if you'll bring back those cows and the man who stole 'em," repeated Buck Johnson. "And I'll give you all the horses and men you think you need."

"I'll do it," replied the two-gun man promptly.

"Good!" cried Buck Johnson, "and you better start to-morrow."

"I shall start to-night—right now."

"Better yet. How many men do you want, and grub for how long?"

"I'll play her a lone hand."

"Alone!" exclaimed Johnson, his confidence visibly cooling. "Alone! Do you think you can make her?"

"I'll be back with those cattle in not more than ten days."

"And the man," supplemented the Señor.

"And the man. What's more, I want that money here when I come in. I don't aim to stay in this country over night."

A grin overspread Buck Johnson's countenance. He understood.

"Climate not healthy for you?" he hazarded. "I guess you'd be safe enough all right with us. But suit yourself. The money will be here."

"That's agreed?" insisted the two-gun man.

"Sure."

"I want a fresh horse—I'll leave mine—he's a good one. I want a little grub."

"All right. Parker'll fit you out."

The stranger rose.

"I'll see you in about ten days."

"Good luck," Señor Buck Johnson wished him.

Chapter IV

THE ACCOMPLISHMENT

The next morning Buck Johnson took a trip down into the "pasture" of five hundred wire-fenced acres.

"He means business," he confided to Jed Parker, on his return. "That cavallo of his is a heap sight better than the Shorty horse we let him take. Jed, you found your man with nerve, all right. How did you do it?"

The two settled down to wait, if not with confidence, at least with interest. Sometimes, remembering the desperate character of the outlaws, their fierce distrust of any intruder, the wildness of the country, Buck Johnson and his foreman inclined to the belief that the stranger had undertaken a task beyond the powers of any one man. Again, remembering the stranger's cool grey eye, the poise of his demeanor, the quickness of his movements, and the two guns with tied holsters to permit of easy withdrawal, they were almost persuaded that he might win.

"He's one of those long-chance fellows," surmised Jed. "He likes excitement. I see that by the way he takes up with my knife play. He'd rather leave his hide on the fence than stay in the corral."

"Well, he's all right," replied Señor Buck Johnson, "and if he ever gets back, which same I'm some doubtful of, his dinero 'll be here for him."

In pursuance of this he rode in to Willets, where

shortly the overland train brought him from Tucson the five thousand dollars in double eagles.

In the meantime the regular life of the ranch went on. Each morning Sang, the Chinese cook, rang the great bell, summoning the men. They ate, and then caught up the saddle horses for the day, turning those not wanted from the corral into the pasture. Shortly they jingled away in different directions, two by two, on the slow Spanish trot of the cowpuncher. All day long thus they would ride, without food or water for man or beast, looking the range, identifying the stock, branding the young calves, examining generally into the state of affairs, gazing always with grave eyes on the magnificent, flaming, changing, beautiful, dreadful desert of the Arizona plains. At evening when the colored atmosphere, catching the last glow, threw across the Chiricahuas its veil of mystery, they jingled in again, two by two, untired, unhasting, the glory of the desert in their deep-set, steady eyes.

And all the day long, while they were absent, the cattle, too, made their pilgrimage, straggling in singly, in pairs, in bunches, in long files, leisurely, ruminantly, without haste. There, at the long troughs filled by the windmill or the blindfolded pump mule, they drank, then filed away again into the mists of the desert. And Señor Buck Johnson, or his foreman, Parker, examined them for their condition, noting the increase, remarking the strays from another range. Later, perhaps, they, too, rode abroad. The same thing happened at nine other ranches from five to ten miles apart, where dwelt other fierce, silent men all under the authority of Buck Johnson.

And when night fell, and the topaz and violet and saffron and amethyst and mauve and lilac had faded suddenly from the Chiricahuas, like a veil that has been rent, and the ramparts had become slate-gray and then black—the soft-breathed night wandered here and there over the desert, and the land fell under an enchantment even stranger than the day's.

So the days went by, wonderful, fashioning the ways and the characters of men. Seven passed. Buck Johnson and his foreman began to look for the stranger. Eight, they began to speculate. Nine, they doubted. On the tenth they gave him up—and he came.

They knew him first by the soft lowing of cattle. Jed Parker, dazzled by the lamp, peered out from the door, and made him out dimly turning the animals into the corral. A moment later his pony's hoofs impacted softly on the baked earth, he dropped from the saddle and entered the room.

"I'm late," said he briefly, glancing at the clock which indicated ten; "but I'm here."

His manner was quick and sharp, almost breathless, as though he had been running.

"Your cattle are in the corral: all of them. Have you the money?"

"I have the money here," replied Buck Johnson, laying his hand against a drawer, "and it's ready for you when you've earned it. I don't care so much for the cattle. What I wanted is the man who stole them. Did you bring him?"

"Yes, I brought him," said the stranger. "Let's see that money."

Buck Johnson threw open the drawer, and drew from it the heavy canvas sack.

"It's here. Now bring in your prisoner."

The two-gun man seemed suddenly to loom large in

the doorway. The muzzles of his revolvers covered the two before him. His speech came short and sharp.

"I told you I'd bring back the cows and the one who rustled them," he snapped. "I've never lied to a man yet. Your stock is in the corral. I'll trouble you for that five thousand. I'm the man who stole your cattle!"

THE REPORTER WHO MADE HIMSELF KING

By Richard Harding Davis

The Old Time Journalist will tell you that the best reporter is the one who works his way up. He holds that the only way to start is as a printer's devil or as an office boy, to learn in time to set type, to graduate from a compositor into a stenographer, and as a stenographer take down speeches at public meetings, and so finally grow into a real reporter, with a fire badge on your left suspender, and a speaking acquaintance with all the greatest men in the city, not even excepting Police Captains.

That is the old time journalist's idea of it. That is the way he was trained, and that is why at the age of sixty he is still a reporter. If you train up a youth in this way, he will go into reporting with too full a knowledge of the newspaper business, with no illusions concerning it, and with no ignorant enthusiasms, but with a keen and justifiable impression that he is not paid enough for what he does. And he will only do what he is paid to do.

Now, you can not pay a good reporter for what he does, because he does not work for pay. He works for his paper. He gives his time, his health, his brains, his sleeping hours, and his eating hours, and sometimes his life to get news for it. He thinks the sun rises only that men may have light by which to read it. But if he has been in a newspaper office from his youth up, he finds out before he becomes a reporter that this is not so, and loses his real value. He should come right out of the University where he has been doing "campus notes" for the college weekly, and be pitchforked out into city work without knowing whether the Battery is at Harlem or Hunter's Point, and with the idea that he is a Moulder of Public Opinion and that the Power of the Press is greater than the Power of Money, and that the few lines he writes are of more value in the Editor's eyes than is the column of advertising on the last page, which they are not. After three years—it is sometimes longer, sometimes not so long—he finds out that he has given his nerves and his youth and his enthusiasm in exchange for a general fund of miscellaneous knowledge, the opportunity of personal encounter with all the greatest and most remarkable men and events that have risen in those three years, and a great fund of resource and patience. He will find that he has crowded the experiences of the lifetime of the ordinary young business man, doctor, or lawyer, or man about town, into three short years; that he has learned to think and to act quickly, to be patient and unmoved when every one else has lost his head, actually or figuratively speaking; to write as fast as another man can talk, and to be able to talk with authority on matters of which other men do not venture even to think until they have read what he has written with a copy-boy at his elbow on the night previous.

It is necessary for you to know this, that you may understand what manner of man young Albert Gordon was.

Young Gordon had been a reporter just three years. He had left Yale when his last living relative died, and had taken the morning train for New York, where they had promised him reportorial work on one of the innumerable Greatest New York Dailies. He arrived at the office at noon, and was sent back over the same road on which he had just come, to Spuyten Duyvil, where a train had been wrecked and everybody of consequence to suburban New York killed. One of the old reporters hurried him to the office again with his "copy," and after he had delivered that, he was sent to the Tombs to talk French to a man in Murderer's Row, who could not talk anything else, but who had shown some international skill in the use of a jimmy. And at eight, he covered a flower-show in Madison Square Garden; and at eleven was sent over the Brooklyn Bridge in a cab to watch a fire and make guesses at the losses to the insurance companies.

He went to bed at one, and dreamed of shattered locomotives, human beings lying still with blankets over them, rows of cells, and banks of beautiful flowers nodding their heads to the tunes of the brass band in the gallery. He decided when he awoke the next morning that he had entered upon a picturesque and exciting career, and as one day followed another, he became more and more convinced of it, and more and more devoted to it. He was twenty then, and he was now twenty-three, and in that time had become a great reporter, and had been to Presidential conventions in Chicago, revolutions in Hayti, Indian outbreaks on the Plains, and midnight meetings of moonlighters in Tennessee, and had seen what work earthquakes, floods, fire, and fever could do in great cities, and had contradicted the President, and borrowed matches from burglars. And now he thought he would like to rest and breathe a bit, and not to work again unless as a

war correspondent. The only obstacle to his becoming
a great war correspondent lay in the fact that there
was no war, and a war correspondent without a war is
about as absurd an individual as a general without an
army. He read the papers every morning on the ele-
vated trains for war clouds; but though there were
many war clouds, they always drifted apart, and peace
smiled again. This was very disappointing to young
Gordon, and he became more and more keenly discouraged.

And then as war work was out of the question, he
decided to write his novel. It was to be a novel of
New York life, and he wanted a quiet place in which
to work on it. He was already making inquiries among
the suburban residents of his acquaintance for just such
a quiet spot, when he received an offer to go to the
Island of Opeki in the North Pacific Ocean, as secretary to the American consul to that place. The gentleman who had been appointed by the President to act
as consul at Opeki, was Captain Leonard T. Travis, a
veteran of the Civil War, who had contracted a severe
attack of rheumatism while camping out at night in
the dew, and who on account of this souvenir of his
efforts to save the Union had allowed the Union he had
saved to support him in one office or another ever
since. He had met young Gordon at a dinner, and had
had the presumption to ask him to serve as his secretary, and Gordon, much to his surprise, had accepted
his offer. The idea of a quiet life in the tropics with
new and beautiful surroundings, and with nothing to do
and plenty of time in which to do it, and to write his
novel besides, seemed to Albert to be just what he
wanted; and though he did not know nor care much
for his superior officer, he agreed to go with him

promptly, and proceeded to say good-by to his friends and to make his preparations. Captain Travis was so delighted with getting such a clever young gentleman for his secretary, that he referred to him to his friends as "my attaché of legation;" nor did he lessen that gentleman's dignity by telling any one that the attaché's salary was to be five hundred dollars a year. His own salary was only fifteen hundred dollars; and though his brother-in-law, Senator Rainsford, tried his best to get the amount raised, he was unsuccessful. The consulship to Opeki was instituted early in the '50's, to get rid of and reward a third or fourth cousin of the President's, whose services during the campaign were important, but whose after-presence was embarrassing. He had been created consul to Opeki as being more distant and unaccessible than any other known spot, and had lived and died there; and so little was known of the island, and so difficult was communication with it, that no one knew he was dead, until Captain Travis, in his hungry haste for office, had uprooted the sad fact. Captain Travis, as well as Albert, had a secondary reason for wishing to visit Opeki. His physician had told him to go to some warm climate for his rheumatism, and in accepting the consulship his object was rather to follow out his doctor's orders at his country's expense, than to serve his country at the expense of his rheumatism.

Albert could learn but very little of Opeki; nothing, indeed, but that it was situated about one hundred miles from the Island of Octavia, which island, in turn, was simply described as a coaling-station three hundred miles distant from the coast of California. Steamers from San Francisco to Yokohama stopped every third week at Octavia, and that was all that either Captain

Travis or his secretary could learn of their new home. This was so very little, that Albert stipulated to stay only as long as he liked it, and to return to the States within a few months if he found such a change of plan desirable.

As he was going to what was an almost undiscovered country, he thought it would be advisable to furnish himself with a supply of articles with which he might trade with the native Opekians, and for this purpose he purchased a large quantity of brass rods, because he had read that Stanley did so, and added to these, brass curtain chains and about two hundred leaden medals similar to those sold by street peddlers during the Constitutional Centennial celebration in New York City.

He also collected even more beautiful but less expensive decorations for Christmas trees, at a wholesale house on Park Row. These he hoped to exchange for furs or feathers or weapons, or for whatever other curious and valuable trophies the Island of Opeki boasted. He already pictured his rooms on his return hung fantastically with crossed spears and boomerangs, feather head-dresses, and ugly idols.

His friends told him that he was doing a very foolish thing, and argued that once out of the newspaper world, it would be hard to regain his place in it. But he thought the novel that he would write while lost to the world at Opeki would serve to make up for his temporary absence from it, and he expressly and impressively stipulated that the editor should wire him if there was a war.

Captain Travis and his secretary crossed the continent without adventure, and took passage from San Francisco on the first steamer that touched at Octavia. They reached that island in three days, and learned with some concern that there was no regular communication with Opeki, and that it would be necessary to charter a sailboat for the trip. Two fishermen agreed to take them and their trunks, and to get them to their destination within sixteen hours if the wind held good. It was a most unpleasant sail. The rain fell with calm, relentless persistence from what was apparently a clear sky; the wind tossed the waves as high as the mast and made Captain Travis ill; and as there was no deck to the big boat, they were forced to huddle up under pieces of canvas, and talked but little. Captain Travis complained of frequent twinges of rheumatism, and gazed forlornly over the gunwale at the empty waste of water.

"If I've got to serve a term of imprisonment on a rock in the middle of the ocean for four years," he said, "I might just as well have done something first to deserve it. This is a pretty way to treat a man who bled for his country. This is gratitude, this is." Albert pulled heavily on his pipe, and wiped the rain and spray from his face and smiled.

"Oh, it won't be so bad when we get there," he said; "they say these Southern people are always hospitable, and the whites will be glad to see any one from the States."

"There will be a round of diplomatic dinners," said the consul, with an attempt at cheerfulness. "I have brought two uniforms to wear at them."

It was seven o'clock in the evening when the rain ceased, and one of the black, half-naked fishermen nodded and pointed at a little low line on the horizon.

"Opeki," he said. The line grew in length until it proved to be an island with great mountains rising to the clouds, and as they drew nearer and nearer, showed a level coast running back to the foot of the mountains and covered with a forest of palms. They next made out a village of thatched huts around a grassy square, and at some distance from the village a wooden structure with a tin roof.

"I wonder where the town is," asked the consul, with a nervous glance at the fishermen. One of them told him that what he saw was the town.

"That?" gasped the consul. "Is that where all the people on the island live?"

The fisherman nodded; but the other added that there were other natives further back in the mountains, but that they were bad men who fought and ate each other. The consul and his attaché of legation gazed at the mountains with unspoken misgivings. They were quite near now, and could see an immense crowd of men and women, all of them black, and clad but in the simplest garments, waiting to receive them. They seemed greatly excited and ran in and out of the huts, and up and down the beach, as wildly as so many black ants. But in the front of the group they distinguished three men who they could see were white, though they were clothed, like the others, simply in a shirt and a short pair of trousers. Two of these three suddenly sprang away on a run and disappeared among the palm-trees; but the third one, when he recognized the American flag in the halyards, threw his straw hat in the water and began turning handsprings over the sand.

"That young gentleman, at least," said Albert, gravely, "seems pleased to see us."

A dozen of the natives sprang into the water and came wading and swimming towards them, grinning and shouting and swinging their arms.

"I don't think it's quite safe, do you?" said the consul, looking out wildly to the open sea. "You see, they don't know who I am."

A great black giant threw one arm over the gunwale and shouted something that sounded as if it were spelt Owah, Owah, as the boat carried him through the surf. "How do you do?" said Gordon, doubtfully. The boat shook the giant off under the wave and beached itself so suddenly that the American consul was thrown forward to his knees. Gordon did not wait to pick him up, but jumped out and shook hands with the young man who had turned handsprings, while the natives gathered about them in a circle and chatted and laughed in delighted excitement.

"I'm awful glad to see you," said the young man, ⌐agerly. "My name's Stedman. I'm from New Haven, ⌐onnecticut. Where are you from?"

"New York," said Albert. "This," he added, pointing solemnly to Captain Travis, who was still on his knees in the boat, "is the American consul to Opeki." The American consul to Opeki gave a wild look at Mr. Stedman of New Haven and at the natives.

"See here, young man," he gasped, "is this all there is of Opeki?"

"The American consul?" said young Stedman, with a gasp of amazement, and looking from Albert to Captain Travis. "Why, I never supposed they would send another here; the last one died about fifteen years ago, and there hasn't been one since. I've been living in the consul's office with the Bradleys, but I'll move out, of course. I'm sure I'm awfully glad to see you. It'll make it so much more pleasant for me."

"Yes," said Captain Travis, bitterly, as he lifted his rheumatic leg over the boat; "that's why we came."

Mr. Stedman did not notice this. He was too much

pleased to be anything but hospitable. "You are soaking wet, aren't you?" he said; "and hungry, I guess. You come right over to the consul's office and get on some other things."

He turned to the natives and gave some rapid orders in their language, and some of them jumped into the boat at this, and began to lift out the trunks, and others ran off towards a large, stout old native, who was sitting gravely on a log, smoking, with the rain beating unnoticed on his gray hair.

"They've gone to tell the King," said Stedman; "but you'd better get something to eat first, and then I'll be happy to present you properly."

"The King," said Captain Travis, with some awe; "is there a king?"

"I never saw a king," Gordon remarked, "and I'm sure I never expected to see one sitting on a log in the rain."

"He's a very good king," said Stedman, confidentially; "and though you mightn't think it to look at him, he's a terrible stickler for etiquette and form. After supper he'll give you an audience; and if you have any tobacco, you had better give him some as a present, and you'd better say it's from the President: he doesn't like to take presents from common people, he's so proud. The only reason he borrows mine is because he thinks I'm the President's son."

"What makes him think that?" demanded the consul, with some shortness. Young Mr. Stedman looked nervously at the consul and at Albert, and said that he guessed some one must have told him.

The consul's office was divided into four rooms with an open court in the middle, filled with palms, and watered somewhat unnecessarily by a fountain.

"I made that," said Stedman, in a modest off-hand way. "I made it out of hollow bamboo reeds connected with a spring. And now I'm making one for the King. He saw this and had a lot of bamboo sticks put up all over the town, without any underground connections, and couldn't make out why the water wouldn't spurt out of them. And because mine spurts, he thinks I'm a magician."

"I suppose," grumbled the consul, "some one told him that too."

"I suppose so," said Mr. Stedman, uneasily.

There was a veranda around the consul's office, and inside the walls were hung with skins, and pictures from illustrated papers, and there was a good deal of bamboo furniture, and four broad, cool-looking beds. The place was as clean as a kitchen. "I made the furniture," said Stedman, "and the Bradleys keep the place in order."

"Who are the Bradleys?" asked Albert.

"The Bradleys are those two men you saw with me," said Stedman; "they deserted from a British man-of-war that stopped here for coal, and they act as my servants. One is Bradley, Sr., and the other, Bradley, Jr."

"Then vessels do stop here occasionally?" the consul said, with a pleased smile.

"Well, not often," said Stedman. "Not so very often; about once a year. The *Nelson* thought this was Octavia, and put off again as soon as she found out her mistake, but the Bradleys took to the bush, and the boat's crew couldn't find them. When they saw your flag, they thought you might mean to send them back, so they ran off to hide again: they'll be back, though, when they get hungry."

The supper young Stedman spread for his guests, as he still treated them, was very refreshing and very good. There was cold fish and pigeon pie, and a hot omelet filled with mushrooms and olives and tomatoes and onions all sliced up together, and strong black coffee. After supper, Stedman went off to see the King, and came back in a little while to say that his Majesty would give them an audience the next day after breakfast. "It is too dark now," Stedman explained; "and it's raining so that they can't make the street lamps burn. Did you happen to notice our lamps? I invented them; but they don't work very well yet. I've got the right idea, though, and I'll soon have the town illuminated all over, whether it rains or not."

The consul had been very silent and indifferent, during supper, to all around him. Now he looked up with some show of interest.

"How much longer is it going to rain, do you think?" he asked.

"Oh, I don't know," said Stedman, critically. "Not more than two months, I should say." The consul rubbed his rheumatic leg and sighed, but said nothing.

The Bradleys returned about ten o'clock, and came in very sheepishly. The consul had gone off to pay the boatmen who had brought them, and Albert in his absence assured the sailors that there was not the least danger of their being sent away. Then he turned into one of the beds, and Stedman took one in another room, leaving the room he had occupied heretofore for the consul. As he was saying good-night, Albert suggested that he had not yet told them how he came to be on a deserted island; but Stedman only laughed and said that that was a long story, and that he would tell him all about it in the morning. So Albert went off to bed without waiting for the consul to return, and fell asleep, wondering at the strangeness of his new life, and assuring himself that if the rain only kept up, he would have his novel finished in a month.

The sun was shining brightly when he awoke, and the palm-trees outside were nodding gracefully in a warm breeze. From the court came the odor of strange flowers, and from the window he could see the ocean brilliantly blue, and with the sun coloring the spray that beat against the coral reefs on the shore.

"Well, the consul can't complain of this," he said, with a laugh of satisfaction; and pulling on a bath-robe, he stepped into the next room to awaken Captain Travis. But the room was quite empty, and the bed undisturbed. The consul's trunk remained just where it had been placed near the door, and on it lay a large sheet of foolscap, with writing on it, and addressed at the top to Albert Gordon. The handwriting was the consul's. Albert picked it up and read it with much anxiety. It began abruptly:—

"The fishermen who brought us to this forsaken spot tell me that it rains here six months in the year, and that this is the first month. I came here to serve my country, for which I fought and bled, but I did not come here to die of rheumatism and pneumonia. I can serve my country better by staying alive; and whether it rains or not, I don't like 't. I have been grossly deceived, and I am going back. Indeed, by the time you get this, I will be on my return trip, as I intend leaving with the men who brought us here as soon as they can get the sail up. My cousin, Senator Rainsford, can fix it all right with the President, and can have me recalled in proper form after I get back. But

of course it would not do for me to leave my post with
no one to take my place, and no one could be more
ably fitted to do so than yourself; so I feel no com-
punctions at leaving you behind. I hereby, therefore,
accordingly appoint you my substitute with full power
to act, to collect all fees, sign all papers, and attend to
all matters pertaining to your office as American consul, and I trust you will worthily uphold the name of
that country and government which it has always been
my pleasure and duty to serve.

"Your sincere friend and superior officer,

"LEONARD T. TRAVIS.

"P.S. I did not care to disturb you by moving my
trunk, so I left it, and you can make what use you
please of whatever it contains, as I shall not want
tropical garments where I am going. What you will
need most, I think, is a waterproof and umbrella.

"P.S. Look out for that young man Stedman. He is
too inventive. I hope you will like your high office;
but as for myself, I am satisfied with little old New
York. Opeki is just a bit too far from civilization to
suit me."

Albert held the letter before him and read it over
again before he moved. Then he jumped to the window. The boat was gone, and there was not a sign of
it on the horizon.

"The miserable old hypocrite!" he cried, half angry
and half laughing. "If he thinks I am going to stay
here alone he is very greatly mistaken. And yet, why
not?" he asked. He stopped soliloquizing and looked
around him, thinking rapidly. As he stood there, Sted-

man came in from the other room, fresh and smiling from his morning's bath.

"Good morning," he said, "where's the consul?"

"The consul," said Albert, gravely, "is before you. In me you see the American consul to Opeki.

"Captain Travis," Albert explained, "has returned to the United States. I suppose he feels that he can best serve his country by remaining on the spot. In case of another war, now, for instance, he would be there to save it again."

"And what are you going to do?" asked Stedman, anxiously. "You will not run away too, will you?"

Albert said that he intended to remain where he was and perform his consular duties, to appoint him his secretary, and to elevate the United States in the opinions of the Opekians above all other nations.

"They may not think much of the United States in England," he said; "but we are going to teach the people of Opeki that America is first on the map, and that there is no second."

"I'm sure it's very good of you to make me your secretary," said Stedman, with some pride. "I hope I won't make any mistakes. What are the duties of a consul's secretary?"

"That," said Albert, "I do not know. But you are rather good at inventing, so you can invent a few. That should be your first duty and you should attend to it at once. I will have trouble enough finding work for myself. Your salary is five hundred dollars a year; and now," he continued, briskly, "we want to prepare for this reception. We can tell the King that Travis was just a guard of honor for the trip, and that I have sent him back to tell the President of my safe arrival. That will keep the President from getting anxious.

There is nothing," continued Albert, "like a uniform to impress people who live in the tropics, and Travis, it so happens, has two in his trunk. He intended to wear them on State occasions, and as I inherit the trunk and all that is in it, I intend to wear one of the uniforms, and you can have the other. But I have first choice, because I am consul."

Captain Travis's consular outfit consisted of one full dress and one undress United States uniform. Albert put on the dress-coat over a pair of white flannel trousers, and looked remarkably brave and handsome. Stedman, who was only eighteen and quite thin, did not appear so well, until Albert suggested his padding out his chest and shoulders with towels. This made him rather warm, but helped his general appearance.

"The two Bradleys must dress up, too," said Albert. "I think they ought to act as a guard of honor, don't you? The only things I have are blazers and jerseys; but it doesn't much matter what they wear, as long as they dress alike."

He accordingly called in the two Bradleys, and gave them each a pair of the captain's rejected white duck trousers, and a blue jersey apiece, with a big white Y on it.

"The students of Yale gave me that," he said to the younger Bradley, "in which to play football, and a great man gave me the other. His name is Walter Camp; and if you rip or soil that jersey, I'll send you back to England in irons; so be careful."

Stedman gazed at his companions in their different costumes, doubtfully. "It reminds me," he said, "of private theatricals. Of the time our church choir played 'Pinafore.'"

"Yes," assented Albert; "but I don't think we look

quite gay enough. I tell you what we need,—medals
You never saw a diplomat without a lot of decorations
and medals."

"Well, I can fix that," Stedman said. "I've got a
trunk-full. I used to be the fastest bicycle-rider in
Connecticut, and I've got all my prizes with me."

Albert said doubtfully that that wasn't exactly the
sort of medal he meant.

"Perhaps not," returned Stedman, as he began fum-
bling in his trunk; "but the King won't know the
difference. He couldn't tell a cross of the Legion of
Honor from a medal for the tug of war."

So the bicycle medals, of which Stedman seemed to
have an innumerable quantity, were strung in profusion
over Albert's uniform, and in a lesser quantity over
Stedman's; while a handful of leaden ones, those sold
on the streets for the Constitutional Centennial, with
which Albert had provided himself, were wrapped up in
a red silk handkerchief for presentation to the King:
with them Albert placed a number of brass rods and
brass chains, much to Stedman's delighted approval.

"That is a very good idea," he said. "Democratic
simplicity is the right thing at home, of course; but
when you go abroad and mix with crowned heads, you
want to show them that you know what's what."

"Well," said Albert, gravely, "I sincerely hope this
crowned head don't know what's what. If he reads
'Connecticut Agricultural State Fair. One mile bicycle
race. First Prize,' on this badge, when we are trying
to make him believe it's a war medal, it may hurt his
feelings."

Bradley, Jr., went ahead to announce the approach
of the American embassy, which he did with so much
manner that the King deferred the audience a half-

hour, in order that he might better prepare to receive his visitors. When the audience did take place, it attracted the entire population to the green spot in front of the King's palace, and their delight and excitement over the appearance of the visitors was sincere and hearty. The King was too polite to appear much surprized, but he showed his delight over his presents as simply and openly as a child. Thrice he insisted on embracing Albert, and kissing him three times on the forehead, which, Stedman assured him in a side whisper, was a great honor; an honor which was not extended to the secretary, although he was given a necklace of animals' claws instead, with which he was better satisfied.

After this reception, the embassy marched back to the consul's office, surrounded by an immense number of the natives, some of whom ran ahead and looked back at them, and crowded so close that the two Bradleys had to poke at those nearest with their guns. The crowd remained outside the office even after the procession of four had disappeared, and cheered. This suggested to Gordon that this would be a good time to make a speech, which he accordingly did, Stedman translating it, sentence by sentence. At the conclusion of this effort, Albert distributed a number of brass rings among the married men present, which they placed on whichever finger fitted best, and departed delighted.

Albert had wished to give the rings to the married women, but Stedman pointed out to him that it would be much cheaper to give them to the married men; for while one woman could only have one husband, one man could have at least six wives.

"And now, Stedman," said Albert, after the mob had gone. "tell me what you are doing on this island."

"It's a very simple story," Stedman said. "I am the representative, or agent, or operator, for the Yokohama Cable Company. The Yokohama Cable Company is a company organized in San Francisco, for the purpose of laying a cable to Yokohama. It is a stock company; and though it started out very well, the stock has fallen very low. Between ourselves, it is not worth over three or four cents. When the officers of the company found out that no one would buy their stock, and that no one believed in them or their scheme, they laid a cable to Octavia, and extended it on to this island. Then they said they had run out of ready money, and would wait until they got more before laying their cable any further. I do not think they ever will lay it any further, but that is none of my business. My business is to answer cable messages from San Francisco, so that the people who visit the home office can see that at least a part of the cable is working. That sometimes impresses them, and they buy stock. There is another chap over in Octavia, who relays all my messages and all my replies to those messages that come to me through him from San Francisco. They never send a message unless they have brought some one to the office whom they want to impress, and who, they think, has money to invest in the Y. C. C. stock, and so we never go near the wire, except at three o'clock every afternoon. And then generally only to say 'How are you?' or 'It's raining,' or something like that. I've been saying 'It's raining' now for the last three months, but to-day I will say that the new consul has arrived. That will be a pleasant surprise for the chap in Octavia, for he must be tired hearing about the weather. He generally answers, 'Here too,' or 'So you said,' or something like that. I don't know what he says to the home office. He's brighter than I am, and that's why they put him between the two ends. He can see that the messages are transmitted more fully and more correctly, in a way to please possible subscribers."

"Sort of copy editor," suggested Albert.

"Yes, something of that sort, I fancy," said Stedman.

They walked down to the little shed on the shore, where the Y. C. C. office was placed, at three that day, and Albert watched Stedman send off his message with much interest. The "chap at Octavia," on being informed that the American consul had arrived at Opeki, inquired, somewhat disrespectfully, "Is it a life sentence?"

"What does he mean by that?" asked Albert.

"I suppose," said his secretary, doubtfully, "that he thinks it a sort of a punishment to be sent to Opeki. I hope you won't grow to think so."

"Opeki is all very well," said Gordon, "or it will be when we get things going our way."

As they walked back to the office, Albert noticed a brass cannon, perched on a rock at the entrance to the harbor. This had been put there by the last consul, but it had not been fired for many years. Albert immediately ordered the two Bradleys to get it in order, and to rig up a flag-pole beside it, for one of his American flags, which they were to salute every night when they lowered it at sundown.

"And when we are not using it," he said, "the King can borrow it to celebrate with, if he doesn't impose on us too often. The royal salute ought to be twenty-one guns, I think; but that would use up too much powder, so he will have to content himself with two."

"Did you notice," asked Stedman that night, as they

sat on the veranda of the consul's house, in the moonlight, "how the people bowed to us as we passed?"

"Yes," Albert said he had noticed it. "Why?"

"Well, they never saluted me," replied Stedman. "That sign of respect is due to the show we made at the reception."

"It is due to us, in any event," said the consul, severely. "I tell you, my secretary, that we, as the representatives of the United States Government, must be properly honored on this island. We must become a power. And we must do so without getting into trouble with the King. We must make them honor him, too, and then as we push him up, we will push ourselves up at the same time."

"They don't think much of consuls in Opeki," said Stedman, doubtfully. "You see the last one was a pretty poor sort. He brought the office into disrepute, and it wasn't really until I came and told them what a fine country the United States was, that they had any opinion of it at all. Now we must change all that."

"That is just what we will do," said Albert. "We will transform Opeki into a powerful and beautiful city. We will make these people work. They must put up a palace for the King, and lay out streets, and build wharves, and drain the town properly, and light it. I haven't seen this patent lighting apparatus of yours, but you had better get to work at it at once, and I'll persuade the King to appoint you commissioner of highways and gas, with authority to make his people toil. And I," he cried, in free enthusiasm, "will organize a navy and a standing army. Only," he added, with a relapse of interest, "there isn't anybody to fight."

"There isn't?" said Stedman, grimly, with a scornful

smile. "You just go hunt up old Messenwah and the Hillmen with your standing army once, and you'll get all the fighting you want."

"The Hillmen?" said Albert.

"The Hillmen are the natives that live up there in the hills," Stedman said, nodding his head towards the three high mountains at the other end of the island, that stood out blackly against the purple, moonlit sky. "There are nearly as many of them as there are Opekians, and they hunt and fight for a living and for the pleasure of it. They have an old rascal named Messenwah for a king, and they come down here about once every three months, and tear things up."

Albert sprang to his feet.

"Oh, they do, do they?" he said, staring up at the mountain tops. "They come down here and tear up things, do they? Well, 1 think we'll stop that, I think we'll stop that! I don't care how many there are. I'll get the two Bradleys to tell me all they know about drilling, to-morrow morning, and we'll drill these Opekians, and have sham battles, and attacks, and repulses, until I make a lot of wild, howling Zulus out of them. And when the Hillmen come down to pay their quarterly visit, they'll go back again on a run. At least some of them will," he added ferociously. "Some of them will stay right here."

"Dear me, dear me!" said Stedman, with awe; "you are a born fighter, aren't you?"

"Well, you wait and see," said Gordon; "may be I am. I haven't studied tactics of war and the history of battles, so that I might be a great war correspondent, without learning something. And there is only one king on this island, and that is old Ollypybus himself. And I'll go over and have a talk with him about it to-morrow."

Young Stedman walked up and down the length of the veranda, in and out of the moonlight, with his hands in his pockets, and his head on his chest. "You have me all stirred up, Gordon," he said; "you seem so confident and bold, and you're not so much older than I am, either."

"My training has been different; that's all," said the reporter.

"Yes," Stedman said bitterly; "I have been sitting in an office ever since I left school, sending news over a wire or a cable, and you have been out in the world, gathering it."

"And now," said Gordon, smiling, and putting his arm around the other boy's shoulders, "we are going to make news ourselves."

"There is one thing I want to say to you before you turn in," said Stedman. "Before you suggest all these improvements on Ollypybus, you must remember that he has ruled absolutely here for twenty years, and that he does not think much of consuls. He has only seen your predecessor and yourself. He likes you because you appeared with such dignity, and because of the presents; but if I were you, I wouldn't suggest these improvements as coming from yourself."

"I don't understand," said Gordon; "who could they come from?"

"Well," said Stedman, "if you will allow me to advise,—and you see I know these people pretty well,— I would have all these suggestions come from the President direct."

"The President!" exclaimed Gordon; "but how? what does the President know or care about Opeki?

and it would take so long——oh, I see, the cable. Is that what you have been doing?" he asked.

"Well, only once," said Stedman, guiltily; "that was when he wanted to turn me out of the consul's office, and I had a cable that very afternoon, from the President, ordering me to stay where I was. Ollypybus doesn't understand the cable, of course, but he knows that it sends messages; and sometimes I pretend to send messages for him to the President; but he began asking me to tell the President to come and pay him a visit, and I had to stop it."

"I'm glad you told me," said Gordon. "The President shall begin to cable to-morrow. He will need an extra appropriation from Congress to pay for his private cablegrams alone."

"And there's another thing," said Stedman. "In all your plans, you've arranged for the people's improvement, but not for their amusement; and they are a peaceful, jolly, simple sort of people, and we must please them."

"Have they no games or amusements of their own?" asked Gordon.

"Well, not what we could call games."

"Very well, then, I'll teach them baseball. Football would be too warm. But that plaza in front of the King's bungalow, where his palace is going to be, is just the place for a diamond. On the whole, though," added the consul, after a moment's reflection, "you'd better attend to that yourself. I don't think it becomes my dignity as American consul to take off my coat and give lessons to young Opekians in sliding to bases; do you? No; I think you'd better do that. The Bradleys will help you, and you had better begin to-morrow. You have been wanting to know what a secretary of legation's duties are, and now you know. It's to organize baseball nines. And after you get yours ready," he added, as he turned into his room for the night, "I'll train one that will sweep yours off the face of the island. For *this* American consul can pitch three curves."

The best-laid plans of men go far astray, sometimes, and the great and beautiful city that was to rise on the coast of Opeki was not built in a day. Nor was it ever built. For before the Bradleys could mark out the foul-lines for the baseball field on the plaza, or teach their standing army the goose step, or lay bamboo pipes for the water-mains, or clear away the cactus for the extension of the King's palace, the Hillmen paid Opeki their quarterly visit.

Albert had called on the King the next morning, with Stedman as his interpreter, as he had said he would, and, with maps and sketches, had shown his Majesty what he proposed to do towards improving Opeki and ennobling her king, and when the King saw Albert's free-hand sketches of wharves with tall ships lying at anchor, and rows of Opekian warriors with the Bradleys at their head, and the design for his new palace, and a royal sedan-chair, he believed that these things were already his, and not still only on paper, and he appointed Albert his Minister of War, Stedman his Minister of Home Affairs, and selected two of his wisest and oldest subjects to serve them as joint advisers. His enthusiasm was even greater than Gordon's, because he did not appreciate the difficulties. He thought Gordon a semi-god, a worker of miracles, and urged the putting up of a monument to him at once in the public plaza, to which Albert objected, on the ground that it would be too suggestive of an idol;

and to which Stedman also objected, but for the less unselfish reason that it would "be in the way of the pitcher's box."

They were feverishly discussing all these great changes, and Stedman was translating as rapidly as he could translate, the speeches of four different men—for the two counsellors had been called in, all of whom wanted to speak at once,—when there came from outside a great shout, and the screams of women, and the clashing of iron, and the pattering footsteps of men running.

As they looked at one another in startled surprise, a native ran into the room, followed by Bradley, Jr., and threw himself down before the King. While he talked, beating his hands and bowing before Ollypybus, Bradley, Jr., pulled his forelock to the consul, and told how this man lived on the far outskirts of the village; how he had been captured while out hunting, by a number of the Hillmen; and how he had escaped to tell the people that their old enemies were on the war path again, and rapidly approaching the village.

Outside, the women were gathering in the plaza, with the children about them, and the men were running from hut to hut, warning their fellows, and arming themselves with spears and swords, and the native bows and arrows.

"They might have waited until we had that army trained," said Gordon, in a tone of the keenest displeasure. "Tell me, quick, what do they generally do when they come?"

"Steal all the cattle and goats, and a woman or two, and set fire to the huts in the outskirts," replied Stedman.

"Well, we must stop them," said Gordon, jumping

up. "We must take out a flag of truce and treat with them. They must be kept off until I have my army in working order. It is most inconvenient. If they had only waited two months, now, or six weeks even, we could have done something; but now we must make peace. Tell the King we are going out to fix things with them, and tell him to keep off his warriors until he learns whether we succeed or fail."

"But, Gordon!" gasped Stedman. "Albert! You don't understand. Why, man, this isn't a street fight or a cane rush. They'll stick you full of spears, dance on your body, and eat you, maybe. A flag of truce!— you're talking nonsense. What do they know of a flag of truce?"

"You're talking nonsense, too," said Albert, "and you're talking to your superior officer. If you are not with me in this, go back to your cable, and tell the man in Octavia that it's a warm day, and that the sun is shining; but if you've any spirit in you,—and I think you have,—run to the office and get my Winchester rifles, and the two shot guns, and my revolvers, and my uniform, and a lot of brass things for presents, and run all the way there and back. And make time. Play you're riding a bicycle at the Agricultural Fair."

Stedman did not hear this last; for he was already off and away, pushing through the crowd, and calling on Bradley, Sr., to follow him. Bradley, Jr., looked at Gordon with eyes that snapped, like a dog that is waiting for his master to throw a stone.

"I can fire a Winchester, sir," he said. "Old Tom can't. He's no good at long range 'cept with a big gun, sir. Don't give him the Winchester. Give it to me, please, sir."

Albert met Stedman in the plaza, and pulled off his

blazer, and put on Captain Travis's—now his—uniform coat, and his white pith helmet.

"Now, Jack," he said, "get up there and tell these people that we are going out to make peace with these Hillmen, or bring them back prisoners of war. Tell them we are the preservers of their homes and wives and children; and you, Bradley, take these presents, and young Bradley, keep close to me, and carry this rifle."

Stedman's speech was hot and wild enough to suit a critical and feverish audience before a barricade in Paris. And when he was through Gordon and Bradley punctuated his oration by firing off the two Winchester rifles in the air, at which the people jumped and fell on their knees, and prayed to their several gods. The fighting men of the village followed the four white men to the outskirts, and took up their stand there as Stedman told them to do, and the four walked on over the roughly hewn road, to meet the enemy.

Gordon walked with Bradley, Jr., in advance. Stedman and old Tom Bradley followed close behind, with the two shotguns, and the presents in a basket.

"Are these Hillmen used to guns?" asked Gordon. Stedman said no, they were not.

"This shotgun of mine is the only one on the island," he explained, "and we never came near enough them, before, to do anything with it. It only carries a hundred yards. The Opekians never make any show of resistance. They are quite content if the Hillmen satisfy themselves with the outlying huts, as long as they leave them and the town alone; so they seldom come to close quarters."

The four men walked on for a half an hour or so, in silence, peering eagerly on every side; but it was not until they had left the woods and marched out into the level stretch of grassy country, that they came upon the enemy. The Hillmen were about forty in number, and were as savage and ugly-looking giants as any in a picture book. They had captured a dozen cows and goats, and were driving them on before them, as they advanced further upon the village. When they saw the four men, they gave a mixed chorus of cries and yells, and some of them stopped, and others ran forward, shaking their spears, and shooting their broad arrows into the ground before them. A tall, gray-bearded, muscular old man, with a skirt of feathers about him, and necklaces of bones and animals' claws around his bare chest, ran in front of them, and seemed to be trying to make them approach more slowly.

"Is that Messenwah?" asked Gordon.

"Yes," said Stedman; "he is trying to keep them back. I don't believe he ever saw a white man before."

"Stedman," said Albert, speaking quickly, "give your gun to Bradley, and go forward with your arms in the air, and waving your handkerchief, and tell them in their language that the King is coming. If they go at you, Bradley and I will kill a goat or two, to show them what we can do with the rifles; and if that don't stop them, we will shoot at their legs; and if that don't stop them—I guess you'd better come back, and we'll all run."

Stedman looked at Albert, and Albert looked at Stedman, and neither of them winced or flinched.

"Is this another of my secretary's duties?" asked the younger boy.

"Yes," said the consul; "but a resignation is always in order. You needn't go if you don't like it. You see, you know the language and I don't, but I know how to shoot, and you don't."

"That's perfectly satisfactory," said Stedman, handing his gun to old Bradley. "I only wanted to know why I was to be sacrificed, instead of one of the Bradleys. It's because I know the language. Bradley, Sr., you see the evil results of a higher education. Wish me luck, please," he said, "and for goodness' sake," he added impressively, "don't waste much time shooting goats."

The Hillmen had stopped about two hundred yards off, and were drawn up in two lines, shouting, and dancing, and hurling taunting remarks at their few adversaries. The stolen cattle were bunched together back of the King. As Stedman walked steadily forward with his handkerchief fluttering, and howling out something in their own tongue, they stopped and listened. As he advanced, his three companions followed him at about fifty yards in the rear. He was one hundred and fifty yards from the Hillmen, before they made out what he said, and then one of the young braves, resenting it as an insult to his chief, shot an arrow at him. Stedman dodged the arrow, and stood his ground without even taking a step backwards, only turning slightly to put his hands to his mouth, and to shout something which sounded to his companions like, "About time to begin on the goats." But the instant the young man had fired, King Messenwah swung his club and knocked him down, and none of the others moved. Then Messenwah advanced before his men to meet Stedman, and on Stedman's opening and shutting his hands to show that he was unarmed, the King threw down his club and spears, and came forward as empty-handed as himself.

"Ah," gasped Bradley, Jr., with his finger trembling on his lever, "let me take a shot at him now." Gordon struck the man's gun up, and walked forward in all the glory of his gold and blue uniform; for both he and Stedman saw now that Messenwah was more impressed by their appearance, and in the fact that they were white men, than with any threats of immediate war. So when he saluted Gordon haughtily, that young man gave him a haughty nod in return, and bade Stedman tell the King that he would permit him to sit down. The King did not quite appear to like this, but he sat down, nevertheless, and nodded his head gravely.

"Now tell him," said Gordon, "that I come from the ruler of the greatest nation on earth, and that I recognize Ollypybus as the only King of this island, and that I come to this little three-penny King with either peace and presents, or bullets and war."

"Have I got to tell him he's a little three-penny King?" said Stedman, plaintively.

"No; you needn't give a literal translation; it can be as free as you please."

"Thanks," said the secretary, humbly.

"And tell him," continued Gordon, "that we will give presents to him and his warriors if he keeps away from Ollypybus, and agrees to keep away always. It he won't do that, try to get him to agree to stay away for three months at least, and by that time we can get word to San Francisco, and have a dozen muskets over here in two months; and when our time of probation is up, and he and his merry men come dancing down the hillside, we will blow them up as high as his mountains. But you needn't tell him that, either. And if he is proud and haughty, and would rather fight, ask him to restrain himself until we show what we can do with our weapons at two hundred yards."

Stedman seated himself in the long grass in front of the King, and with many revolving gestures of his arms, and much pointing at Gordon, and profound nods and bows, retold what Gordon had dictated. When he had finished, the King looked at the bundle of presents, and at the guns, of which Stedman had given a very wonderful account, but answered nothing.

"I guess," said Stedman, with a sigh, "that we will have to give him a little practical demonstration to help matters. I am sorry, but I think one of those goats has got to die. It's like vivisection. The lower order of animals have to suffer for the good of the higher."

"Oh," said Bradley, Jr., cheerfully, "I'd just as soon shoot one of those niggers as one of the goats."

So Stedman bade the King tell his men to drive a goat towards them, and the King did so, and one of the men struck one of the goats with his spear, and it ran clumsily across the plain.

"Take your time, Bradley," said Gordon. "Aim low, and if you hit it, you can have it for supper."

"And if you miss it," said Stedman, gloomily, "Messenwah may have us for supper."

The Hillmen had seated themselves a hundred yards off, while the leaders were debating, and they now rose curiously and watched Bradley, as he sank upon one knee, and covered the goat with his rifle. When it was about one hundred and fifty yards off, he fired, and the goat fell over dead.

And then all the Hillmen, with the King himself, broke away on a run, towards the dead animal, with much shouting. The King came back alone, leaving his people standing about and examining the goat. He was much excited, and talked and gesticulated violently.

"He says—" said Stedman; "he says—"

"What? yes; go on."

"He says—goodness me!—what do you think he says?"

"Well, what does he say?" cried Gordon, in great excitement. "Don't keep it all to yourself."

"He says," said Stedman, "that we are deceived. That he is no longer King of the Island of Opeki, that he is in great fear of us, and that he has got himself into no end of trouble. He says he sees that we are indeed mighty men, that to us he is as helpless as the wild boar before the javelin of the hunter."

"Well, he's right," said Gordon. "Go on."

"But that which we ask is no longer his to give. He has sold his kingship and his right to this island to another king, who came to him two days ago in a great canoe, and who made noises as we do,—with guns, I suppose he means,—and to whom he sold the island for a watch that he has in a bag around his neck. And that he signed a paper, and made marks on a piece of bark, to show that he gave up the island freely and forever."

"What does he mean?" said Gordon. "How can he give up the island? Ollypybus is the king of half of it, anyway, and he knows it."

"That's just it," said Stedman. "That's what frightens him. He said he didn't care about Ollypybus, and didn't count him in when he made the treaty, because he is such a peaceful chap that he knew he could thrash him into doing anything he wanted him to do. And now that you have turned up and taken

Ollypybus's part, he wishes he hadn't sold the island, and wishes to know if you are angry."

"Angry? of course I'm angry," said Gordon, glaring as grimly at the frightened monarch as he thought was safe. "Who wouldn't be angry? Who do you think these people were who made a fool of him, Stedman? Ask him to let us see this watch."

Stedman did so, and the King fumbled among his necklaces until he had brought out a leather bag tied round his neck with a cord, and containing a plain stem-winding silver watch marked on the inside "Munich."

"That doesn't tell anything," said Gordon. "But it's plain enough. Some foreign ship of war has settled on this place as a coaling-station, or has annexed it for colonization, and they've sent a boat ashore, and they've made a treaty with this old chap, and forced him to sell his birthright for a mess of porridge. Now, that's just like those monarchical pirates, imposing upon a poor old black."

Old Bradley looked at him impudently.

"Not at all," said Gordon; "it's quite different with us; we don't want to rob him of Ollypybus, or to annex their lands. All we want to do is to improve it, and have the fun of running it for them and meddling in their affairs of state. Well, Stedman," he said, "what shall we do?"

Stedman said that the best and only thing to do was to threaten to take the watch away from Messenwah, but to give him a revolver instead, which would make a friend of him for life, and to keep him supplied with cartridges only as long as he behaved himself, and then to make him understand that, as Ollypybus had not given his consent to the loss of the island,

Messenwah's agreement, or treaty, or whatever it was, did not stand, and that he had better come down the next day, early in the morning, and join in a general consultation. This was done, and Messenwah agreed willingly to their proposition, and was given his revolver and shown how to shoot it, while the other presents were distributed among the other men, who were as happy over them as girls with a full dance-card.

"And now, to-morrow," said Stedman, "understand, you are all to come down unarmed, and sign a treaty with great Ollypybus, in which he will agree to keep to one half of the island, if you keep to yours, and there must be no more wars or goat stealing, or this gentleman on my right and I will come up and put holes in you just as the gentleman on the left did with the goat."

Messenwah and his warriors promised to come early, and saluted reverently as Gordon and his three companions walked up together very proudly and stiffly.

"Do you know how I feel?" said Gordon.

"How?" asked Stedman.

"I feel as I used to do in the city, when the boys in the street were throwing snowballs, and I had to go by with a high hat on my head and pretend not to know they were behind me. I always felt a cold chill down my spinal column, and I could feel that snowball, whether it came or not, right in the small of my back. And I can feel one of those men pulling his bow, now, and the arrow sticking out of my right shoulder."

"Oh, no, you can't," said Stedman. "They are too much afraid of those rifles. But I do feel sorry for any of those warriors whom old man Messenwah doesn't like, now that he has that revolver. He isn't the sort to practise on goats."

There was great rejoicing when Stedman and Gordon told their story to the King, and the people learned that they were not to have their huts burned and their cattle stolen. The armed Opekians formed a guard around the ambassadors and escorted them to their homes with cheers and shouts, and the women ran at their side and tried to kiss Gordon's hand.

"I'm sorry I can't speak the language, Stedman," said Gordon, "or I would tell them what a brave man you are. You are too modest to do it yourself, even if I dictated something for you to say. As for me," he said, pulling off his uniform, "I am thoroughly disgusted and disappointed. It never occurred to m until it was all over, that this was my chance to be . war correspondent. It wouldn't have been much of a war, but then I would have been the only one on the spot, and that counts for a great deal. Still, my time may come."

"We have a great deal on hand for to-morrow," said Gordon that evening, "and we had better turn in early."

And so the people were still singing and rejoicing down in the village, when the two conspirators for the peace of the country went to sleep for the night. It seemed to Gordon as though he had hardly turned his pillow twice to get the coolest side, when some one touched him, and he saw, by the light of the dozen glow-worms in the tumbler by his bedside, a tall figure at its foot.

"It's me—Bradley," said the figure.

"Yes," said Gordon, with the haste of a man to

show that sleep has no hold on him; "exactly; what is it?"

"There is a ship of war in the harbor," Bradley answered in a whisper. "I heard her anchor chains rattle when she came to, and that woke me. I could hear that if I were dead. And then I made sure by her lights; she's a great boat, sir, and I can know she's a ship of war by the challenging, when they change the watch. I thought you'd like to know, sir."

Gordon sat up and clutched his knees with his hands. "Yes, of course," he said; "you are quite right. Still, I don't see what there is to do."

He did not wish to show too much youthful interest, but though fresh from civilization, he had learned how far from it he was, and he was curious to see this sign of it that had come so much more quickly than he had anticipated.

"Wake Mr. Stedman, will you?" said he, "and we will go and take a look at her."

"You can see nothing but the light," said Bradley, as he left the room; "it's a black night, sir."

Stedman was not new from the sight of men and ships of war, and came in half dressed and eager.

"Do you suppose it's the big canoe Messenwah spoke of?" he said.

"I thought of that," said Gordon.

The three men fumbled their way down the road to the plaza, and saw, as soon as they turned into it, the great outlines and the brilliant lights of an immense vessel, still more immense in the darkness, and glowing like a strange monster of the sea, with just a suggestion here and there, where the lights spread, of her cabins and bridges. As they stood on the shore.

shivering in the cool night wind, they heard the bells strike over the water.

"It's two o'clock," said Bradley, counting.

"Well, we can do nothing, and they cannot mean to do much to-night," Albert said. "We had better get some more sleep, and, Bradley, you keep watch and tell us as soon as day breaks."

"Aye, aye, sir," said the sailor.

"If that's the man-of-war that made the treaty with Messenwah, and Messenwah turns up to-morrow, it looks as if our day would be pretty well filled up," said Albert, as they felt their way back to the darkness.

"What do you intend to do ?" asked his secretary, with a voice of some concern.

"I don't know," Albert answered gravely, from the blackness of the night. "It looks as if we were getting ahead just a little too fast; doesn't it? Well," he added, as they reached the house, "let's try to keep in step with the procession, even if we can't be drum-majors and walk in front of it." And with this cheering tone of confidence in their ears, the two diplomats went soundly asleep again.

The light of the rising sun filled the room, and the parrots were chattering outside, when Bradley woke him again.

"They are sending a boat ashore, sir," he said excitedly, and filled with the importance of the occasion. "She's a German man-of-war, and one of the new model. A beautiful boat, sir; for her lines were laid in Glasgow, and I can tell that, no matter what flag she flies. You had best be moving to meet them: the village isn't awake yet."

Albert took a cold bath and dressed leisurely; then he made Bradley, Jr., who had slept through it all, get up breakfast, and the two young men ate it and drank their coffee comfortably and with an air of confidence that deceived their servants, if it did not deceive themselves. But when they came down the path, smoking and swinging their sticks, and turned into the plaza, their composure left them like a mask, and they stopped where they stood. The plaza was enclosed by the natives gathered in whispering groups, and depressed by fear and wonder. On one side were crowded all the Messenwah warriors, unarmed, and as silent and disturbed as the Opekians. In the middle of the plaza some twenty sailors were busy rearing and bracing a tall flagstaff that they had shaped from a royal palm, and they did this as unconcernedly and as contemptuously, and with as much indifference to the strange groups on either side of them, as though they were working on a barren coast, with nothing but the startled sea-gulls about them. As Albert and Stedman came upon the scene, the flagpole was in place and the halliards hung from it with a little bundle of bunting at the end of one of them.

"We must find the King at once," said Gordon. He was terribly excited and angry. "It is easy enough to see what this means. They are going through the form of annexing this island to the other lands of the German government. They are robbing old Ollypybus of what is his. They have not even given him a silver watch for it."

The King was in his bungalow, facing the plaza. Messenwah was with him, and an equal number of each of their councils. The common danger had made them lie down together in peace; but they gave a murmur of relief as Gordon strode into the room with no ceremony, and greeted them with a curt wave of the hand.

"Now then, Stedman, be quick," he said. "Explain to them what this means; tell them that I will protect them; that I am anxious to see that Ollypybus is not cheated; that we will do all we can for them."

Outside, on the shore, a second boat's crew had landed a group of officers and a file of marines. They walked in all the dignity of full dress across the plaza to the flagpole, and formed in line on the three sides of it, with the marines facing the sea. The officers, from the captain with a prayer-book in his hand, to the youngest middy, were as indifferent to the frightened natives about them as the other men had been. The natives, awed and afraid, crouched back among their huts, the marines and the sailors kept their eyes front, and the German captain opened his prayer-book. The debate in the bungalow was over.

"If you only had your uniform, sir," said Bradley, Sr., miserably.

"This is a little bit too serious for uniforms and bicycle medals," said Gordon. "And these men are used to gold lace."

He pushed his way through the natives, and stepped confidently across the plaza. The youngest middy saw him coming, and nudged the one next him with his elbow, and he nudged the next, but none of the officers moved, because the captain had begun to read.

"One minute, please," called Gordon.

He stepped out into the hollow square formed by the marines, and raised his helmet to the captain.

"Do you speak English or French?" Gordon said in French; "I do not understand German."

The captain lowered the book in his hands and

gazed reflectively at Gordon through his spectacles, and made no reply.

"If I understand this," said the younger man, trying to be very impressive and polite, "you are laying claim to this land, in behalf of the German government."

The captain continued to observe him thoughtfully, and then said, "That iss so," and then asked, "Who are you?"

"I represent the King of this island, Ollypybus, whose people you see around you. I also represent the United States Government that does not tolerate a foreign power near her coast, since the days of President Monroe and before. The treaty you have made with Messenwah is an absurdity. There is only one king with whom to treat, and he—"

The captain turned to one of his officers and said something, and then, after giving another curious glance at Gordon, raised his book and continued reading, in a deep, unruffled monotone. The officer whispered an order, and two of the marines stepped out of line, and dropping the muzzles of their muskets, pushed Gordon back out of the enclosure, and left him there with his lips white, and trembling all over with indignation. He would have liked to have rushed back into the lines and broken the captain's spectacles over his sun-tanned nose and cheeks, but he was quite sure this would only result in his getting shot, or in his being made ridiculous before the natives, which was almost as bad; so he stood still for a moment, with his blood choking him, and then turned and walked back to where the King and Stedman were whispering together. Just as he turned, one of the men pulled the halyards, the ball of bunting ran up into the air, bobbed, twitched, and turned, and broke into the folds of the

German flag. At the same moment the marines raised their muskets and fired a volley, and the officers saluted and the sailors cheered.

"Do you see that?" cried Stedman, catching Gordon's humor, to Ollypybus; "that means that you are no longer king, that strange people are coming here to take your land, and to turn your people into servants, and to drive you back into the mountains. Are you going to submit? are you going to let that flag stay where it is?"

Messenwah and Ollypybus gazed at one another with fearful, helpless eyes. "We are afraid," Ollypybus cried; "we do not know what we should do."

"What do they say?"

"They say they do not know what to do."

"I know what I'd do," cried Gordon. "If I were not an American consul, I'd pull down their old flag, and put a hole in their boat and sink her."

"Well, I'd wait until they get under way, before you do either of those things," said Stedman soothingly. "That captain seems to be a man of much determination of character."

"But I will pull it down," cried Gordon. "I will resign, as Travis did. I am no longer consul. You can be consul if you want to. I promote you. I am going up a step higher. I mean to be king. Tell those two," he ran on excitedly, "that their only course and only hope is in me; that they must make me ruler of the island until this thing is over; that I will resign again as soon as it is settled, but that some one must act at once, and if they are afraid to, I am not, only they must give me authority to act for them. They must abdicate in my favor."

"Are you in earnest?" gasped Stedman.

"Don't I talk as if I were?" demanded Gordon, wiping the perspiration from his forehead.

"And can I be consul?" said Stedman, cheerfully.

"Of course. Tell them what I propose to do."

Stedman turned and spoke rapidly to the two kings. The people gathered closer to hear.

The two rival monarchs looked at one another in silence for a moment, and then both began to speak at once, their counsellors interrupting them and mumbling their guttural comments with anxious earnestness. It did not take them very long to see that they were all of one mind, and then they both turned to Gordon and dropped on one knee, and placed his hands on their foreheads, and Stedman raised his cap.

"They agree," he explained, for it was but pantomime to Albert. "They salute you as a ruler; they are calling you Tellaman, which means peacemaker. The Peacemaker, that is your title. I hope you will deserve it, but I think they might have chosen a more appropriate one."

"Then I'm really King?" demanded Albert, decidedly, "and I can do what I please? They give me full power. Quick, do they?"

"Yes, but don't do it," begged Stedman, "and just remember I am American consul now, and that is a much superior being to a crowned monarch; you said so yourself."

Albert did not reply to this, but ran across the plaza followed by the two Bradleys. The boats had gone.

"Hoist that flag beside the brass cannon," he cried, "and stand ready to salute it when I drop this one."

Bradley, Jr., grasped the halliards of the flag, which he had forgotten to raise and salute in the morning in all the excitement of the arrival of the man-of-war.

Bradley, Sr., stood by the brass cannon, blowing gently on his lighted fuse. The Peacemaker took the halliards of the German flag in his two hands, gave a quick, sharp tug, and down came the red, white and black piece of bunting, and the next moment young Bradley sent the stars and stripes up in their place. As it rose, Bradley's brass cannon barked merrily like a little bull-dog, and the Peacemaker cheered.

"Why don't you cheer, Stedman?" he shouted. "Tell those people to cheer for all they are worth. What sort of an American consul are you?"

Stedman raised his arm half-heartedly to give the time, and opened his mouth; but his arm remained fixed and his mouth open, while his eyes stared at the retreating boat of the German man-of-war. In the stern sheets of this boat, the stout German captain was struggling unsteadily to his feet; he raised his arm and waved it to some one on the great man-of-war, as though giving an order. The natives looked from Stedman to the boat, and even Gordon motion-less, watching. They had not very long to wait. There was a puff of white smoke, and a flash, and then a loud report, and across the water came a great black ball skipping lightly through and over the waves, as easily as a flat stone thrown by a boy. It seemed to come very slowly. At least it came slowly enough for every one to see that it was coming directly towards the brass cannon. The Bradleys certainly saw this, for they ran as fast as they could, and kept on running. The ball caught the cannon under its mouth, and tossed it in the air, knocking the flagpole into a dozen pieces, and passing on through two of the palm-covered huts.

"Great Heavens, Gordon!" cried Stedman; "they are firing on us."

But Gordon's face was radiant and wild.

"Firing on *us!*" he cried. "On *us!* Don't you see? Don't you understand? What do *we* amount to? They have fired on the American flag. Don't you see what that means? It means war. A great international war. And I am a war correspondent at last!" He ran up to Stedman and seized him by the arm so tightly that it hurt.

"By three o'clock," he said, "they will know in the office what has happened. The country will know it to-morrow when the paper is on the street; people will read it all over the world. The Emperor will hear of it at breakfast; the President will cable for further particulars. He will get them. It is the chance of a lifetime, and we are on the spot!"

Stedman did not hear this; he was watching the broadside of the ship to see another puff of white smoke, but there came no such sign. The two rowboats were raised, there was a cloud of black smoke from the funnel, a creaking of chains sounding faintly across the water, and the ship started at half speed and moved out of the harbor. The Opekians and the Hillmen fell on their knees, or to dancing, as best suited their sense of relief, but Gordon shook his head.

"They are only going to land the marines," he said; "perhaps they are going to the spot they stopped at before, or to take up another position further out at sea. They will land men and then shell the town, and the land forces will march here and cooperate with the vessel, and everybody will be taken prisoner or killed. We have the center of the stage, and we are making history."

"I'd rather read it than make it," said Stedman,
"You've got us in a senseless, silly position, Gordon,
and a mighty unpleasant one. And for no reason that
I can see, except to make copy for your paper."

"Tell those people to get their things together,"
said Gordon, "and march back out of danger into the
woods. Tell Ollypybus I am going to fix things all
right; I don't know just how yet, but I will, and now
come after me as quickly as you can to the cable office.
I've got to tell the paper all about it."

It was three o'clock before the "chap at Octavia"
answered Stedman's signalling. Then Stedman delivered Gordon's message, and immediately shut off all
connection, before the Octavia operator could question him. Gordon dictated his message in this way:—

"Begin with the date line, 'Opeki, June 22.'

"At seven o'clock this morning, the captain and
officers of the German man-of-war, *Kaiser*, went
through the ceremony of annexing this island in the
name of the German Emperor, basing their right to
do so on an agreement made with a leader of a
wandering tribe, known as the Hillmen. King Ollypybus, the present monarch of Opeki, delegated his
authority, as also did the leader of the Hillmen, to
King Tallaman, or the Peacemaker, who tore down
the German flag, and raised that of the United States
in its place. At the same moment the flag was saluted
by the battery. This salute, being mistaken for an
attack on the *Kaiser*, was answered by that vessel.
Her first shot took immediate effect, completely destroying the entire battery of the Opekians, cutting
down the American flag, and destroying the houses
of the people—"

"There was only one brass cannon and two huts," expostulated Stedman.

"Well, that was the whole battery, wasn't it?" asked Gordon, "and two huts is plural. I said houses of the people. I couldn't say two houses of the people. Just you send this as you get it. You are not an American consul at the present moment. You are an under-paid agent of a cable company, and you send my stuff as I write it. The American residents have taken refuge in the consulate—that's us," explained Gordon, "and the English residents have sought refuge in the woods— that's the Bradleys. King Tellaman—that's me—declares his intention of fighting against the annexation. The forces of the Opekians are under the command of Captain Thomas Bradley—I guess I might as well made him a colonel—of Colonel Thomas Bradley, of the English army.

"The American consul says—Now, what do you say, Stedman? Hurry up, please," asked Gordon, "and say something good and strong."

"You get me all mixed up," complained Stedman, plaintively. "Which am I now, a cable operator or the American consul?"

"Consul, of course. Say something patriotic and about your determination to protect the interests of your government, and all that." Gordon bit the end of his pencil impatiently, and waited.

"I won't do anything of the sort, Gordon," said Steadman; "you are getting me into an awful lot of trouble, and yourself too. I won't say a word."

"The American consul," read Gordon, as his pencil wriggled across the paper, "refuses to say anything for publication until he has communicated with the authorities at Washington, but from all I can learn he sympathizes entirely with Tellaman. Your correspondent has just returned from an audience with King Tellaman, who asks him to inform the American people that the Monroe doctrine will be sustained as long as he rules this island. I guess that's enough to begin with," said Gordon. "Now send that off quick, and then get away from the instrument before the man in Octavia begins to ask questions. I am going out to precipitate matters."

Gordon found the two kings sitting dejectedly side by side, and gazing grimly upon the disorder of the village, from which the people were taking their leave as quickly as they could get their few belongings piled upon the ox-carts. Gordon walked amongst them, helping them in every way he could, and tasting, in their subservience and gratitude, the sweets of sovereignty. When Stedman had locked up the cable office and rejoined him, he bade him tell Messenwah to send three of his youngest men and fastest runners back to the hills to watch for the German vessel and see where she was attempting to land her marines.

"This is a tremendous chance for descriptive writing, Stedman," said Gordon, enthusiastically, "all this confusion and excitement, and the people leaving their homes and all that. It's like the people getting out of Brussels before Waterloo, and then the scene at the foot of the mountains, while they are camping out there, until the Germans leave. I never had a chance like this before."

It was quite dark by six o'clock, and none of the three messengers had as yet returned. Gordon walked up and down the empty plaza and looked now at the horizon for the man-of-war, and again down the road back of the village. But neither the vessel nor the messengers, bearing word of her, appeared. The night passed without any incident, and in the morning Gordon's impatience became so great that he walked out to where the villagers were in camp and passed on half way up the mountain, but he could see no sign of the man-of-war. He came back more restless than before, and keenly disappointed.

"If something don't happen before three o'clock, Stedman," he said, "our second cablegram will have to consist of glittering generalities and a lengthy interview with King Tellaman, by himself."

Nothing did happen. Ollypybus and Messenwah began to breathe more freely. They believed the new king had succeeded in frightening the German vessel away forever. But the new king upset their hopes by telling them that the Germans had undoubtedly already landed, and had probably killed the three messengers.

"Now then," he said, with pleased expectation, as Stedman and he seated themselves in the cable office at three o'clock, "open it up and let's find out what sort of an impression we have made."

Stedman's face, as the answer came in to his first message of greeting, was one of strangely marked disapproval.

"What does he say?" demanded Gordon, anxiously.

"He hasn't done anything but swear yet," answered Stedman, grimly.

"What is he swearing about?"

"He wants to know why I left the cable yesterday. He says he has been trying to call me up for the last twenty-four hours ever since I sent my message at three o'clock. The home office is jumping mad, and want me discharged. They won't do that, though," he said, in a cheerful aside, "because they haven't paid me my salary for the last eight months. He says—great Scott! this will please you, Gordon—he says that there have been over two hundred queries for matter from papers all over the United States, and from Europe. Your paper beat them on the news, and now the home office is packed with San Francisco reporters, and the telegrams are coming in every minute, and they have been abusing him for not answering them, and he says that I'm a fool. He wants as much as you can send, and all the details. He says all the papers will have to put 'By Yokohama Cable Company' on the top of each message they print, and that that is advertising the company, and is sending the stock up. It rose fifteen points on 'change in San Francisco to-day, and the president and the other officers are buying—"

"Oh, I don't want to hear about their old company," snapped out Gordon, pacing up and down in despair. "What am I to do? that's what I want to know. Here 1 have the whole country stirred up and begging for news. On their knees for it, and a cable all to myself and the only man on the spot, and nothing to say. I'd just like to know how long that German idiot intends to wait before he begins shelling this town and killing people. He has put me in a most absurd position."

"Here's a message for you, Gordon," said Stedman, with business-like calm. "Albert Gordon, Correspondent," he read: "Try American consul. First message O.K.; beat the country; can take all you send. Give names of foreign residents massacred, and fuller account blowing up palace. Dodge."

The expression on Gordon's face as this message was

slowly read off to him, had changed from one of gratified pride to one of puzzled consternation.

"What's he mean by foreign residents massacred, and blowing up of palace?" asked Stedman, looking over his shoulder anxiously. "Who is Dodge?"

"Dodge is the night editor," said Gordon, nervously. "They must have read my message wrong. You sent just what I gave you, didn't you?" he asked.

"Of course I did," said Stedman, indignantly.

"I didn't say anything about the massacre of anybody, did I?" asked Gordon. "I hope they are not improving on my account. What *am* I to do? This is getting awful. I'll have to go out and kill a few people myself. Oh, why don't that Dutch captain begin to do something! What sort of a fighter does he call himself? He wouldn't shoot at a school of porpoises. He's not—"

"Here comes a message to Leonard T. Travis, American consul, Opeki," read Stedman. "It's raining messages to-day. 'Send full details of massacre of American citizens by German sailors.' Secretary of—great Scott!" gasped Stedman, interrupting himself and gazing at his instrument with horrified fascination—"the Secretary of State."

"That settles it," roared Gordon, pulling at his hair and burying his face in his hands. "I have *got* to kill some of them now."

"Albert Gordon, Correspondent," read Stedman, impressively, like the voice of Fate. "Is Colonel Thomas Bradley commanding native forces at Opeki, Colonel Sir Thomas Kent-Bradley of Crimean war fame? Correspondent London *Times*, San Francisco Press Club."

"Go on, go on!" said Gordon, desperately. "I'm
getting used to it now. Go on!"

"American consul, Opeki," read Stedman. "Home
Secretary desires you to furnish list of names English
residents killed during shelling of Opeki by ship of
war *Kaiser*, and estimate of amount property destroyed.
Stoughton, British Embassy, Washington."

"Stedman!" cried Gordon, jumping to his feet,
"there's a mistake here somewhere. These people
cannot all have made my message read like that.
Some one has altered it, and now I have got to make
these people here live up to that message, whether they
like being massacred and blown up or not. Don't
answer any of those messages, except the one from
Dodge; tell him things have quieted down a bit, and
that I'll send four thousand words on the flight of the
natives from the village, and their encampment at
the foot of the mountains, and of the exploring party
we have sent out to look for the German vessel; and
now I am going out to make something happen."

Gordon said that he would be gone for two hours
at least, and as Stedman did not feel capable of receiv-
ing any more nerve-stirring messages, he cut off all
connection with Octavia, by saying, "Good-by for
two hours," and running away from the office. He
sat down on a rock on the beach, and mopped his face
with his handkerchief.

"After a man has taken nothing more exciting than
weather reports from Octavia for a year," he solilo-
quized, "it's a bit disturbing to have all the crowned
heads of Europe and their secretaries calling upon you
for details of a massacre that never came off."

At the end of two hours Gordon returned from the
consulate with a mass of manuscript in his hand

"Here's three thousand words," he said desperately. "I never wrote more and said less in my life. It will make them weep at the office. I had to pretend that they knew all that had happened so far; they apparently do know more than we do, and I have filled it full of prophecies of more trouble ahead, and with interviews with myself and the two ex-Kings. The only news element in it is, that the messengers have returned to report that the German vessel is not in sight, and that there is no news. They think she has gone for good. Suppose she has, Stedman," he groaned, looking at him helplessly, "what *am* I going to do?"

"Well, as for me," said Stedman, "I'm afraid to go near that cable. It's like playing with a live wire. My nervous system won't stand many more such shocks as those they gave us this morning."

Gordon threw himself down dejectedly in a chair in the office, and Stedman approached his instrument gingerly, as though it might explode.

"He's swearing again," he explained sadly, in answer to Gordon's look for inquiry. "He wants to know when I am going to stop running away from the wire. He has a stack of messages to send, he says, but I guess he'd better wait and take your copy first; don't you think so?"

"Yes, I do," said Gordon. "I don't want any more messages than I've had. That's the best I can do," he said, as he threw his manuscript down beside Stedman. "And they can keep on cabling until the wire burns red hot, and they won't get any more."

There was silence in the office for some time, while Stedman looked over Gordon's copy, and Gordon stared dejectedly out at the ocean.

"This is pretty poor stuff, Gordon," said Stedman. "It's like giving people milk when they want brandy."

"Don't you suppose I know that?" growled Gordon. "It's the best I can do, isn't it? It's not my fault that we are not all dead now. I can't massacre foreign residents if there are no foreign residents, but I can commit suicide though, and I'll do it if something don't happen."

There was a long pause, in which the silence of the office was only broken by the sound of the waves beating on the coral reefs outside. Stedman raised his head wearily.

"He's swearing again," he said; "he says this stuff of yours is all nonsense. He says stock in the Y. C. C. has gone up to one hundred and two, and that owners are unloading and making their fortunes, and that this sort of descriptive writing is not what the company want."

"What's he think I'm here for?" cried Gordon. "Does he think I pulled down the German flag and risked my neck half a dozen times and had myself made King just to boom his Yokohama cable stock? Confound him! You might at least swear back. Tell him just what the situation is in a few words. Here, stop that rigmarole to the paper, and explain to your home office that we are awaiting developments, and that, in the meanwhile, they must put up with the best we can send them. Wait; send this to Octavia."

Gordon wrote rapidly, and read what he wrote as rapidly as it was written.

"Operator, Octavia. You seem to have misunderstood my first message. The facts in the case are these. A German man-of-war raised a flag on this island. It was pulled down and the American flag raised in its place and saluted by a brass cannon. The German-man-of-war fired once at the flag and knocked it down, and then steamed away and has not been seen since. Two huts were upset, that is all the damage done; the battery consisted of the one brass cannon before mentioned. No one, either native or foreign, has been massacred. The English residents are two sailors. The American residents are the young man who is sending you this cable and myself. Our first message was quite true in substance, but perhaps misleading in detail. I made it so because I fully expected much more to happen immediately. Nothing has happened, or seems likely to happen, and that is the exact situation up to date. Albert Gordon."

"Now," he asked after a pause, "what does he say to that?"

"He doesn't say anything," said Stedman.

"I guess he has fainted. Here it comes," he added in the same breath. He bent toward his instrument, and Gordon raised himself from his chair and stood beside him as he read it off. The two young men hardly breathed in the intensity of their interest.

"Dear Stedman," he slowly read aloud. "You and your young friend are a couple of fools. If you had allowed me to send you the messages awaiting transmission here to you, you would not have sent me such a confession of guilt as you have just done. You had better leave Opeki at once or hide in the hills. I am afraid I have placed you in a somewhat compromising position with the company, which is unfortunate, especially as, if I am not mistaken, they owe you some back pay. You should have been wiser in your day, and bought Y. C. C. stock when it was down to five cents, as 'yours truly' did. You re not, Stedman, as bright a boy as some. And as for your friend, the war correspondent, he has queered himself for life. You see, my dear Stedman, after I had sent off your first message, and demands for further details came pouring in, and I could not get you at the wire to supply them, I took the liberty of sending some on myself."

"Great Heavens!" gasped Gordon.

Stedman grew very white under his tan, and the perspiration rolled on his cheeks.

"Your message was so general in its nature, that it allowed my imagination full play, and I sent on what I thought would please the papers, and, what was much more important to me, would advertise the Y. C. C. stock. This I have been doing while waiting for material from you. Not having a clear idea of the dimensions or population of Opeki, it is possible that I have done you and your newspaper friend some injustice. I killed off about a hundred American residents, two hundred English, because I do not like the English, and a hundred French. I blew up old Ollypybus and his palace with dynamite, and shelled the city, destroying some hundred thousand dollars' worth of property, and then I waited anxiously for your friend to substantiate what I had said. This he has most unkindly failed to do. I am very sorry, but much more so for him than for myself, for I, my dear friend, have cabled on to a man in San Francisco, who is one of the directors of the Y. C. C., to sell all my stock, which he has done at one hundred and two, and he is keeping the money until I come. And I leave Octavia this afternoon to reap my just reward. I am in about twenty thousand dollars on your little war, and I feel grateful. So much so that I will inform you that the ship of war *Kaiser* has arrived at San Francisco, for which port she sailed directly from Opeki. Her captain has explained the real situation, and offered to make every amend for the accidental indignity shown to our flag. He says he aimed at the cannon, which was trained on his vessel, and which had first fired on him. But you must know, my dear Stedman, that before his arrival, war vessels belonging to the several powers mentioned in my revised dispatches, had started for Opeki at full speed, to revenge the butchery of the foreign residents. A word, my dear young friend, to the wise is sufficient. I am indebted to you to the extent of twenty thousand dollars, and in return I give you this kindly advice. Leave Opeki. If there is no other way, swim. But leave Opeki."

The sun, that night, as it sank below the line when the clouds seemed to touch the sea, merged them both into a blazing, blood-red curtain, and colored the most wonderful spectacle that the natives of Opeki had ever seen. Six great ships of war, stretching out over a league of sea, stood blackly out against the red background, rolling and rising, and leaping forward, flinging back smoke and burning sparks up into the air behind them, and throbbing and panting like living creatures in their race for revenge. From the south, came a three-decked vessel, a great island of floating steel, with a flag as red as the angry sky behind it, snapping in the wind. To the south of it plunged two long-low-lying torpedo boats, flying the French tri-color, and still further to the north towered three magnificent hulls of the White Squadron. Vengeance was written on every curve and line, on each straining engine rod, and on each polished gun muzzle.

And in front of these, a clumsy fishing boat rose and fell on each passing wave. Two sailors sat in the stern, holding the rope and tiller, and in the bow, with their backs turned forever toward Opeki, stood two young boys, their faces lit by the glow of the setting sun and stirred by the sight of the great engines of war plunging past them on their errand of vengeance.

"Stedman," said the elder boy, in an awe-struck whisper, and with a wave of his hand, "we have not lived in vain."

A LODGING FOR THE NIGHT

By Robert Louis Stevenson

It was late in November, 1456. The snow fell over Paris with rigorous, relentless persistency; sometimes the wind made a sally and scattered it in flying vortices; sometimes there was a lull, and flake after flake descended out of the black night air, silent, circuitous, interminable. To poor people, looking up under moist eyebrows, it seemed a wonder where it all came from. Master Francis Villon had propounded an alternative that afternoon, at a tavern window: was it only Pagan Jupiter plucking geese upon Olympus? or were the holy angels moulting? He was only a poor Master of Arts, he went on; and as the question somewhat touched upon divinity, he durst not venture to conclude. A silly old priest from Montargis, who was among the company, treated the young rascal to a bottle of wine in honor of the jest and grimaces with which it was accompanied, and swore on his own white beard that he had been just such another irreverent dog when he was Villon's age.

The air was raw and pointed, but not far below freezing; and the flakes were large, damp, and adhesive. The whole city was sheeted up. An army might have marched from end to end and not a footfall given the alarm. If there were any belated birds in heaven, they saw the island like a large white patch, and the bridges

(By special arrangement with Charles Scribner's Sons)

like slim white spars, on the black ground of the river.
High up overhead the snow settled among the tracery
of the cathedral towers. Many a niche was drifted
full; many a statue wore a long white bonnet on its
grotesque or sainted head. The gargoyles had been
transformed into great false noses, drooping towards
the point. The crockets were like upright pillows
swollen on one side. In the intervals of the wind,
there was a dull sound of dripping about the precincts
of the church.

The cemetery of St. John had taken its own share
of the snow. All the graves were decently covered;
tall white housetops stood around in grave array;
worthy burghers were long ago in bed, benightcapped
like their domiciles; there was no light in all the neigh-
borhood but a little peep from a lamp that hung
swinging in the church choir, and tossed the shadows
to and fro in time to its oscillations. The clock was
hard on ten when the patrol went by with halberds
and a lantern, beating their hands; and they saw
nothing suspicious about the cemetery of St. John.

Yet there was a small house, backed up against the
cemetery wall, which was still awake, and awake to
evil purpose, in that snoring district. There was not
much to betray it from without; only a stream of
warm vapor from the chimney-top, a patch where
the snow melted on the roof, and a few half-obliterated
footprints at the door. But within, behind the shut-
tered windows, Master Francis Villon, the poet, and
some of the thievish crew with whom he consorted,
were keeping the night alive and passing round the
bottle.

A great pile of living embers diffused a strong and
ruddy glow from the arched chimney. Before this

straddled Dom Nicolas, the Picardy monk, with his
skirts picked up and his fat legs bared to the comfortable warmth. His dilated shadow cut the room in half;
and the firelight only escaped on either side of his
broad person, and in a little pool between his outspread
feet. His face had the beery, bruised appearance of
the continual drinker's; it was covered with a network
of congested veins, purple in ordinary circumstances,
but now pale violet, for even with his back to the fire
the cold pinched him on the other side. His cowl
had half fallen back, and made a strange excrescence
on either side of his bull neck. So he straddled, grum-
bling, and cut the room in half with the shadow of
his portly frame.

On the right, Villon and Guy Tabary were huddled
together over a scrap of parchment; Villon making
a ballade which he was to call the "Ballade of Roast
Fish," said Tabary spluttering admiration at his
shoulder. The poet was a rag of a man, dark, little,
and lean, with hollow cheeks and thin black locks. He
carried his four-and-twenty years with feverish animation. Greed had made folds about his eyes, evil
smiles had puckered his mouth. The wolf and pig
struggled together in his face. It was an eloquent,
sharp, ugly, earthly countenance. His hands were small
and prehensile, with fingers knotted like a cord; and
they were continually flickering in front of him in violent and expressive pantomime. As for Tabary, a
broad, complacent, admiring imbecility breathed from
his squash nose and slobbering lips: he had become
a thief, just as he might have become the most decent
of burgesses, by the imperious chance that rules the
lives of human geese and human donkeys.

At the monk's other hand, Montigny and Thevenin

Pensete played a game of chance. About the first there clung some flavor of good birth and training, as about a fallen angel; something long, lithe, and courtly in the person; something aquiline and darkling in the face. Thevenin, poor soul, was in great feather: he had done a good stroke of knavery that afternoon in the Faubourg St. Jacques, and all night he had been gaining from Montigny. A flat smile illuminated his face; his bald head shone rosily in a garland of red curls; his little protuberant stomach shook with silent chucklings as he swept in his gains.

"Doubles or quits?" said Thevenin.

Montigny nodded grimly.

"*Some may prefer to dine in state,*" wrote Villon, "*On bread and cheese on silver plate.* Or, or—help me out, Guido!"

Tabary giggled.

"*Or parsley on a golden dish,*" scribbled the poet.

The wind was freshening without; it drove the snow before it, and sometimes raised its voice in a victorious whoop, and made sepulchral grumblings in the chimney. The cold was growing sharper as the night went on. Villon, protruding his lips, imitated the gust with something between a whistle and a groan. It was an eerie, uncomfortable talent of the poet's, much detested by the Picardy monk.

"Can't you hear it rattle in the gibbet?" said Villon. "They are all dancing the devil's jig on nothing, up there. You may dance, my gallants, you'll be none the warmer! Whew! what a gust! Down went somebody just now! A medlar the fewer on the three-legged medlar-tree!—I say, Dom Nicolas, it'll be cold to-night on the St. Denis Road?" he asked.

Dom Nicolas winked both his big eyes, and seemed

to choke upon his Adam's apple. Montfaucon, the great grisly Paris gibbet, stood hard by the St. Denis Road, and the pleasantry touched him on the raw. As for Tabary, he laughed immoderately over the medlars; he had never heard anything more light-hearted; and he held his sides and crowed. Villon fetched him a fillip on the nose, which turned his mirth into an attack of coughing.

"Oh, stop that row," said Villon, "and think of rhymes to 'fish.'"

"Doubles or quits," said Montigny doggedly.

"With all my heart," quoth Thevenin.

"Is there any more in that bottle?" asked the monk.

"Open another," said Villon. "How do you ever hope to fill that big hogshead, your body, with little things like bottles? And how do you expect to get to heaven? How many angels, do you fancy, can be spared to carry up a single monk from Picardy? Or do you think yourself another Elias—and they'll send the coach for you?"

"*Hominibus impossible,*" replied the monk as he filled his glass.

Tabary was in ecstasies.

Villon filliped his nose again.

"Laugh at my jokes, if you like," he said.

"It was very good," objected Tabary.

Villon made a face at him. "Think of rhymes to 'fish,'" he said. "What have you to do with Latin? You'll wish you knew none of it at the great assizes, when the devil calls for Guido Tabary, clericus—the devil with the hump-back and red-hot finger-nails. Talking of the devil," he added in a whisper, "look at Montigny!"

All three peered covertly at the gamester. He did

not seem to be enjoying his luck. His mouth was a little to a side; one nostril nearly shut, and the other much inflated. The black dog was on his back, as people say, in terrifying nursery metaphor; and he breathed hard under the gruesome burthen.

"He looks as if he could knife him," whispered Tabary, with round eyes.

The monk shuddered, and turned his face and spread his open hands to the red embers. It was the cold that thus affected Dom Nicolas, and not any excess of moral sensibility.

"Come now," said Villon—"about this ballade. How does it run so far?" And beating time with his hand, he read it aloud to Tabary.

They were interrupted at the fourth rhyme by a brief and fatal movement among the gamesters. The round was completed, and Thevenin was just opening his mouth to claim another victory, when Montigny leaped up, swift as an adder, and stabbed him to the heart. The blow took effect before he had time to utter a cry, before he had time to move. A tremor or two convulsed his frame; his hands opened and shut, his heels rattled on the floor; then his head rolled backward over one shoulder with the eyes wide open; and Thevenin Pensete's spirit had returned to Him who made it.

Every one sprang to his feet; but the business was over in two twos. The four living fellows looked at each other in rather a ghastly fashion; the dead man contemplating a corner of the roof with a singular and ugly leer.

"My God!" said Tabary; and he began to pray in Latin.

Villon broke out into hysterical laughter. He came

a step forward and ducked a ridiculous bow at Thevenin, and laughed still louder. Then he sat down suddenly, all of a heap, upon a stool, and continued
laughing bitterly, as though he would shake himself to
pieces.

Montigny recovered his composure first.

"Let's see what he has about him," he remarked,
and he picked the dead man's pockets with a practised hand, and divided the money into four equal
portions on the table. "There's for you," he said.

The monk received his share with a deep sigh, and
a single stealthy glance at the dead Thevenin, who was
beginning to sink into himself and topple sideways
off the chair.

"We're all in for it," cried Villon, swallowing his
mirth. "It's a hanging job for every man jack of us
that's here—not to speak of those who aren't." He
made a shocking gesture in the air with his raised
right hand, and put out his tongue and threw his head
on one side, so as to counterfeit the appearance of
one who has been hanged. Then he pocketed his share
of the spoil, and executed a shuffle with his feet as if
to restore the circulation.

Tabary was the last to help himself; he made a dash
at the money, and retired to the other end of the
apartment.

Montigny stuck Thevenin upright in the chair, and
drew out the dagger, which was followed by a jet of
blood.

"You fellows had better be moving," he said, as he
wiped the blade on his victim's doublet.

"I think we had," returned Villon, with a gulp.
"Damn his fat head!" he broke out. "It sticks in
my throat like phlegm. What right has a man to have

red hair when he is dead?" And he fell all of a heap again upon the stool, and fairly covered his face with his hands.

Montigny and Dom Nicolas laughed aloud, even Tabary feebly chiming in.

"Cry baby," said the monk.

"I always said he was a woman," added Montigny, with a sneer. "Sit up, can't you?" he went on, giving another shake to the murdered body. "Tread out the fire, Nick!"

But Nick was better employed; he was quietly taking Villon's purse, as the poet sat, limp and trembling, on the stool where he had been making a ballade not three minutes before. Montigny and Tabary dumbly demanded a share of the booty, which the monk silently promised as he passed the little bag into the bosom of his gown. In many ways an artistic nature unfits a man for practical existence.

No sooner had the theft been accomplished than Villon shook himself, jumped to his feet, and began helping to scatter and extinguish the embers. Meanwhile Montigny opened the door and cautiously peered into the street. The coast was clear; there was no meddlesome patrol in sight. Still it was judged wiser to slip out severally; and as Villon was himself in a hurry to escape from the neighbourhood of the dead Thevenin, and the rest were in a still greater hurry to get rid of him before he should discover the loss of his money, he was the first by general consent to issue forth into the street.

The wind had triumphed and swept all the clouds from heaven. Only a few vapours, as thin as moonlight, fleeted rapidly across the stars. It was bitter cold; and by a common optical effect, things seemed almost more definite than in the broadest daylight. The sleeping city was absolutely still; a company of white hoods, a field full of little alps, below the twinkling stars. Villon cursed his fortune. Would it were still snowing! Now, wherever he went, he left an indelible trail behind him on the glittering streets; wherever he went he was still tethered to the house by the cemetery of St. John; wherever he went he must weave, with his own plodding feet, the rope that bound him to the crime and would bind him to the gallows. The leer of the dead man came back to him with a new significance. He snapped his fingers as if to pluck up his own spirits, and choosing a street at random, stepped boldly forward in the snow.

Two things preoccupied him as he went: the aspect of the gallows at Montfaucon in this bright, windy phase of the night's existence, for one; and for another, the look of the dead man with his bald head and garland of red curls. Both struck cold upon his heart, and he kept quickening his pace as if he could escape from unpleasant thoughts by mere fleetness of foot. Sometimes he looked back over his shoulder with a sudden nervous jerk; but he was the only moving thing in the white streets, except when the wind swooped round a corner and threw up the snow, which was beginning to freeze, in spouts of glittering dust.

Suddenly he saw, a long way before him, a black clump and a couple of lanterns. The clump was in motion, and the lanterns swung as though carried by men walking. It was a patrol. And though it was merely crossing his line of march he judged it wiser to get out of eyeshot as speedily as he could. He was not in the humor to be challenged, and he was conscious of making a very conspicuous mark upon the snow. Just on his left hand there stood a great hotel, with some turrets and a large porch before the door; it was half ruinous, he remembered, and had long stood empty; and so he made three steps of it, and jumped into the shelter of the porch. It was pretty dark inside, after the glimmer of the snowy streets, and he was groping forward with outspread hands, when he stumbled over some substance which offered an indescribable mixture of resistances, hard and soft, firm and loose. His heart gave a leap, and he sprang two steps back and stared dreadfully at the obstacle. Then he gave a little laugh of relief. It was only a woman, and she dead. He knelt beside her to make sure upon this latter point. She was freezing cold, and rigid like a stick. A little ragged finery fluttered in the wind about her hair, and her cheeks had been heavily rouged that same afternoon. Her pockets were quite empty; but in her stocking, underneath the garter, Villon found two of the small coins that went by the name of whites. It was little enough; but it was always something; and the poet was moved with a deep sense of pathos that she should have died before she had spent her money. That seemed to him a dark and pitiable mystery; and he looked from the coins in his hand to the dead woman, and back again to the coins, shaking his head over the riddle of man's life Henry V. of England, dying at Vincennes just after he had conquered France, and this poor jade cut off by a cold draught in a great man's doorway, before she had time to spend her couple of whites—it seemed a cruel way to carry on the world. Two whites would have taken such a little while to squander; and yet it would have been one more good taste in the mouth, one more smack of the lips, before the devil got the soul, and the body was left to birds and vermin. He would like to use all his tallow before the light was blown out and the lantern broken.

While these thoughts were passing through his mind, he was feeling, half mechanically, for his purse. Suddenly his heart stopped beating; a feeling of cold scales passed up the back of his legs, and a cold blow seemed to fall upon his scalp. He stood petrified for a moment; then he felt again with one feverish movement; and then his loss burst upon him, and he was covered at once with perspiration. To spendthrifts money is so living and actual—it is such a thin veil between them and their pleasures! There is only one limit to their fortune—that of time; and a spendthrift with only a few crowns is the Emperor of Rome until they are spent. For such a person to lose his money is to suffer the most shocking reverse, and fall from heaven to hell, from all to nothing, in a breath. And all the more if he has put his head in the halter for it; if he may be hanged to-morrow for that same purse, so dearly earned, so foolishly departed! Villon stood and cursed; he threw the two whites into the street; he shook his fist at heaven; he stamped, and was not horrified to find himself trampling the poor corpse. Then he began rapidly to retrace his steps towards the house beside the cemetery. He had forgotten all fear of the patrol, which was long gone by at any rate, and had no idea but that of his lost purse. It was in vain that he looked right and left upon the snow: nothing was to be seen. He had not dropped it in the streets. Had it fallen in the house? He would have liked dearly to go in and see; but the idea of the grisly occupant unmanned him. And he saw besides, as he drew near, that their efforts to put out the fire had been unsuccessful; on the contrary, it had broken into a blaze, and a changeful light played in the chinks of door and window, and revived his terror for the authorities and Paris gibbet.

He returned to the hotel with the porch, and groped about upon the snow for the money he had thrown away in his childish passion. But he could only find one white; the other had probably struck sideways and sunk deeply in. With a single white in his pocket, all his projects for a rousing night in some wild tavern vanished utterly away. And it was not only pleasure that fled laughing from his grasp; positive discomfort, positive pain, attacked him as he stood ruefully before the porch. His perspiration had dried upon him; and although the wind had now fallen, a binding frost was setting in stronger with every hour, and he felt benumbed and sick at heart. What was to be done? Late as was the hour, improbable as was success, he would try the house of his adopted father, the chaplain of St. Benoit.

He ran there all the way, and knocked timidly. There was no answer. He knocked again and again, taking heart with every stroke; and at last steps were heard approaching from within. A barred wicket fell open in the iron-studded door, and emitted a gush of yellow light.

"Hold up your face to the wicket," said the chaplain from within.

"It's only me," whimpered Villon.

"Oh, it's only you, is it?" returned the chaplain; and he cursed him with foul unpriestly oaths for disturbing him at such an hour, and bade him be off to hell, where he came from.

"My hands are blue to the wrist," pleaded Villon;

"my feet are dead and full of twinges; my nose aches with the sharp air; the cold lies at my heart. I may be dead before morning. Only this once, father, and before God, I will never ask again!"

"You should have come earlier," said the ecclesiastic coolly. "Young men require a lesson now and then." He shut the wicket and retired deliberately into the interior of the house.

Villon was beside himself; he beat upon the door with his hands and feet, and shouted hoarsely after the chaplain.

"Wormy old fox!" he cried. "If I had my hand under your twist, I would send you flying headlong into the bottomless pit."

A door shut in the interior, faintly audible to the poet down long passages. He passed his hand over his mouth with an oath. And then the humor of the situation struck him, and he laughed and looked lightly up to heaven, where the stars seemed to be winking over his discomfiture.

What was to be done? It looked very like a night in the frosty streets. The idea of the dead woman popped into his imagination, and gave him a hearty fright; what had happened to her in the early night might very well happen to him before morning. And he so young! and with such immense possibilities of disorderly amusement before him! He felt quite pathetic over the notion of his own fate, as if it had been some one else's, and made a little imaginative vignette of the scene in the morning when they should find his body.

He passed all his chances under review, turning the white between his thumb and forefinger. Unfortunately he was on bad terms with some old friends who would once have taken pity on him in such a plight. He had lampooned them in verses; he had beaten and cheated them; and yet, now, when he was in so close a pinch, he thought there was at least one who might perhaps relent. It was a chance. It was worth trying at least, and he would go and see.

On the way, two little accidents happened to him which colored his musings in a very different manner. For, first, he fell in with the track of a patrol, and walked in it for some hundred yards, although it lay out of his direction. And this spirited him up; at least he had confused his trail; for he was still possessed with the idea of people tracking him all about Paris over the snow, and collaring him next morning before he was awake. The other matter affected him quite differently. He passed a street corner, where, not so long before, a woman and her child had been devoured by wolves. This was just the kind of weather, he reflected, when wolves might take it into their heads to enter Paris again; and a lone man in these deserted streets would run the chance of something worse than a mere scare. He stopped and looked upon the place with an unpleasant interest— it was a center where several lanes intersected each other, and held his breath to listen, lest he should detect some galloping black things on the snow or hear the sound of howling between him and the river. He remembered his mother telling him the story and pointing out the spot, while he was yet a child. His mother! If he only knew where she lived, he might make sure at least of shelter. He determined he would inquire upon the morrow; nay, he would go and see her too, poor old girl! So thinking, he arrived at his destination—his last hope for the night.

The house was quite dark, like its neighbors; and yet after a few taps, he heard a movement overhead, a door opening, and a cautious voice asking who was there. The poet named himself in a loud whisper, and waited, not without some trepidation, the result. Nor had he to wait long. A window was suddenly opened, and a pailful of slops splashed down upon the doorstep. Villon had not been unprepared for something of the sort, and had put himself as much in shelter as the nature of the porch admitted; but for all that, he was deplorably drenched below the waist. His hose began to freeze almost at once. Death from cold and exposure stared him in the face; he remembered he was of phthisical tendency, and began coughing tentatively. But the gravity of the danger steadied his nerves. He stopped a few hundred yards from the door where he had been so rudely used, and reflected with his finger to his nose. He could only see one way of getting a lodging, and that was to take it. He had noticed a house not far away, which looked as if it might be easily broken into, and thither he betook himself promptly, entertaining himself on the way with the idea of a room still hot, with a table still loaded with the remains of supper, where he might pass the rest of the black hours and whence he should issue, on the morrow, with an armful of valuable plate. He even considered on what viands and what wines he should prefer; and as he was calling the roll of his favorite dainties, roast fish presented itself to his mind with an odd mixture of amusement and horror.

"I shall never finish that ballade," he thought to himself; and then, with another shudder at the recollection, "Oh, damn his fat head!" he repeated fervently, and spat upon the snow.

The house in question looked dark at first sight; but as Villon made a preliminary inspection in search of the handiest point of attack, a little twinkle of light caught his eye from behind a curtained window.

"The devil!" he thought. "People awake! Some student or some saint, confound the crew! Can't they get drunk and lie in bed snoring like their neighbors? What's the good of curfew, and poor devils of bell-ringers jumping at a rope's end in bell-towers? What's the use of day, if people sit up all night? The gripes to them!" He grinned as he saw where his logic was leading him. "Every man to his business, after all," added he, "and if they're awake, by the Lord, I may come by a supper honestly for once, and cheat the devil."

He went boldly to the door and knocked with an assured hand. On both previous occasions, he had knocked timidly and with some dread of attracting notice; but now when he had just discarded the thought of a burglarious entry, knocking at a door seemed a mighty simple and innocent proceeding. The sound of his blows echoed through the house with thin, phantasmal reverberations, as tho it were quite empty; but these had scarcely died away before a measured tread drew near, a couple of bolts were withdrawn, and one wing was opened broadly, as tho no guile or fear of guile were known to those within. A tall figure of a man, muscular and spare, but a little bent, confronted Villon. The head was massive in bulk, but finely sculptured; the nose blunt at the bottom, but refining upward to where it joined a pair of strong and honest eyebrows; the mouth and eyes surrounded with delicate markings, and the whole face based upon a thick white beard, boldly and squarely trimmed.

Seen as it was by the light of a flickering hand-lamp, it looked perhaps nobler than it had a right to do; but it was a fine face, honorable rather than intelligent, strong, simple, and righteous.

"You knock late, sir," said the old man in resonant, courteous tones.

Villon cringed and brought up many servile words of apology; at a crisis of this sort the beggar was uppermost in him, and the man of genius hid his head with confusion.

"You are cold," repeated the old man, "and hungry? Well, step in." And he ordered him into the house with a noble enough gesture.

"Some great seigneur," thought Villon, as his host, setting down the lamp on the flagged pavement of the entry, shot the bolts once more into their places.

"You will pardon me if I go in front," he said, when this was done; and he preceded the poet upstairs into a large apartment, warmed with a pan of charcoal and lit by a great lamp hanging from the roof. It was very bare of furniture: only some gold plate on a sideboard; some folios; and a stand of armor between the windows. Some smart tapestry hung upon the walls, representing the crucifixion of our Lord in one piece, and in another a scene of shepherds and shepherdesses by a running stream. Over the chimney was a shield of arms.

"Will you seat yourself," said the old man, "and forgive me if I leave you? I am alone in my house to-night, and if you are to eat I must forage for you myself."

No sooner was his host gone than Villon leaped from the chair on which he had just seated himself, and began examining the room, with the stealth and passion of a cat. He weighed the gold flagons in his hands, opened all the folios, and investigated the arms upon the shield, and the stuff with which the seats were lined. He raised the window curtains, and saw that the windows were set with rich stained glass in figures, so far as he could see, of martial import. Then he stood in the middle of the room, drew a long breath, and retaining it with puffed cheeks, looked round and round him, turning on his heels, as if to impress every feature of the apartment on his memory.

"Seven pieces of plate," he said. "If there had been ten, I would have risked it. A fine house, and a fine old master, so help me all the saints!"

And just then, hearing the old man's tread returning along the corridor, he stole back to his chair, and began humbly toasting his wet legs before the charcoal pan.

His entertainer had a plate of meat in one hand and a jug of wine in the other. He set down the plate upon the table, motioning Villon to draw in his chair, and going to the sideboard, brought back two goblets which he filled.

"I drink your better fortune," he said, gravely touching Villon's cup with his own.

"To our better acquaintance," said the poet, growing bold. A mere man of the people would have been awed by the courtesy of the old seigneur, but Villon was hardened in that matter, he had made mirth for great lords before now, and found them as black rascals as himself. And so he devoted himself to the viands with a ravenous gusto, while the old man, leaning backward, watched him with steady, curious eyes.

"You have blood on your shoulder, my man," he said.

Montigny must have laid his wet right hand upon him as he left the house. He cursed Montigny in his heart.

"It was none of my shedding," he stammered.

"I had not supposed so," returned his host quietly. "A brawl?"

"Well, something of that sort," Villon admitted with a quaver.

"Perhaps a fellow murdered?"

"Oh, no, not murdered," said the poet, more and more confused. "It was all fair play—murdered by accident. I had no hand in it, God strike me dead!" he added fervently.

"One rogue fewer, I dare say," observed the master of the house.

"You may dare to say that," agreed Villon, infinitely relieved. "As big a rogue as there is between here and Jerusalem. He turned up his toes like a lamb. But it was a nasty thing to look at. I dare say you've seen dead men in your time, my lord?" he added glancing at the armor.

"Many," said the old man. "I have followed the wars, as you imagine."

Villon laid down his knife and fork, which he had just taken up again.

"Were any of them bald?" he asked.

"Oh, yes, and with hair as white as mine."

"I don't think I should mind the white so much," said Villon. "His was red." And he had a return of his shuddering and tendency to laughter, which he drowned with a great draught of wine. "I'm a little put out when I think of it," he went on. "I knew him—damn him! And then the cold gives a man fancies—or the fancies give a man cold, I don't know which."

"Have you any money?" asked the old man.

"I have one white," returned the poet, laughing. "I got it out of a dead jade's stocking in a porch. She was as dead as Cæsar, poor wench, and as cold as a church, with bits of ribbon sticking in her hair. This is a hard world in winter for wolves and wenches and poor rogues like me."

"I," said the old man, "am Enguerrand de la Feuillée, seigneur de Brisetout, bailly du Patatrac. Who and what may you be?"

Villon rose and made a suitable reverence. "I am called Francis Villon," he said, "a poor Master of Arts of this university. I know some Latin, and a deal of vice. I can make chansons, ballades, lais, virelais, and roundels, and I am very fond of wine. I was born in a garret, and I shall not improbably die upon the gallows. I may add, my lord, that from this night forward I am your lordship's very obsequious servant to command."

"No servant of mine," said the knight; "my guest for this evening, and no more."

"A very grateful guest," said Villon politely, and he drank in dumb show to his entertainer.

"You are shrewd," began the old man, tapping his forehead, "very shrewd; you have learning; you are a clerk; and yet you take a small piece of money off a dead woman in the street. Is it not a kind of theft?"

"It is a kind of theft much practised in the wars, my lord."

"The wars are the field of honor," returned the old

man proudly. "There a man plays his life upon the cast; he fights in the name of his lord the king, his Lord God, and all their lordships the holy saints and angels."

"Put it," said Villon, "that I were really a thief should I not play my life also, and against heavier odds?"

"For gain but not for honor."

"Gain?" repeated Villon with a shrug. "Gain! The poor fellow wants supper, and takes it. So does the soldier in a campaign. Why, what are all these requisitions we hear so much about? If they are not gain to those who take them, they are loss enough to the others. The men-at-arms drink by a good fire, while the burgher bites his nails to buy them wine and wood. I have seen a good many plowmen swinging on trees about the country; ay, I have seen thirty on one elm, and a very poor figure they made; and when I asked some one how all these came to be hanged, I was told it was because they could not scrape together enough crowns to satisfy the men-at-arms."

"These things are a necessity of war, which the low-born must endure with constancy. It is true that some captains drive overhard; there are spirits in every rank not easily moved by pity; and indeed many follow arms who are no better than brigands."

"You see," said the poet, "you cannot separate the soldier from the brigand; and what is a thief but an isolated brigand with circumspect manners? I steal a couple of mutton chops, without so much as disturbing people's sleep; the farmer grumbles a bit, but sups none the less wholesomely on what remains. You come up blowing gloriously on a trumpet, take away the whole sheep, and beat the farmer pitifully into the bargain. I have no trumpet; I am only Tom, Dick, or Harry; I am a rogue and a dog, and hanging's too good for me—with all my heart; but just ask the farmer which of us he prefers, just find out which of us he lies awake to curse on cold nights."

"Look at us two," said his lordship. "I am old, strong, and honored. If I were turned from my house to-morrow, hundreds would be proud to shelter me. Poor people would go out and pass the night in the streets with their children, if I merely hinted that I wished to be alone. And I find you up, wandering homeless, and picking farthings off dead women by the wayside! I fear no man and nothing; I have seen you tremble and lose countenance at a word. I wait God's summons contentedly in my own house, or, if it please the king to call me out again, upon the field of battle. You look for the gallows; a rough, swift death, without hope or honor. Is there no difference between these two?"

"As far as to the moon," Villon acquiesced. "But if I had been born lord of Brisetout, and you had been the poor scholar Francis, would the difference have been any the less? Should not I have been warming my knees at this charcoal pan, and would not you have been groping for farthings in the snow? Should not I have been the soldier, and you the thief?"

"A thief?" cried the old man. "I a thief! If you understood your words, you would repent them."

Villon turned out his hands with a gesture of inimitable impudence. "If your lordship had done me the honor to follow my argument!" he said.

"I do you too much honor in submitting to your presence," said the knight. "Learn to curb your tongue when you speak with old and honorable men.

or some one hastier than I may reprove you in a sharper fashion." And he rose and paced the lower end of the apartment, struggling with anger and antipathy. Villon surreptitiously refilled his cup, and settled himself more comfortably in the chair, crossing his knees and leaning his head upon one hand and the elbow against the back of the chair. He was now replete and warm; and he was in nowise frightened for his host, having gaged him as justly as was possible between two such different characters. The night was far spent, and in a very comfortable fashion after all; and he felt morally certain of a safe departure on the morrow.

"Tell me one thing," said the old man, pausing in his walk. "Are you really a thief?"

"I claim the sacred rights of hospitality," returned the poet. "My lord, I am."

"You are very young," the knight continued.

"I should never have been so old," replied Villon, showing his fingers, "if I had not helped myself with these ten talents. They have been my nursing mothers and my nursing fathers."

"You may still repent and change."

"I repent daily," said the poet. "There are few people more given to repentance than poor Francis. As for change, let somebody change my circumstances. A man must continue to eat, if it were only that he may continue to repent."

"The change must begin in the heart," returned the old man solemnly.

"My dear lord," answered Villon, "do you really fancy that I steal for pleasure? I hate stealing, like any other piece of work or of danger. My teeth chatter when I see a gallows. But I must eat, I must

drink, I must mix in society of some sort. What the
devil! Man is not a solitary animal—*Cui Deus fœmi-
nam tradit*. Make me king's pantler—make me abbot
of St. Denis; make me bailly of the Patatrac; and
then I shall be changed indeed. But as long as you
leave me the poor scholar Francis Villon, without a
farthing, why, of course, I remain the same."

"The grace of God is all-powerful."

"I should be a heretic to question it," said Francis.
"It has made you lord of Brisetout and bailly of the
Patatrac; it has given me nothing but the quick wits
under my hat and these te. toe upon my hands. May
I help myself to wine? I thank you respectfully. By
God's grace, you have a very superior vintage."

The lord of Brisetout walked to and fro with his
hands behind his back. Perhaps he was not yet quite
settled in his mind about the parallel between thieves
and soldiers; perhaps Villon had interested him by
some cross-thread of sympathy; perhaps his wits were
simply muddled by so much unfamiliar reasoning; but
whatever the cause, he somehow yearned to convert the
young man to a better way of thinking, and could not
make up his mind to drive him forth again into the
street.

"There is something more than I can understand in
this," he said at length. "Your mouth is full of subtleties, and the devil has led you very far astray; but
the devil is only a very weak spirit before God's truth,
and all his subtleties vanish at a word of true honor,
like darkness at morning. Listen to me once more.
I learned long ago that a gentleman should live chival-
rously and lovingly to God, and the king, and his lady;
and though I have seen many strange things done, I
·ave still striven to command my ways upon that rule.

It is not only written in all noble histories, but in
every man's heart, if he will take care to read. You
speak of food and wine, and I know very well that
hunger is a difficult trial to endure; but you do not
speak of other wants; you say nothing of honor, of
faith to God and other men, of courtesy, of love without reproach. It may be that I am not very wise—and
yet I think I am—but you seem to me like one who
has lost his way and made a great error in life. You
are attending to the little wants, and you have totally
forgotten the great and only real ones, like a man who
should be doctoring toothache on the Judgment Day.
For such things as honor and love and faith are not
only nobler than food and drink, but indeed I think we
desire them more, and suffer more sharply for their
absence. I speak to you as I think you will most easily
understand me. Are you not, while careful to fill your
belly, disregarding another appetite in your heart, which
spoils the pleasure of your life and keeps you continually wretched?"

Villon was sensibly nettled under all this sermon-
izing. "You think I have no sense of honor!" he
cried. "I'm poor enough, God knows! It's hard to
see rich people with their gloves, and you blowing in
your hands. An empty belly is a bitter thing, altho
you speak so lightly of it. If you had had as many
as I, perhaps you would change your tune. Anyway
I'm a thief—make the most of that—but I'm not a
devil from hell, God strike me dead. I would have
you to know I've an honor of my own, as good as
yours, though I don't prate about it all day long, as if
it was a God's miracle to have any. It seems quite
natural to me; I keep it in its box till it's wanted.
Why now, look you here, how long have I been in this

room with you? Did you not tell me you were alone in the house? Look at your gold plate! You're strong, if you like, but you're old and unarmed, and I have my knife. What did I want but a jerk of the elbow and here would have been you with the cold steel in your bowels, and there would have been me, linking in the streets, with an armful of golden cups! Did you suppose I hadn't wit enough to see that? And I scorned the action. There are your damned goblets, as safe as in a church; there are you, with your heart ticking as good as new; and here am I, ready to go out again as poor as I came in, with my one white that you threw in my teeth! And you think I have no sense of honor —God strike me dead!"

The old man stretched out his right arm. "I will tell you what you are," he said. "You are a rogue, my man, an impudent and black-hearted rogue and vagabond. I have passed an hour with you. Oh! believe me, I feel myself disgraced! And you have eaten and drunk at my table. But now I am sick at your presence; the day has come, and the night-bird should be off to his roost. Will you go before, or after?"

"Which you please," returned the poet, rising. "I believe you to be strictly honorable." He thoughtfully emptied his cup. "I wish I could add you were intelligent," he went on, knocking on his head with his knuckles. "Age! age! the brains stiff and rheumatic."

The old man preceded him from a point of self-respect. Villon followed, whistling, with his thumbs in his girdle.

"God pity you," said the lord of Brisetout at the door.

"Good-bye, papa," returned Villon with a yawn. "Many thanks for the cold mutton."

The door closed behind him. The dawn was breaking over the white roofs. A chill, uncomfortable morning ushered in the day. Villon stood and heartily stretched himself in the middle of the road.

"A very dull old gentleman," he thought. "I wonder what his goblets may be worth."

FRIENDS IN SAN ROSARIO

By O. Henry

The west-bound stopped at San Rosario on time at 3:20 a. m. A man with a thick black-leather wallet under his arm left the train and walked rapidly up the main street of the town. There were other passengers who also got off at San Rosario, but they either slouched limberly over to the railroad eating-house or the Silver Dollar saloon, or joined the groups of idlers about the station.

Indecision had no part in the movements of the man with the wallet. He was short in stature, but strongly built, with very light, closely trimmed hair, smooth, determined face, and aggressive, gold-rimmed nose glasses. He was well dressed in the prevailing Eastern style. His air denoted a quiet but conscious reserve force, if not actual authority.

After walking a distance of three squares he came to the center of the town's business area. Here another street of importance crossed the main one, forming the hub of San Rosario's life and commerce. Upon one corner stood the post-office. Upon another Rubensky's Clothing Emporium. The other two diagonally opposing corners were occupied by the town's two banks, the First National and the Stockmen's National. Into the First National Bank of San Rosario the newcomer walked, never slowing his brisk step until he stood at the cashier's window. The bank opened for business at nine, and the working force was already assembled, each member preparing his department for the day's business. The cashier was examining the mail when he noticed the stranger standing at his window.

"Bank doesn't open 'til nine," he remarked, curtly, but without feeling. He had had to make that statement so often to early birds since San Rosario adopted city banking hours.

"I am well aware of that," said the other man, in cool, brittle tones. "Will you kindly receive my card?"

The cashier drew the small, spotless parallelogram inside the bars of his wicket, and read:

> ## J. F. C. NETTLEWICK
> National Bank Examiner

"Oh—er—will you walk around inside, Mr.—er—Nettlewick. Your first visit—didn't know your business, of course. Walk right around, please."

The examiner was quickly inside the sacred precincts of the bank, where he was ponderously introduced to each employee in turn by Mr. Edlinger, the cashier—a middle-aged gentleman of deliberation, discretion, and method.

"I was kind of expecting Sam Turner round again, pretty soon," said Mr. Edlinger. "Sam's been examining us now for about four years. I guess you'll find us all right, tho, considering the tightness in business. Not overly much money on hand, but able to stand the storms, sir, stand the storms."

"Mr. Turner and I have been ordered by the Con

troller to exchange districts," said the examiner, in his decisive, formal tones. "He is covering my old territory in southern Illinois and Indiana. I will take the cash first, please."

Perry Dorsey, the teller, was already arranging his cash on the counter for the examiner's inspection. He knew it was right to a cent, and he had nothing to fear, but he was nervous and flustered. So was every man in the bank. There was something so icy and swift, so impersonal and uncompromising about this man that his very presence seemed an accusation. He looked to be a man who would never make nor overlook an error.

Mr. Nettlewick first seized the currency, and with a rapid, almost juggling motion, counted it by packages. Then he spun the sponge cup toward him and verified the count by bills. His thin, white fingers flew like some expert musician's upon the keys of a piano. He dumped the gold upon the counter with a crash, and the coins whined and sang as they skimmed across the marble slab from the tips of his nimble digits. The air was full of fractional currency when he came to the halves and quarters. He counted the last nickel and dime. He had the scales brought, and he weighed every sack of silver in the vault. He questioned Dorsey concerning each of the cash memoranda—certain checks, charge slips, etc., carried over from the previous day's work—with unimpeachable courtesy, yet with something so mysteriously momentous in his frigid manner, that the teller was reduced to pink cheeks and a stammering tongue.

This newly imported examiner was so different from Sam Turner. It had been Sam's way to enter the bank with a shout, pass the cigars, and tell the latest stories he had picked up on his rounds. His customary greeting to Dorsey had been, "Hello, Perry! Haven't skipped out with the boodle yet, I see." Turner's way of counting the cash had been different, too. He would finger the packages of bills in a tired kind of way, and then go into the vault and kick over a few sacks of silver, and the thing was done. Halves and quarters and dimes? Not for Sam Turner. "No chicken feed for me," he would say when they were set before him. "I'm not in the agricultural department." But, then, Turner was a Texan, an old friend of the bank's president, and had known Dorsey since he was a baby.

While the examiner was counting the cash, Major Thomas B. Kingman—known to every one as "Major Tom"—the president of the First National, drove up to the side door with his old dun horse and buggy, and came inside. He saw the examiner busy with the money, and, going into the little "pony corral," as he called it, in which his desk was railed off, he began to look over his letters.

Earlier, a little incident had occurred that even the sharp eyes of the examiner had failed to notice. When he had begun his work at the cash counter, Mr. Edlinger had winked significantly at Roy Wilson, the youthful bank messenger, and nodded his head slightly toward the front door. Roy understood, got his hat and walked leisurely out, with his collector's book under his arm. Once outside, he made a beeline for the Stockmen's National. That bank was also getting ready to open. No customers had, as yet, presented themselves.

"Say, you people!" cried Roy, with the familiarity of youth and long acquaintance, "you want to get a move on you. There's a new bank examiner over at the First, and he's a stem-winder. He's counting nickels on Perry, and he's got the whole outfit bluffed. Mr. Edlinger gave me the tip to let you know."

Mr. Buckley, president of the Stockmen's National—a stout, elderly man, looking like a farmer dressed for Sunday—heard Roy from his private office at the rear and called him.

"Has Major Kingman come down to the bank yet?" he asked of the boy.

"Yes, sir, he was just driving up as I left," said Roy.

"I want you to take him a note. Put it into his own hands as soon as you get back."

Mr. Buckley sat down and began to write.

Roy returned and handed to Major Kingman the envelop containing the note. The major read it, folded it, and slipped it into his vest pocket. He leaned back in his chair for a few moments as if he were meditating deeply, and then rose and went into the vault. He came out with the bulky, old-fashioned leather note case stamped on the back in gilt letters, "Bills Discounted." In this were the notes due the bank with their attached securities, and the major, in his rough way, dumped the lot upon his desk and began to sort them over.

By this time Nettlewick had finished his count of the cash. His pencil fluttered like a swallow over the sheet of paper on which he had set his figures. He opened his black wallet, which seemed to be also a kind of secret memorandum book, made a few rapid figures in it, wheeled and transfixed Dorsey with the glare of his spectacles. That look seemed to say: "You're safe this time, but——"

"Cash all correct," snapped the examiner. He made

a dash for the individual bookkeeper, and, for a few minutes there was a fluttering of ledger leaves and a sailing of balance sheets through the air.

"How often do you balance your pass-books?" he demanded, suddenly.

"Er—once a month," faltered the individual book-keeper, wondering how many years they would give him.

"All right," said the examiner, turning and charging upon the general bookkeeper, who had the statements of his foreign banks and their reconcilement memo-randa ready. Everything there was found to be all right. Then the stub book of the certificates of deposit. Flutter—flutter—zip—zip—check! All right. List of over-drafts, please. Thanks. H'm-m. Un-signed bills of the bank, next. All right.

Then came the cashier's turn, and easy-going Mr. Edlinger rubbed his nose and polished his glasses nervously under the quick fire of questions concerning the circulation, undivided profits, bank real estate, and stock ownership.

Presently Nettlewick was aware of a big man tower-ing above him at his elbow—a man sixty years of age, rugged and hale, with a rough, grizzled beard, a mass of gray hair, and a pair of penetrating blue eyes that confronted the formidable glasses of the examiner without a flicker.

"Er—Major Kingman, our president—er—Mr. Net-tlewick," said the cashier.

Two men of very different types shook hands. One was a finished product of the world of straight lines, conventional methods, and formal affairs. The other was something freer, wider, and nearer to nature. Tom Kingman had not been cut to any pattern. He had been mule-driver, cowboy, ranger, soldier, sheriff, prospector and cattleman. Now, when he was bank president, his old comrades from the prairies, of the saddle, tent, and trail, found no change in him. He had made his fortune when Texas cattle were at the high tide of value, and had organized the First National Bank of San Rosario. In spite of his largeness of heart and sometimes unwise generosity toward his old friends, the bank had prospered, for Major Tom Kingman knew men as well as he knew cattle. Of late years the cattle business had known a depression, and the major's bank was one of the few whose losses had not been great.

"And now," said the examiner, briskly, pulling out his watch, "the last thing is the loans. We will take them up now, if you please."

He had gone through the First National at almost record-breaking speed—but thoroly, as he did everything. The running order of the bank was smooth and clean, and that had facilitated his work. There was but one other bank in the town. He received from the Government a fee of twenty-five dollars for each bank that he examined. He should be able to go over those loans and discounts in half an hour. If so, he could examine the other bank immediately afterward, and catch the 11:45, the only other train that day in the direction he was working. Otherwise, he would have to spend the night and Sunday in this uninteresting Western town. That was why Mr. Nettlewick was rushing matters.

"Come with me, sir," said Major Kingman, in his deep voice, that united the Southern drawl with the rhythmic twang of the West; "We will go over them together. Nobody in the bank knows those notes as

I do. Some of 'em are a little wobbly on their legs, and some are mavericks without extra many brands on their backs, but they'll most all pay out at the round-up."

The two sat down at the president's desk. First, the examiner went through the notes at lightning speed, and added up their total, finding it to agree with the amount of loans carried on the book of daily balances. Next, he took up the larger loans, inquiring scrupulously into the condition of their endorsers or securities. The new examiner's mind seemed to course and turn and make unexpected dashes hither like a bloodhound seeking a trail. Finally he pushed aside all the notes except a few, which he arranged in a neat pile before him, and began a dry, formal little speech.

"I find, sir, the condition of your bank to be very good, considering the poor crops and the depression in the cattle interests of your state. The clerical work seems to be done accurately and punctually. Your past-due paper is moderate in amount, and promises only a small loss. I would recommend the calling in of your large loans, and the making of only sixty and ninety day or call loans until general business revives. And now, there is one thing more, and I will have finished with the bank. Here are six notes aggregating something like $40,000. They are secured, according to their faces, by various stocks, bonds, shares, etc., to the value of $70,000. Those securities are missing from the notes to which they should be attached. I suppose you have them in the safe or vault. You will permit me to examine them."

Major Tom's light-blue eyes turned unflinchingly toward the examiner.

"No, sir," he said, in a low but steady tone; "those securities are neither in the safe nor the vault. I have taken them. You may hold me personally responsible for their absence."

Nettlewick felt a slight thrill. He had not expected this. He had struck a momentous trail when the hunt was drawing to a close.

"Ah!" said the examiner. He waited a moment, and then continued: "May I ask you to explain more definitely?"

"The securities were taken by me," repeated the major. "It was not for my own use, but to save an old friend in trouble. Come in here, sir, and we'll talk it over."

He led the examiner into the bank's private office at the rear, and closed the door. There was a desk, and a table, and half-a-dozen leather-covered chairs. On the wall was the mounted head of a Texas steer with horns five feet from tip to tip. Opposite hung the major's old cavalry saber that he had carried at Shiloh and Fort Pillow.

Placing a chair for Nettlewick, the major seated himself by the window, from which he could see the post-office and the carved limestone front of the Stockman's National. He did not speak at once, and Nettlewick felt, perhaps, that the ice should be broken by something so near its own temperature as the voice of official warning.

"Your statement," he began, "since you have failed to modify it, amounts, as you must know, to a very serious thing. You are aware, also, of what my duty must compel me to do. I shall have to go before the United States Commissioner and make——"

"I know, I know," said Major Tom, with a wave

of his hand. "You don't suppose I'd run a bank without being posted on national banking laws and the revised statutes! Do your duty. I'm not asking any favors. But I spoke of my friend. I did want you to hear me tell you about Bob."

Nettlewick settled himself in his chair. There would be no leaving San Rosario for him that day. He would have to telegraph to the Controller of the Currency; he would have to swear out a warrant before the United States Commissioner for the arrest of Major Kingman; perhaps he would be ordered to close the bank on account of the loss of the securities. It was not the first crime the examiner had unearthed. Once or twice the terrible upheaval of human emotions that his investigations had loosed had almost caused a ripple in his official calm. He had seen bank men kneel and plead and cry like women for a chance— an hour's time—the overlooking of a single error. One cashier had shot himself at his desk before him. None of them had taken it with the dignity and coolness of this stern old Westerner. Nettlewick felt that he owed it to him at least to listen if he wished to talk. With his elbow on the arm of his chair, and his square chin resting upon the fingers of his right hand, the bank examiner waited to hear the confession of the president of the First National Bank of San Rosario.

"When a man's your friend," began Major Tom, somewhat didactically, "for forty years, and tried by water, fire, earth, and cyclones, when you can do him a little favor you feel like doing it."

("Embezzle for him $70,000 worth of securities," thought the examiner.)

"We were cowboys together, Bob and I," con

tinued the major, speaking slowly, and deliberately, and musingly, as if his thoughts were rather with the past then the critical present, "and we prospected together for gold and silver over Arizona, New Mexico, and a good part of California. We were both in the war of 'sixty-one, but in different commands. We've fought Indians and horse thieves side by side; we've starved for weeks in a cabin in the Arizona mountains, buried twenty feet deep in snow; we've ridden herd together when the wind blew so hard the lightning couldn't strike—well, Bob and I have been through some rough spells since the first time we met in the branding camp of the old Anchor-Bar ranch. And during that time we've found it necessary more than once to help each other out of tight places. In those days it was expected of a man to stick to his friend, and he didn't ask any credit for it. Probably next day you'd need him to get at your back and help stand off a band of Apaches, or put a tourniquet on your leg above a rattlesnake bite and ride for whisky. So, after all, it was give and take, and if you didn't stand square with your pardner, why, you might be shy one when you needed him. But Bob was a man who was willing to go further than that. He never played a limit.

"Twenty years ago I was sheriff of this county and I made Bob my chief deputy. That was before the boom in cattle when we both made our stake. I was sheriff and collector, and it was a big thing for me then. I was married, and we had a boy and a girl— a four and a six year old. There was a comfortable house next to the courthouse, furnished by the county, rent free, and I was saving money. Bob did most of the office work. Both of us had seen rough times and plenty of rustling and danger, and I tell you it was great to hear the rain and the sleet dashing against the windows of nights, and be warm and safe and comfortable, and know you could get up in the morning and be shaved and have folks call you 'mister.' And then, I had the finest wife and kids that ever struck the range, and my old friend with me enjoying the first fruits of prosperity and white shirts, and I guess I was happy. Yes, I was happy about that time."

The major sighed and glanced casually out of the window. The bank examiner changed his position, and leaned his chin upon his other hand.

"One winter," continued the major, "the money for the county taxes came pouring in so fast that I didn't have time to take the stuff to the bank for a week. I just shoved the checks into a cigar box and the money into a sack, and locked them in the big safe that belonged in the sheriff's office.

"I had been overworked that week, and was about sick, anyway. My nerves were out of order, and my sleep at night didn't seem to rest me. The doctor had some scientific name for it, and I was taking medicine. And so, added to the rest, I went to bed at night with that money on my mind. Not that there was much need of being worried, for the safe was a good one, and nobody but Bob and I knew the combination. On Friday night there was about $6,500 in cash in the bag. On Saturday morning I went to the office as usual. The safe was locked, and Bob was writing at his desk. I opened the safe, and the money was gone. I called Bob, and roused everybody in the courthouse to announce the robbery. It struck me that

Bob took it pretty quiet, considering how much it reflected upon both him and me.

"Two days went by and we never got a clue. It couldn't have been burglars, for the safe had been opened by the combination in the proper way. People must have begun to talk, for one afternoon in comes Alice—that's my wife—and the boy and girl, and Alice stamps her foot, and her eyes flash, and she cries out, 'The lying wretches—Tom, Tom!' and I catch her in a faint, and bring her 'round little by little, and she lays her head down and cries and cries for the first time since she took Tom Kingman's name and fortunes. And Jack and Zilla—the youngsters—they were always wild as tigers' cubs to rush at Bob and climb all over him whenever they were allowed to come to the courthouse—they stood and kicked their little shoes, and herded together like scared partridges. They were having their first trip down into the shadows of life. Bob was working at his desk, and he got up and went out without a word. The grand jury was in session then, and the next morning Bob went before them and confessed that he stole the money. He said he lost it in a poker game. In fifteen minutes they had found a true bill and sent me the warrant to arrest the man with whom I'd been closer than a thousand brothers for many a year.

"I did it, and then I said to Bob, pointing: 'There's my house, and here's my office, and up there's Maine, and out that way is California, and over there is Florida—and that's your range 'til court meets. You're in my charge, and I take the responsibility. You be here when you're wanted.'

" 'Thanks, Tom,' he said, kind of carelessly; 'I was sort of hoping you wouldn't lock me up. Court meets

next Monday, so, if you don't object, I'll just loaf
around the office until then. I've got one favor to
ask, if it isn't too much. If you'd let the kids come
out in the yard once in a while and have a romp I'd
like it.'

"'Why not?' I answered him. 'They're welcome,
and so are you. And come to my house the same as
ever.' You see, Mr. Nettlewick, you can't make a
friend of a thief, but neither can you make a thief of
a friend, all at once."

The examiner made no answer. At that moment
was heard the shrill whistle of a locomotive pulling
into the depot. That was the train on the little,
narrow-gage road that struck into San Rosario from
the south. The major cocked his ear and listened for
a moment, and looked at his watch. The narrow-
gage was in on time—10:35. The major continued:

"So Bob hung around the office, reading the papers
and smoking. I put another deputy to work in his
place, and, after a while, the first excitement of the
case wore off.

"One day when we were alone in the office Bob came
over to where I was sitting. He was looking sort of
grim and blue—the same look he used to get when
he'd been up watching for Indians all night or herd-
riding.

"'Tom,' says he, 'it's harder than standing off red-
skins; it's harder than lying in the lava desert forty
miles from water; but I'm going to stick it out to
the end. You know that's been my style. But if
you'd 'ip me the smallest kind of a sign—if you'd
just say, "Bob I understand," why, it would make it
lots easier.'

"I was surprised. 'I don't know what you mean,

Bob,' I said. 'Of course, you know that I'd do anything under the sun to help you that I could. But
you've got me guessing.'

"'All right, Tom,' was all he said, and he went
back to his newspaper and lit another cigar.

"It was the night before the court met when I
found out what he meant. I went to bed that night
with the same old, light-headed, nervous feeling come
back upon me. I dropped off to sleep about midnight. When I woke I was standing half dressed in
one of the courthouse corridors. Bob was holding
one of my arms, our family doctor the other, and
Alice was shaking me and half crying. She had sent
for the doctor without my knowing it, and when he
came they had found me out of bed and missing, and
had begun a search.

"'Sleep-walking,' said the doctor.

"All of us went back to the house, and the doctor
told us some remarkable stories about the strange
things people had done while in that condition. I
was feeling rather chilly after my trip out, and, as
my wife was out of the room at the time, I pulled
open the door of an old wardrobe that stood in the
room and dragged out a big quilt I had seen in there.
With it tumbled out the bag of money for stealing
which Bob was to be tried—and convicted—in the
morning.

"'How the jumping rattlesnakes did that get there?'
I yelled, and all hands must have seen how surprised
I was. Bob knew in a flash.

"'You darned old snoozer,' he said, with the old-
time look on his face, 'I saw you put it there. I
watched you open the safe and take it out, and I

followed you. I looked through the window and saw you hide it in that wardrobe.'

" 'Then, you blankety-blank, flop-eared, sheep-headed coyote, what did you say you took it for?'

" 'Because,' said Bob, simply, 'I didn't know you were asleep.'

"I saw him glance toward the door of the room where Jack and Zilla were, and I knew then what it meant to be a man's friend from Bob's point of view."

Major Tom paused, and again directed his glance out of the window. He saw someone in the Stockmen's National Bank reach and draw a yellow shade down the whole length of its plate-glass, big front window, altho the position of the sun did not seem to warrant such a defensive movement against its rays.

Nettlewick sat up straight in his chair. He had listened patiently, but without consuming interest, to the major's story. It had impressed him as irrelevant to the situation, and it could certainly have no effect upon the consequences. Those Western people, he thought, had an exaggerated sentimentality. They were not business-like. They needed to be protected from their friends. Evidently the major had concluded. And what he had said amounted to nothing.

"May I ask," said the examiner, "if you have anything further to say that bears directly upon the question of those abstracted securities?"

"Abstracted securities, sir!" Major Tom turned suddenly in his chair, his blue eyes flashing upon the examiner. "What do you mean, sir?"

He drew from his coat pocket a batch of folded papers held together by a rubber band, tossed them into Nettlewick's hands, and rose to his feet.

"You'll find those securities there, sir, every stock,

bond, and share of 'em, I took them from the notes while you were counting the cash. Examine and compare them for yourself."

The major led the way back into the banking room. The examiner, astounded, perplexed, nettled, at sea, followed. He felt that he had been made the victim of something that was not exactly a hoax, but that left him in the shoes of one who had been played upon, used, and then discarded, without even an inkling of the game. Perhaps, also, his official position had been irreverently juggled with. But there was nothing he could take hold of. An official report of the matter would be an absurdity. And, somehow, he felt that he would never know anything more about the matter than he did then.

Frigidly, mechanically, Nettlewick examined the securities, found them to tally with the notes, gathered his black wallet, and rose to depart.

"I will say," he protested, turning the indignant glare of his glasses upon Major Kingman, "that your statements—your misleading statements, which you have not condescended to explain—do not appear to be quite the thing, regarded either as business or humor. I do not understand such motives or actions."

Major Tom looked at him serenely and not unkindly.

"Son," he said, "there are plenty of things in the chaparral, and on the prairies, and up the cañons that you don't understand. But I want to thank you for listening to a garrulous old man's prosy story. We old Texans love to talk about our adventures and our old comrades, and the home folks have long ago learned to run when we begin with 'Once upon a time,' so we have to spin our yarns to the stranger within our gates."

The major smiled, but the examiner only bowed coldly, and abruptly quitted the bank. They saw him travel diagonally across the street in a straight line and enter the Stockmen's National Bank.

Major Tom sat down at his desk and drew from his vest pocket the note Roy had given him. He had read it once, but hurriedly, and now, with something like a twinkle in his eyes, he read it again. These were the words he read:

DEAR TOM:

I hear there's one of Uncle Sam's grayhounds going through you, and that means that we'll catch him inside of a couple of hours, maybe. Now, I want you to do something for me. We've got just $2,200 in the bank, and the law requires that we have $20,-000. I let Ross and Fisher have $18,000 late yesterday afternoon to buy up that Gibson bunch of cattle. They'll realize $40,000 in less than thirty days on the transaction, but that won't make my cash on hand look any prettier to that bank examiner. Now, I can't show him those notes, for they're just plain notes of hand without any security in sight, but you know very well that Pink Ross and Jim Fisher are two of the finest white men God ever made, and they'll do the square thing. You remember Jim Fisher—he was the one who shot that faro dealer in El Paso. I wired Sam Bradshaw's bank to send me $20,000, and it will get in on the narrow-gage at 10:35. You can't let a bank examiner in to count $2,200 and close your doors. Tom, you hold that examiner. Hold him. Hold him if you have to rope him and sit on his head. Watch our front window after the narrow-gage gets in, and when we've got the cash inside we'll pull down the shade for a signal. Don't turn him loose till then. I'm counting on you, Tom.

Your Old Pard,

Bob Buckley,

Prest. Stockmen's National.

The major began to tear the note into small pieces and throw them into his waste basket. He gave a satisfied little chuckle as he did so.

"Confounded old reckless cowpuncher!" he growled, contentedly, "that pays him some on account for what he tried to do for me in the sheriff's office twenty years ago."

THE FOURTH MAN

By John Russell

The raft might have been taken for a swath of cut
sedge or a drifting tangle of roots as it slid out of the
shadowy river mouth at dawn and dipped into the first
ground swell. But while the sky brightened and the
breeze came fresh offshore it picked a way among
shoals and swampy islets with purpose and direction,
and when at last the sun leaped up and cleared his
bright eye of the morning mist it had passed the wide
entrance to the bay and stood to open sea.

It was a curious craft for such a venture, of a type
that survives here and there in the obscure corners of
the world. The coracle maker would have scorned it.
The first navigating pithecanthrope built nearly as well
with his log and bush. A mat of pandanus leaves
served for its sail and a paddle of niaouli wood for its
helm. But it had a single point of real seaworthiness.
Its twin floats, paired as a catamaran, were woven of
reed bundles and bamboo sticks upon triple rows of
bladders. It was light as a bladder itself, elastic, fit
to ride any weather. One other quality this raft possessed which recommended it beyond all comfort and
all safety to its present crew. It was very nearly invisible. They had only to unstep its mast and lie flat
in the cup of its soggy platform and they could not be
spied half a mile away.

Four men occupied the raft. Three of them were white. Their bodies had been scored with brambles and blackened with dried blood, and on wrist and ankle they bore the dark and wrinkled stain of the gyves. The hair upon them was long and matted. They wore only the rags of blue canvas uniforms. But they were whites, members of the superior race—members of a highly superior race according to those philosophers who rate the criminal aberration as a form of genius.

The fourth was the man who had built the raft and was now sailing it. There was nothing superior about him. His skin was a layer of soot. His prognathous jaw carried out the angle of a low forehead. No line of beauty redeemed his lean limbs and knobby joints. Nature had set upon him her plainest stamp of inferiority, and his only attempts to relieve it were the twist of bark about his middle and the prong of pig ivory through the cartilage of his nose. Altogether a very ordinary specimen of one of the lowest branches of the human family—the Canaques of New Caledonia.

The three whites sat together well forward, and so they had sat in silence for hours. But at sunrise, as if some spell had been raised by the clang of that great copper gong in the east, they stirred and breathed deep of the salt air and looked at one another with hope in their haggard faces, and then back toward the land which was now no more than a gray-green smudge behind them. . . . "Friends," said the eldest, whose temples were bound with a scrap of crimson scarf, "Friends—the thing is done."

With a gesture like conjuring he produced from the breast of his tattered blouse three cigarets, fresh and round, and offered them.

"Nippers!" cried the one at his right. "True nippers —name of a little good man! And here? Doctor, I always said you were a marvel. See if they be not new from the box!"

Dr. Dubosc smiled. Those who had known him in very different circumstances about the boulevards, the lobbies, the clubs, would have known him again and in spite of all disfigurement by that smile. And here, at the bottom of the earth, it had set him still apart in the prisons, the cobalt mines, the chain gangs of a community not much given to mirth. Many a crowded lecture hall at Montpellier had seen him touch some intellectual firework with just such a twinkle behind his bristly gray brows, with just such a thin curl of lip.

"By way of celebration," he explained. "Consider. There are seventy-five evasions from Nouméa every six months, of which not more than one succeeds. I had the figures myself from Dr. Pierre at the infirmary. He is not much of a physician, but a very honest fellow. Could anybody win on that percentage without dissipating? I ask you."

"Therefore you prepared for this?"

"It is now three weeks since I bribed the night guard to get these same nippers."

The other regarded him with admiration. Sentiment came readily upon this beardless face, tender and languid, but overdrawn, with eyes too large and soft and oval too long. It was one of those faces familiar enough to the police which might serve as model for an angel were it not associated with some revolting piece of deviltry. Fenayrou himself had been condemned "to perpetuity" as an incorrigible.

"Is not our doctor a wonder?" he inquired as he handed a cigarette along to the third white man. "He

thinks of everything. You should be ashamed to
grumble. See—we are free, after all. Free!"

The third was a gross, pock-marked man with hair-
less lids known sometimes as Niniche, Trois Huit, Le
Tordeur, but chiefly among copains as Perroquet—a
name derived perhaps from his beaked nose, or from
some perception of his jailbird character. He was a
garroter by profession, accustomed to rely upon his
fists only for the exchange of amenities. Dubosc might
indulge a fancy and Fenayrou seek to carry it as a pose,
but The Parrot remained a gentleman of strictly serious turn. There is perhaps a tribute to the practical
spirit of penal administration in the fact that while
Dubosc was the most dangerous of these three and
Fenayrou the most depraved, Perroquet was the one
with the official reputation, whose escape would be
signaled first among the "Wanted." He accepted the
cigaret because he was glad to get it, but he said nothing until Dubosc passed a tin box of matches and the
first gulp of picadura filled his lungs. . . .

"Wait till you've got your two feet on a pave, my
boy. That will be the time to talk of freedom. What?
Suppose there came a storm."

"It is not the season of storms," observed Dubosc.

But The Parrot's word had given them a check.
Such spirits as these, to whom the land had been a
horror, would be slow to feel the terror of the sea.
Back there they had left the festering limbo of a con-
vict colony, oblivion. Out here they had reached the
rosy threshold of the big round world again. They
were men raised from the dead, charged with all the
furious appetites of lost years, with the savor of life
strong and sweet on their lips. And yet they paused
and looked about in quickened perception, with the

clutch at the throat that takes the landsman on big waters. The spaces were so wide and empty. The voices in their ears were so strange and murmurous. There was a threat in each wave that came from the depths, a sinister vibration. None of them knew the sea. None knew its ways, what tricks it might play, what traps it might spread—more deadly than those of the jungle.

The raft was running now before a brisk chop with alternate spring and wallow, while the froth bubbled in over the prow and ran down among them as they sat. "Where is that cursed ship that was to meet us here?" demanded Fenayrou.

"It will meet us right enough." Dubosc spoke carelessly, tho behind the blown wisp of his cigaret he had been searching the outer horizon with keen glance. "This is the day, as agreed. We will be picked up off the mouth of the river."

"You say," growled Perroquet. "But where is any river now? Or any mouth? Sacred name! this wind will blow us to China if we keep on."

"We dare not lie in any closer. There is a government launch at Torrien. Also the traders go armed hereabouts, ready for chaps like us. And don't imagine that the native trackers have given us up. They are likely to be following still in their proas."

"So far!"

Fenayrou laughed, for The Parrot's dread of their savage enemies had a morbid tinge.

"Take care, Perroquet. They will eat you yet."

"Is it true?" demanded the other, appealing to Dubosc. "I have heard it is even permitted these devils to keep all runaways they can capture—Name of God! —to fatten on."

"An idle tale," smiled Dubosc. "They prefer the reward. But one hears of convicts being badly mauled. There was a forester who made a break from Baie du Sud and came back lacking an arm. Certainly these people have not lost the habit of cannibalism."

"Piecemeal," chuckled Fenayrou. "They will only sample you, Perroquet. Let them make a stew of your brains. You would miss nothing."

But The Parrot swore.

"Name of a name—what brutes!" he said, and by a gesture recalled the presence of that fourth man who was of their party and yet so completely separated from them that they had almost forgotten him.

The Canaque was steering the raft. He sat crouched at the stern, his body glistening like varnished ebony with spray. He held the steering paddle, immobile as an image, his eyes fixed upon the course ahead.

There was no trace whatever of expression on his face, no hint of what he thought or felt or whether he thought or felt anything. He seemed not even aware of their regard, and each one of them experienced somehow that twinge of uneasiness with which the white always confronts his brother of color—this enigma brown or yellow or black he is fated never wholly to understand or to fathom. . . .

"It occurs to me," said Fenayrou, in a pause, "that our friend here who looks like a shiny boot is able to steer us God knows where. Perhaps to claim the reward."

"Reassure yourself," answered Dubosc. "He steers by my order. Besides, it is a simple creature—an infant, truly, incapable of any but the most primitive reasoning."

"Is he incapable of treachery?"

"Of any that would deceive us. Also, he is bound
by his duty. I made my bargain with his chief, up
the river, and this one is sent to deliver us on board
our ship. It is the only interest he has in us."

"And he will do it?"

"He will do it. Such is the nature of the native."

"I am glad you feel so," returned Fenayrou, adjusting himself indolently among the drier reeds and
nursing the last of his cigaret. "For my part I
wouldn't trust a figurehead like that for two sous.
Mazette! What a monkey face!"

"Brute!" repeated Perroquet, and this man, sprung
from some vile river-front slum of Argenteuil, whose
home had been the dock pilings, the grog shop, and
the jail, even this man viewed the black Canaque from
an immeasurable distance with the look of hatred and
contempt. . . .

Under the heat of the day the two younger convicts
lapsed presently into dozing. But Dubosc did not doze.
His tormented soul peered out behind its mask as he
stood to sweep the sky line again under shaded hand.
His theory had been so precise, the fact was so different.
He had counted absolutely on meeting the ship—some
small schooner, one of those flitting, half-piratical traders of the copra islands that can be hired like cabs in a
dark street for any questionable enterprise. Now there
was no ship, and there was no cross-roads where one
might sit and wait. Such a craft as the catamaran
could not be made to lie to.

The doctor foresaw ugly complications for which he
had not prepared and whereof he must bear the burden.
The escape had been his own conception, directed by
him from the start. He had picked his companions de-

liberately from the whole forced labor squad, Perroquet for his great strength, Fenayrou as a ready echo. He had made it plain since their first dash from the mine, during their skirmish with the military guards, their subsequent wanderings in the brush with bloodhounds and trackers on the trail—through every crisis—that he alone should be the leader.

For the others, they had understood well enough which of their number was the chief beneficiary. Those mysterious friends on the outside that were reaching half around the world to further their release had never heard of such individuals as Fenayrou and The Parrot. Dubosc was the man who had pulled the wires: that brilliant physician whose conviction for murder had followed so sensationally, so scandalously, upon his sweep of academic and social honors. There would be clacking tongues in many a Parisian salon, and white faces in some, when news should come of his escape. Ah, yes, for example, they knew the highflyer of the band, and they submitted—so long as he led them to victory. They submitted, while reserving a depth of jealousy, the inevitable remnant of caste persisting still in this democracy of stripes and shame.

By the middle of the afternoon the doctor had taken certain necessary measures.

"Ho," said Fenayrou sleepily. "Behold our colors at the masthead. What is that for, comrade?"

The sail had been lowered and in its place streamed the scrap of crimson scarf that had served Dubosc as a turban.

"To help them sight us when the ship comes."

"What wisdom!" cried Fenayrou. "Always he thinks of everything, our doctor: everything—"

He stopped with the phrase on his lips and his hand

outstretched toward the center of the platform. Here, in a damp depression among the reeds, had lain the wicker-covered bottle of green glass in which they carried their water. It was gone.

"Where is that flask?" he demanded. "The sun has grilled me like a bone."

"You will have to grill some more," said Dubosc grimly. "This crew is put on rations."

Fenayrou stared at him wide-eyed, and from the shadow of a folded mat The Parrot thrust his purpled face. "What do you sing me there? Where is that water?"

"I have it," said Dubosc.

They saw, in fact, that he held the flask between his knees, along with their single packet of food in its wrapping of cocoanut husk.

"I want a drink," challenged Perroquet.

"Reflect a little. We must guard our supplies like reasonable men. One does not know how long we may be floating here." . . .

Fell a silence among them, heavy and strained, in which they heard only the squeaking of frail basketwork as their raft labored in the wash. Slow as was their progress, they were being pushed steadily outward and onward, and the last cliffs of New Caledonia were no longer even a smudge in the west, but only a hazy line. And still they had seen no moving thing upon the great round breast of the sea that gleamed in its corselet of brass plates under a brazen sun. "So that is the way you talk now?" began The Parrot, half choking. "You do not know how long? But you were sure enough when we started."

"I am still sure," returned Dubosc. "The ship will come. Only she cannot stay for us in one spot. She will be cruising to and fro until she intercepts us. We must wait."

"Ah, good! We must wait. And in the meantime, what? Fry here in the sacred heat with our tongues hanging out while you deal us drop by drop—hein?"

"Perhaps."

"But no!" The garroter clenched his hands. "Blood of God, there is no man big enough to feed me with a spoon!"

Fenayrou's chuckle came pat, as it had more than once, and Dubosc shrugged.

"You laugh!" cried Perroquet, turning in fury. "But how about this lascar of a captain that lets us put to sea unprovided? What? He thinks of everything, does he? He thinks of everything! . . . Sacred farceur—let me hear you laugh again!"

Somehow Fenayrou was not so minded.

"And now he bids us be reasonable," concluded The Parrot. "Tell that to the devils in hell. You and your cigarets, too. Bah—comedian!"

"It is true," muttered Fenayrou, frowning. "A bad piece of work for a captain of runaways."

But the doctor faced mutiny with his thin smile.

"All this alters nothing. Unless we would die very speedily, we must guard our water."

"By whose fault?"

"Mine," acknowledged the doctor. "I admit it. What then? We can't turn back. Here we are. Here we must stay. We can only do our best with what we have."

"I want a drink," repeated The Parrot, whose throat was afire since he had been denied.

"You can claim your share, of course. But take

warning of one thing. After it is gone do not think to sponge on us—on Fenayrou and me."

"He would be capable of it, the pig!" exclaimed Fenayrou, to whom this thrust had been directed. "I know him. See here, my old, the doctor is right. Fair for one, fair for all."

"I want a drink."

Dubosc removed the wooden plug from the flask.

"Very well," he said quietly.

With the delicacy that lent something of legerdemain to all his gestures, he took out a small canvas wallet, the crudest equivalent of the professional black bag, from which he drew a thimble. Meticulously he poured a brimming measure, and Fenayrou gave a shout at the grumbler's fallen jaw as he accepted that tiny cup between his big fingers. Dubosc served Fenayrou and himself with the same amount before he recorked the bottle.

"In this manner we should have enough to last us three days—maybe more—with equal shares among the three of us." . . .

Such was his summing of the demonstration, and it passed without comment, as a matter of course in the premises, that he should count as he did—ignoring that other who sat alone at the stern of the raft, the black Canaque, the fourth man.

Perroquet had been outmaneuvered, but he listened sullenly while for the hundredth time Dubosc recited his easy and definite plan for their rescue, as arranged with his secret correspondents.

"That sounds very well," observed The Parrot, at last. "But what if these jokers only mock themselves of you? What if they have counted it good riddance to let you rot here? And us? Sacred name, that would be a famous jest! To let us wait for a ship and they have no ship!"

"Perhaps the doctor knows better than we how sure a source he counts upon," suggested Fenayrou slyly.

"That is so," said Dubosc, with great good humor. "My faith, it would not be well for them to fail me. Figure to yourselves that there is a safety vault in Paris full of papers to be opened at my death. Certain friends of mine could hardly afford to have some little confessions published that would be found there. . . . Such a tale as this, for instance—"

And to amuse them he told an indecent anecdote of high life, true or fictitious, it mattered nothing, so he could make Fenayrou's eyes glitter and The Parrot growl in wonder. Therein lay his means of ascendancy over such men, the knack of eloquence and vision. Harried, worn, oppressed by fears that he could sense so much more sharply than they, he must expend himself now in vulgar marvels to distract these ruder minds. He succeeded so far that when the wind fell at sunset they were almost cheerful, ready to believe that the morning would bring relief. They dined on dry biscuit and another thimbleful of water apiece and took watch by amiable agreement. And through that long, clear night of stars, whenever the one of the three who lay awake between his comrades chanced to look aft, he could see the vague blot of another figure—the naked Canaque, who slumbered there apart. . . .

It was an evil dawning. Fenayrou, on the morning trick, was aroused by a foot as hard as a hoof, and started up at Perroquet's wrathful face, with the doctor's graver glance behind.

"Idler! Good-for-nothing! Will you wake at least

before I smash your ribs? Name of God, here is a way to stand watch!"

"Keep off!" cried Fenayrou wildly. "Keep off. Don't touch me!"

"Eh, and why not, fool? Do you know that the ship could have missed us? A ship could have passed us a dozen times while you slept!"

"Bourrique!"

"Vache!"

They spat the insults of the prison while Perroquet knotted his great fist over the other, who crouched away catlike, his mobile mouth twisted to a snarl. Dubosc stood aside in watchful calculation until against the angry red sunrise in which they floated there flashed the naked red gleam of steel. Then he stepped between.

"Enough. Fenayrou, put up that knife."

"The dog kicked me!"

"You were at fault," said Dubosc sternly. "Perroquet!"

"Are we all to die that he may sleep?" stormed The Parrot.

"The harm is done. Listen now, both of you. Things are bad enough already. We may need all our energies Look about."

They looked and saw the far, round horizon and the empty desert of the sea and their own long shadows that slipped slowly before them over its smooth, slow heaving, and nothing else. The land had sunk away from them in the night—some one of the chance currents that sweep among the islands had drawn them none could say where or how far. The trap had been sprung. "Good God, how lonely it is!" breathed Fenayrou in a hush.

No more was said. They dropped their quarrel. Silently they shared their rations as before, made shift to eat something with their few drops of water, and sat down to pit themselves one against another in the vital struggle that each could feel was coming—a sort of tacit test of endurance.

A calm had fallen, as it does between trades in this flawed belt, an absolute calm. The air hung weighted. The sea showed no faintest crinkle, only the maddening, unresting heave and fall in polished undulations on which the lances of the sun broke and drove in under their eyelids as white-hot splinters; a savage sun that kindled upon them with the power of a burning glass, that sucked the moisture from poor human bits of jelly and sent them crawling to the shelter of their mats and brought them out again, gasping, to shrivel anew. The water, the world of water, seemed sleek and thick as oil. They came to loathe it and the rotting smell of it, and when the doctor made them dip themselves overside they found little comfort. It was warm, sluggish, slimed. But a curious thing resulted.

While they clung along the edge of the raft they all faced inboard, and there sat the black Canaque. He did not join them. He did not glance at them. He sat hunkered on his heels in the way of the native, with arms hugging his knees. He stayed in his place at the stern, motionless under that shattering sun gazing out into vacancy. Whenever they raised their eyes they saw him. He was the only thing to see.

"Here is one who appears to enjoy himself quite well," remarked Dubosc.

"I was thinking so myself," said Fenayrou.

"The animal!" rumbled Perroquet.

They observed him, and for the first time with direct interest, with thought of him as a fellow being—with the beginning of envy.

"He does not seem to suffer."

"What is going on in his brain? What does he dream of there? One would say he despises us."

"The beast!"

"Perhaps he is waiting for us to die," suggested Fenayrou with a harsh chuckle. "Perhaps he is waiting for the reward. He would not starve on the way home, at least. And he could deliver us—piecemeal."

They studied him.

"How does he do it, doctor? Has he no feeling?"

"I have been wondering," said Dubosc. "It may be that his fibers are tougher—his nerves."

"Yet we have had water and he none."

"But look at his skin, fresh and moist."

"And his belly, fat as a football!"

The Parrot hauled himself aboard.

"Don't tell me this black beast knows thirst!" he cried with a strange excitement. "Is there any way he could steal our supplies?"

"Certainly not."

"Then, name of a dog, what if he has supplies of his own hidden about?"

The same monstrous notion struck them all, and the others swarmed to help. They knocked the black aside. They searched the platform where he had sat, burrowing among the rushes, seeking some secret cache, another bottle or a gourd. They found nothing.

"We were mistaken," said Dubosc.

But Perroquet had a different expression for disappointment. He turned on the Canaque and caught him by the kinky mop of the hair and proceeded to give him what is known as gruel in the cobalt mines. This was a little specialty of The Parrot's. He paused only when he himself was breathless and exhausted and threw the limp, unresisting body from him.

"There, lump of dirt! That will teach you. Maybe you're not so chipper now, my boy—hein? Not quite so satisfied with your luck. Pig! That will make you feel." . . .

It was a ludicrous, a wanton, a witless thing. But the others said nothing. The learned Dubosc made no protest. Fenayrou had none of his usual jests at the garroter's stupidity. They looked on as at the satisfaction of a common grudge. The white trampled the black with or without cause, and that was natural. And the black crept away into his place with his hurts and his wrongs and made no sign and struck no blow. And that was natural too.

The sun declined into a blazing furnace whereof the gates stood wide, and they prayed to hasten it and cursed because it hung enchanted. But when it was gone their blistered bodies still held the heat like things incandescent. The night closed down over them like a purple bowl, glazed and impermeable. They would have divided the watches again, though none of them thought of sleep, but Fenayrou made a discovery.

"Idiots!" he rasped. "Why should we look and look? A whole navy of ships cannot help us now. If we are becalmed, why so are they!"

The Parrot was singularly put out.

"Is this true?" he asked Dubosc.

"Yes, we must hope for a breeze first."

"Then, name of God, why didn't you tell us so? Why did you keep on playing out the farce?"

He pondered it for a time. "See here," he said. "You are wise, eh? You are very wise. You know things we do not and you keep them to yourself." He leaned forward to peer into the doctor's face. "Very good. But if you think you're going to use that cursed smartness to get the best of us in any way—see here, my zig, I pull your gullet out like the string of an orange. . . . Like that. What?"

Fenayrou gave a nervous giggle and Dubosc shrugged, but it was perhaps about this time that he began to regret his intervention in the knife play.

For there was no breeze and there was no ship.

By the third morning each had sunk within himself, away from the rest. The doctor was lost in a profound depression, Perroquet in dark suspicion, and Fenayrou in bodily suffering, which he supported ill. Only two effective ties still bound their confederacy. One was the flask which Dubosc had slung at his side by a strip of the wickerwork. Every move he made with it, every drop he poured, was followed by burning eyes. And he knew and he had no advantage of them in knowing that the will to live was working its relentless formula aboard that raft. Under his careful saving there still remained nearly half of their original store.

The other bond, as it had come to be by strange mutation, was the presence of the black Canaque.

There was no forgetting the fourth man now, no overlooking of him. He loomed upon their consciousness, more formidable, more mysterious, more exasperating with every hour. Their own powers were ebbing. The naked savage had yet to give the slightest sign of complaint or weakness.

During the night he had stretched himself out on

the platform as before, and after a time he had slept. Through the hours of darkness and silence while each of the whites wrestled with despair, this black man had slept as placidly as a child, with easy, regular breathing. Since then he had resumed his place aft. And so he remained, unchanged, a fixed fact and a growing wonder.

The brutal rage of Perroquet, in which he had vented his distorted hate of the native, had been followed by superstitious doubts.

"Doctor," he said at last, in awed huskiness, "is this a man or a fiend?"

"It is a man."

"A miracle," put in Fenayrou.

But the doctor lifted a finger in a way his pupils would have remembered.

"It is a man," he repeated, "and a very poor and wretched example of a man. You will find no lower type anywhere. Observe his cranial angle, the high ears, the heavy bones of his skull. He is scarcely above the ape. There are educated apes more intelligent."

"Ah? Then what?"

"He has a secret," said the doctor.

That was a word to transfix them.

"A secret! But we see him—every move he makes, every instant. What chance for a secret?"

The doctor rather forgot his audience, betrayed by chagrin and bitterness.

"How pitiful!" he mused. "Here are we three— children of the century, products of civilization—I fancy none would deny that, at least. And here is this man who belongs before the Stone Age. In a set trial of fitness, of wits, of resource, is he to win? Pitiful!"

"What kind of secret?" demanded Perroquet fuming.

"I cannot say," admitted Dubosc, with a baffled gesture. "Possibly some method of breathing, some peculiar posture that operates to cheat the sensations of the body. Such things are known among primitive peoples—known and carefully guarded—like the properties of certain drugs, the uses of hypnotism and complex natural laws. Then, again, it may be psychologic—a mental attitude persistently held. Who knows? . . .

"To ask him? Useless. He will not tell. Why should he? We scorn him. We give him no share with us. We abuse him. He simply falls back on his own expedients. He simply remains inscrutable—as he has always been and will always be. He never tells those innermost secrets. They are the means by which he has survived from the depth of time, by which he may yet survive when all our wisdom is dust."

"I know several very excellent ways of learning secrets," said Fenayrou as he passed his dry tongue over his lips. "Shall I begin?"

Dubosc came back with a start and looked at him.

"It would be useless. He could stand any torture you could invent. No, that is not the way."

"Listen to mine," said Perroquet, with sudden violence. "Me, I am wearied of the gab. You say he is a man? Very well. If he is a man, he must have blood in his veins. That would be, anyway, good to drink."

"No," returned Dubosc. "It would be hot. Also it would be salt. For food—perhaps. But we do not need food."

"Kill the animal, then, and throw him over!"

"We gain nothing."

"Well, sacred name, what do you want?"

"To beat him!" cried the doctor, curiously agitated. "To beat him at the game—that's what I want! For our own sakes, for our racial pride, we must, we must. To outlast him, to prove ourselves his masters. By better brain, by better organization and control. Watch him, watch him, friends—that we may ensnare him, that we may detect and defeat him in the end!"

But the doctor was miles beyond them.

"Watch?" growled The Parrot. "I believe you, old windbag. It is all one watch. I sleep no more and leave any man alone with that bottle."

To this the issue finally sharpened. Such craving among such men could not be stayed much longer by driblets. They watched. They watched the Canaque. They watched each other. And they watched the falling level in their flask—until the tension gave.

Another dawn upon the same dead calm, rising like a conflagration through the puddled air, cloudless, hopeless! Another day of blinding, slow-drawn agony to meet. And Dubosc announced that their allowance must be cut to half a thimbleful.

There remained perhaps a quarter of a liter—a miserable reprieve of bare life among the three of them, but one good swallow for a yearning throat.

At sight of the bottle, at the tinkle of its limpid content, so cool and silvery green inside the glass, Fenayrou's nerve snapped. . . .

"More!" he begged, with pleading hands. "I die. More!"

When the doctor refused him he groveled among the reeds, then rose suddenly to his knees and tossed his arms abroad with a hoarse cry:

"A ship! A ship!"

The others span about. They saw the thin unbroken ring of this greater and more terrible prison to which they had exchanged: and that was all they saw, though they stared and stared. They turned back to Fenayrou and found him in the act of tilting the bottle. A cunning slash of his knife had loosed it from its sling at the doctor's side. . . . Even now he was sucking at the mouth, spilling the precious liquid—

With one sweep Perroquet caught up their paddle and flattened him, crushed him.

Springing across the prostrate man, Dubosc snatched the flask upright and put the width of the raft between himself and the big garroter who stood wide-legged, his bloodshot eyes alight, rumbling in his chest.

"There is no ship," said The Parrot. "There will be no ship. We are done. Because of you and your rotten promises that brought us here—doctor, liar, ass!"

Dubosc stood firm.

"Come a step nearer and I break bottle and all over your head."

They stood regarding each other, and Perroquet's brows gathered in a slow effort of thought.

"Consider," urged Dubosc with his quaint touch of pedantry. "Why should you and I fight? We are rational men. We can see this trouble through and win yet. Such weather cannot last forever. Besides, here are only two of us to divide the water now."

"That is true," nodded The Parrot. "That is true, isn't it? Fenayrou kindly leaves us his share. An inheritance—what? A famous idea. I'll take mine now."

Dubosc probed him keenly.

"My share, at once, if you please." insisted Perroquet, with heavy docility. "Afterward, we shall see. Afterward."

The doctor smiled his grim and wan little smile.

"So be it."

Without relinquishing the flask he brought out his canvas wallet once more—that wallet which replaced the professional black bag—and rolled out the thimble by some swift sleight of his flexible fingers while he held Perroquet's glance with his own.

"I will measure it for you."

He poured the thimbleful and handed it over quickly, and when Perroquet had tossed it off he filled again and again.

"Four—five," he counted. "That is enough."

But The Parrot's big grip closed quietly around his wrist at the last offering and pinioned him and held him helpless.

"No, it is not enough. Now I will take the rest. Ha, wise man! Have I fooled you at last?"

There was no chance to struggle, and Dubosc did not try, only stayed smiling up at him, waiting.

Perroquet took the bottle.

"The best man wins," he remarked. "Eh, my zig? A bright notion—of yours. The—best—"

His lips moved, but no sound issued. A look of the most intense surprize spread upon his round face. He stood swaying a moment, and collapsed like a huge hinged toy when the string is cut.

Dubosc stooped and caught the bottle again, looking down at his big adversary, who sprawled in brief convulsion and lay still, a bluish scum oozing between his teeth. . . .

"Yes, the best man wins," repeated the doctor, and laughed as he in turn raised the flask for a draft.

"The best wins!" echoed a voice in his ear.

Fenayrou, writhing up and striking like a wounded snake, drove the knife home between his shoulders.

The bottle fell and rolled to the middle of the platform, and there, while each strove vainly to reach it, it poured out its treasure in a tiny stream that trickled away and was lost.

It may have been minutes or hours later—for time has no count in emptiness—when next a sound proceeded from that frail slip of a raft, hung like a mote between sea and sky. It was a phrase of song, a wandering strain in half tones and fluted accidentals, not unmelodious. The black Canaque was singing. He sang without emotion or effort, quite casually and softly to himself. So he might sing by his forest hut to ease some hour of idleness. Clasping his knees and gazing out into space, untroubled, unmoved, enigmatic to the end, he sang—he sang.

And, after all, the ship came.

She came in a manner befitting the sauciest little tops'l schooner between Nukahiva and the Pelews—as her owner often averred and none but the envious denied—in a manner worthy, too, of that able Captain Jean Guibert, the merriest little scamp that ever cleaned a pearl bank or snapped a cargo of labor from a scowling coast. Before the first whiff out of the west came the *Petite Suzanne*, curtsying and skipping along with a flash of white frill by her forefoot, and brought up startled and stood shaking her skirts and keeping herself quite daintily to windward.

"And 'ere they are sure enough, by dam!" said the polyglot Captain Jean in the language of commerce and profanity. "Zose passengers for us, hey? They ɔeen here all the time, not ten mile off—I bet you, Marteau. Ain't it 'ell? What you zink, my gar?"

His second, a tall and excessively bony individual of gloomy outlook, handed back the glasses.

"More bad luck. I never approved of this job. And now—see?—we have had our voyage for nothing. What misfortune!"

"Marteau, if that good Saint Pierre gives you some day a gold 'arp still you would holler bad luck—bad job!" retorted Captain Jean. "Do I 'ire you to stand zere and cry about ze luck? Get a boat over, and quicker zan zat!"

M. Marteau aroused himself sufficiently to take command of the boat's crew that presently dropped away to investigate. . . .

"It is even as I thought," he called up from the quarter when he returned with his report. "I told you how it would be, Captain Jean."

"Hey?" cried the captain, bouncing at the rail. "Have you got zose passengers yet, *enfant de salaud?*"

"I have not," said Marteau in the tone of lugubrious triumph. There was nothing in the world that could have pleased him quite so much as this chance to prove Captain Jean the loser on a venture. "We are too late. Bad luck, bad luck—that calm. What misforκune! They are all dead!"

"Will you mind your business?" shouted the skipper.

"But still, the gentlemen are dead—"

"What is zat to me? All ze better, they will cost ɔozing to feed."

"But how—"

"Hogsheads, my gar," said Captain Jean paternally. "Zose hogsheads in the afterhold. Fill them nicely with brine, and zere we are!" And, having drawn all possible satisfaction from the other's amazement, he sprang the nub of his joke with a grin. "Ze gentlemen's passage is all paid, Marteau. Before we left Sydney, Marteau. I contrac' to bring back three escape' convicts, and so by 'ell I do—in pickle! And now if you'll kindly get zose passengers aboard like I said an' bozzer less about ze goddam luck, I be much oblige'. Also, zere is no green on my eye, Marteau, and you can dam' well smoke it!"

Marteau recovered himself with difficulty in time to recall another trifling detail. "There is a fourth man on board that raft, Captain Jean. He is a Canaque—still alive. What shall we do with him?"

"A Canaque?" snapped Captain Jean. "A Canaque! I had no word in my contrac' about any Canaque. . . . Leave him zere. . . . He is only a dam' nigger. He'll do well enough where he is."

And Captain Jean was right, perfectly right, for while the *Petite Suzanne* was taking aboard her grisly cargo the wind freshened from the west, and just about the time she was shaping away for Australia the "dam' nigger" spread his own sail of pandanus leaves and twirled his own helm of niaouli wood and headed the catamaran eastward, back toward New Caledonia.

Feeling somewhat dry after his exertion, he plucked at random from the platform a hollow reed with a sharp end and, stretching himself at full length in his accustomed place at the stern, he thrust the reed down into one of the bladders underneath and drank his fill of sweet water. . . .

He had a dozen such storage bladders remaining, built into the floats at intervals above the water line—quite enough to last him safely home again.

THE MOST DANGEROUS GAME

By Richard Connell

"Off there to the right—somewhere—is a large island," said Whitney. "It's rather a mystery—"

"What island is it?" Rainsford asked.

"The old charts call it 'Ship-Trap Island,'" Whitney replied. "A suggestive name, isn't it? Sailors have a curious dread of the place. I don't know why. Some superstition—"

"Can't see it," remarked Rainsford, trying to peer through the dank tropical night that was palpable as it pressed its thick warm blackness in upon the yacht.

"You've good eyes," said Whitney, with a laugh, "and I've seen you pick off a moose moving in the brown fall bush at four hundred yards, but even you can't see four miles or so through a moonless Carribbean night."

"Nor four yards," admitted Rainsford. "Ugh! It's like moist black velvet."

"It will be light in Rio," promised Whitney. "We should make it in a few days. I hope the jaguar guns have come from Purdey's. We should have some good hunting up the Amazon. Great sport, hunting."

"The best sport in the world," agreed Rainsford.

"For the hunter," amended Whitney. "Not for the jaguar."

"Don't talk rot, Whitney," said Rainsford. "You're a big-game hunter, not a philosopher. Who cares how a jaguar feels?"

"Perhaps the jaguar does," observed Whitney.

"Bah! They've no understanding."

"Even so, I rather think they understand one thing —fear. The fear of pain and the fear of death."

"Nonsense," laughed Rainsford. "This hot weather is making you soft, Whitney. Be a realist. The world is made up of two classes—the hunters and the huntees. Luckily, you and I are hunters. Do you think we've passed that island yet?"

"I can't tell in the dark. I hope so."

"Why?" asked Rainsford.

"The place has a reputation—a bad one."

"Cannibals?" suggested Rainsford.

"Hardly. Even cannibals wouldn't live in such a God-forsaken place. But it's gotten into sailor lore, somehow. Didn't you notice that the crew's nerves seemed a bit jumpy to-day?"

"They were a bit strange, now you mention it. Even Captain Nielsen—"

"Yes, even that tough-minded old Swede, who'd go up to the devil himself and ask him for a light. Those fishy blue eyes held a look I never saw there before. All I could get out of him was: 'This place has an evil name among sea-faring men, sir.' Then he said to me, very gravely: 'Don't you feel anything?'—as if the air about us was actually poisonous. Now, you mustn't laugh when I tell you this—I did feel something like a sudden chill.

"There was no breeze. The sea was as flat as a plate-glass window. We were drawing near the island then. What I felt was a—a mental chill; a sort of sudden dread."

"Pure imagination," said Rainsford. "One superstitious sailor can taint the whole ship's company with his fear."

"Maybe. But sometimes I think sailors have an extra sense that tells them when they are in danger. Sometimes I think evil is a tangible thing—with wave lengths, just as sound and light have. An evil place can, so to speak, broadcast vibrations of evil. Anyhow, I'm glad we're getting out of this zone. Well, I think I'll turn in now, Rainsford."

"I'm not sleepy," said Rainsford. "I'm going to smoke another pipe up on the after deck."

"Good night, then, Rainsford. See you at breakfast."

"Right. Good night, Whitney."

There was no sound in the night as Rainsford sat there, but the muffled throb of the engine that drove the yacht swiftly through the darkness, and the swish and ripple of the wash of the propeller.

Rainsford, reclining in a steamer chair, indolently puffed on his favorite brier. The sensuous drowsiness of the night was on him. "It's so dark," he thought, "that I could sleep without closing my eyes; the night would be my eyelids—"

An abrupt sound startled him. Off to the right he heard it, and his ears, expert in such matters, could not be mistaken. Again he heard the sound, and again. Somewhere, off in the blackness, some one had fired a gun three times.

Rainsford sprang up and moved quickly to the rail, mystified. He strained his eyes in the direction from which the reports had come, but it was like trying to see through a blanket. He leaped upon the rail and balanced himself there, to get greater elevation; his pipe, striking a rope, was knocked from his mouth. He lunged for it; a short, hoarse cry came from his lips as he realized he had reached too far and had lost his balance. The cry was pinched off short as the blood-warm waters of the Caribbean Sea closed over his head.

He struggled up to the surface and tried to cry out, but the wash from the speeding yacht slapped him in the face and the salt water in his open mouth made him gag and strangle. Desperately he struck out with strong strokes after the receding lights of the yacht, but he stopped before he had swum fifty feet. A certain cool-headedness had come to him; it was not the first time he had been in a tight place. There was a chance that his cries could be heard by some one aboard the yacht, but that chance was slender, and grew more slender as the yacht raced on. He wrestled himself out of his clothes, and shouted with all his power. The lights of the yacht became faint and ever-vanishing fireflies; then they were blotted out entirely by the night.

Rainsford remembered the shots. They had come from the right, and doggedly he swam in that direction, swimming with slow, deliberate strokes, conserving his strength. For a seemingly endless time he fought the sea. He began to count his strokes; he could do possibly a hundred more and then—

Rainsford heard a sound. It came out of the darkness, a high, screaming sound, the sound of an animal in an extremity of anguish and terror.

He did not recognize the animal that made the sound; he did not try to; with fresh vitality he swam toward the sound. He heard it again; then it was cut short by another noise, crisp, staccato.

"Pistol shot," muttered Rainsford, swimming on.

Ten minutes of determined effort brought another sound to his ears—the most welcome he had ever heard—the muttering and growling of the sea breaking on a rocky shore. He was almost on the rocks before he saw them; on a night less calm he would have been shattered against them. With his remaining strength he dragged himself from the swirling waters. Jagged crags appeared to jut into the opaqueness, he forced himself upward, hand over hand. Gasping, his hands raw, he reached a flat place at the top. Dense jungle came down to the very edge of the cliffs. What perils that tangle of trees and underbrush might hold for him did not concern Rainsford just then. All he knew was that he was safe from his enemy, the sea, and that utter weariness was on him. He flung himself down at the jungle edge and tumbled headlong into the deepest sleep of his life.

When he opened his eyes he knew from the position of the sun that it was late in the afternoon. Sleep had given him new vigor; a sharp hunger was picking at him. He looked about him, almost cheerfully.

"Where there are pistol shots, there are men. Where there are men, there is food," he thought. But what kind of men, he wondered, in so forbidding a place? An unbroken front of snarled and ragged jungle fringed the shore.

He saw no sign of a trail through the closely knit web of weeds and trees; it was easier to go along the shore, and Rainsford floundered along by the water. Not far from where he had landed, he stopped.

Some wounded thing, by the evidence a large animal,

had thrashed about in the underbrush; the jungle weeds were crushed down and the moss was lacerated; one patch of weeds was stained crimson. A small, glittering object not far away caught Rainsford's eye and he picked it up. It was an empty cartridge.

"A twenty-two," he remarked. "That's odd. It must have been a fairly large animal too. The hunter had his nerve with him to tackle it with a light gun. It's clear that the brute put up a fight. I suppose the first three shots I heard was when the hunter flushed his quarry and wounded it. The last shot was when he trailed it here and finished it."

He examined the ground closely and found what he had hoped to find—the print of hunting boots. They pointed along the cliff in the direction he had been going. Eagerly he hurried along, now slipping on a rotten log or a loose stone, but making headway; night was beginning to settle down on the island.

Bleak darkness was blacking out the sea and jungle when Rainsford sighted the lights. He came upon them as he turned a crook in the coast line, and his first thought was that he had come upon a village, for there were many lights. But as he forged along he saw to his great astonishment that all the lights were in one enormous building—a lofty structure with pointed towers plunging upward into the gloom. His eyes made out the shadowy outlines of a palatial château; it was set on a high bluff, and on three sides of it cliffs dived down to where the sea licked greedy lips in the shadows.

"Mirage," thought Rainsford. But it was no mirage, he found, when he opened the tall spiked iron gate. The stone steps were real enough; the massive door with a leering gargoyle for a knocker was real enough; yet about it all hung an air of unreality.

He lifted the knocker, and it creaked up stiffly, as if it had never before been used. He let it fall, and it startled him with its booming loudness. He thought he heard steps within; the door remained closed. Again Rainsford lifted the heavy knocker, and let it fall. The door opened then, opened as suddenly as if it were on a spring, and Rainsford stood blinking in the river of glaring gold light that poured out. The first thing Rainsford's eyes discerned was the largest man Rainsford had ever seen—a gigantic creature, solidly made and black-bearded to the waist. In his hand the man held a long-barreled revolver, and he was pointing it straight at Rainsford's heart.

Out of the snarl of beard two small eyes regarded Rainsford.

"Don't be alarmed," said Rainsford, with a smile which he hoped was disarming. "I'm no robber. I fell off a yacht. My name is Sanger Rainsford of New York City."

The menacing look in the eyes did not change. The revolver pointed as rigidly as if the giant were a statue. He gave no sign that he understood Rainsford's words, or that he had even heard them. He was dressed in uniform, a black uniform trimmed with gray astrakhan.

"I'm Sanger Rainsford of New York," Rainsford began again. "I fell off a yacht. I am hungry."

The man's only answer was to raise with his thumb the hammer of his revolver. Then Rainsford saw the man's free hand go to his forehead in a military salute, and he saw him click his heels together and stand at attention. Another man was coming down the broad marble steps, an erect, slender man in evening clothes. He advanced to Rainsford and held out his hand.

In a cultivated voice marked by a slight accent that gave it added precision and deliberateness, he said: "It is a very great pleasure and honor to welcome Mr. Sanger Rainsford, the celebrated hunter, to my home."

Automatically Rainsford shook the man's hand.

"I've read your book about hunting snow leopards in Tibet, you see," explained the man. "I am General Zaroff."

Rainsford's first impression was that the man was singularly handsome; his second was that there was an original, almost bizarre quality about the general's face. He was a tall man past middle age, for his hair was a vivid white; but his thick eyebrows and pointed military mustache was as black as the night from which Rainsford had come. His eyes, too, were black and very bright. He had high cheek bones, a sharp-cut nose, a spare, dark face, the face of a man used to giving orders, the face of an aristocrat. Turning to the giant in uniform, the general made a sign. The giant put away his pistol, saluted, withdrew.

"Ivan is an incredibly strong fellow," remarked the general, "but he has the misfortune to be deaf and dumb. A simple fellow, but, I'm afraid, like all his race, a bit of a savage."

"Is he Russian?"

"He is a Cossack," said the general, and his smile showed red lips and pointed teeth. "So am I."

"Come," he said, "we shouldn't be chatting here. We can talk later. Now you want clothes, food, rest.

You shall have them. This is a most restful spot."

Ivan had reappeared, and the general spoke to him with lips that moved but gave forth no sound.

"Follow Ivan, if you please, Mr. Rainsford," said the general. "I was about to have my dinner when you came. I'll wait for you. You'll find that my clothes will fit you, I think."

It was to a huge, beam-ceilinged bedroom with a canopied bed big enough for six men that Rainsford followed the silent giant. Ivan laid out an evening suit, and Rainsford, as he put it on, noticed that it came from a London tailor who ordinarily cut and sewed for none below the rank of duke.

The dining room to which Ivan conducted him was in many ways remarkable. There was a medieval magnificence about it; it suggested a baronial hall of feudal times with its oaken panels, its high ceiling, its vast refectory table where twoscore men could sit down to eat. About the hall were the mounted heads of many animals—lions, tigers, elephants, moose, bears; larger or more perfect specimens Rainsford had never seen. At the great table the general was sitting, alone.

"You'll have a cocktail, Mr. Rainsford," he suggested. The cocktail was surpassingly good; and, Rainsford noted, the table appointments were of the finest—the linen, the crystal, the silver, the china.

They were eating *borsch*, the rich, red soup with whipped cream so dear to Russian palates. Half apologetically General Zaroff said: "We do our best to preserve the amenities of civilization here. Please forgive any lapses. We are well off the beaten track, you know. Do you think the champagne has suffered from its long ocean trip?"

"Not in the least," declared Rainsford. He was finding the general a most thoughtful and affable host, a true cosmopolite. But there was one small trait of the general's that made Rainsford uncomfortable. Whenever he looked up from his plate he found the general studying him, appraising him narrowly.

"Perhaps," said General Zaroff, "you were surprised that I recognized your name. You see, I read all books on hunting published in English, French, and Russian. I have but one passion in my life, Mr. Rainsford, and it is the hunt."

"You have some wonderful heads here," said Rainsford as he ate a particularly well cooked filet mignon. "That Cape buffalo is the largest I ever saw."

"Oh, that fellow. Yes, he was a monster."

"Did he charge you?"

"Hurled me against a tree," said the general. "Fractured my skull. But I got the brute."

"I've always thought," said Rainsford, "that the Cape buffalo is the most dangerous of all big game."

For a moment the general did not reply; he was smiling his curious red-lipped smile. Then he said slowly: "No. You are wrong, sir. The Cape buffalo is not the most dangerous big game." He sipped his wine. "Here in my preserve on this island," he said in the same slow tone, "I hunt more dangerous game."

Rainsford expressed his surprize. "Is there big game on this island?"

The general nodded. "The biggest."

"Really?"

"Oh, it isn't here naturally, of course. I have to stock the island."

"What have you imported, general?" Rainsford asked. "Tigers?"

The general smiled. "No," he said. "Hunting tigers ceased to interest me some years ago. I exhausted their possibilities, you see. No thrill left in tigers, no real danger. I live for danger, Mr. Rainsford."

The general took from his pocket a gold cigaret case and offered his guest a long black cigaret with a silver tip; it was perfumed and gave off a smell like incense.

"We will have some capital hunting, you and I," said the general. "I shall be most glad to have your society."

"But what game—" began Rainsford.

"I'll tell you," said the general. "You will be amused, I know. I think I may say, in all modesty, that I have done a rare thing. I have invented a new sensation. May I pour you another glass of port, Mr. Rainsford?"

"Thank you, general."

The general filled both glasses, and said: "God makes some men poets. Some He makes kings, some beggars. Me He made a hunter. My hand was made for the trigger, my father said. He was a very rich man with a quarter of a million acres in the Crimea, and he was an ardent sportsman. When I was only five years old he gave me a little gun, specially made in Moscow for me, to shoot sparrows with. When I shot some of his prize turkeys with it, he did not punish me; he complimented me on my marksmanship. I killed my first bear in the Caucasus when I was ten. My whole life has been one prolonged hunt. I went into the army—it was expected of noblemen's sons—and for a time commanded a division of Cossack cavalry, but my real interest was always the hunt.

I have hunted every kind of game in every land. It would be impossible for me to tell you how many animals I have killed."

The general puffed at his cigaret.

"After the debacle in Russia I left the country, for it was imprudent for an officer of the Czar to stay there.   Many noble Russians lost everything.   I, luckily, had invested heavily in American securities, so I shall never have to open a tea room in Monte Carlo or drive a taxi in Paris.   Naturally, I continued to hunt—grizzlies in your Rockies, crocodiles in the Ganges, rhinoceroses in East Africa.   It was in Africa that the Cape buffalo hit me and laid me up for six months.   As soon as I recovered I started for the Amazon to hunt jaguars, for I had heard they were unusually cunning.   They weren't."   The Cossack sighed.   "They were no match at all for a hunter with his wits about him, and a high-powered rifle.   I was bitterly disappointed.   I was lying in my tent with a splitting headache one night when a terrible thought pushed its way into my mind.   Hunting was beginning to bore me!   And hunting, remember, had been my life.   I have heard that in America business men often go to pieces when they give up the business that has been their life."

"Yes, that's so," said Rainsford.

The general smiled.   "I had no wish to go to pieces," he said.   "I must do something.   Now, mine is an analytical mind, Mr. Rainsford.   Doubtless that is why I enjoy the problems of the chase."

"No doubt, General Zaroff."

"So," continued the general, "I asked myself why the hunt no longer fascinated me.   You are much younger than I am, Mr. Rainsford, and have not hunted as much, but you perhaps can guess the answer."

"What was it?"

"Simply this: hunting had ceased to be what you call 'a sporting proposition.' It had become too easy. I always got my quarry. Always. There is no greater bore than perfection."

The general lit a fresh cigaret.

"No animal had a chance with me any more. That is no boast; it is a mathematical certainty. The animal had nothing but his legs and his instinct. Instinct is no match for reason. When I thought of this it was a tragic moment for me, I can tell you."

Rainsford leaned across the table, absorbed in what his host was saying.

"It came to me as an inspiration what I must do," the general went on.

"And that was?"

The general smiled the quiet smile of one who has faced an obstacle and surmounted it with success. "I had to invent a new animal to hunt," he said.

"A new animal? You're joking."

"Not at all," said the general. "I never joke about hunting. I needed a new animal. I found one. So I bought this island, built this house, and here I do my hunting. The island is perfect for my purposes—there are jungles with a maze of trails in them, hills, swamps—"

"But the animal, General Zaroff?"

"Oh," said the general, "it supplies me with the most exciting hunting in the world. No other hunting compares with it for an instant. Every day I hunt, and I never grow bored now, for I have a quarry with which I can match my wits."

Rainsford's bewilderment showed in his face.

"I wanted the ideal animal to hunt," explained the general. "So I said: 'What are the attributes of an ideal quarry?' And the answer was, of course: 'It must have courage, cunning, and, above all, it must be able to reason.'"

"But no animal can reason," objected Rainsford.

"My dear fellow," said the general, "there is one that can."

"But you can't mean—" gasped Rainsford.

"And why not?"

"I can't believe you are serious, General Zaroff. This is a grisly joke."

"Why should I not be serious? I am speaking of hunting."

"Hunting? Good God, General Zaroff, what you speak of is murder."

The general laughed with entire good nature. He regarded Rainsford quizzically. "I refuse to believe that so modern and civilized a young man as you seem to be harbors romantic ideas about the value of human life. Surely your experiences in the war—"

"Did not make me condone cold-blooded murder," finished Rainsford stiffly.

Laughter shook the general. "How extraordinarily droll you are!" he said. "One does not expect nowadays to find a young man of the educated class, even in America, with such a naive, and, if I may say so, mid-Victorian point of view. It's like finding a snuffbox in a limousine. Ah, well, doubtless you had Puritan ancestors. So many Americans appear to have had. I'll wager you'll forget your notions when you go hunting with me. You've a genuine new thrill in store for you, Mr. Rainsford."

"Thank you, I'm a hunter, not a murderer."

"Dear me," said the general, quite unruffled, "again that unpleasant word. But I think I can show you that your scruples are quite ill founded."

"Yes?"

"Life is for the strong, to be lived by the strong, and, if needs be, taken by the strong. The weak of the world were put here to give the strong pleasure. I am strong. Why should I not use my gift? If I wish to hunt, why should I not? I hunt the scum of the earth—sailors from tramp ships—lascars, blacks, Chinese, whites, mongrels—a thorobred horse or hound is worth more than a score of them."

"But they are men," said Rainsford hotly.

"Precisely," said the general. "That is why I use them. It gives me pleasure. They can reason, after a fashion. So they are dangerous."

"But where do you get them?"

The general's left eyelid fluttered down in a wink. "This island is called Ship Trap," he answered. "Sometimes an angry god of the high seas sends them to me. Sometimes, when Providence is not so kind, I help Providence a bit. Come to the window with me."

Rainsford went to the window and looked out toward the sea.

"Watch! Out there!" exclaimed the general, pointing into the night. Rainsford's eyes saw only blackness, and then, as the general pressed a button, far out to sea Rainsford saw the flash of lights.

The general chuckled. "They indicate a channel," he said, "where there's none: giant rocks with razor edges crouch like a sea monster with wide-open jaws.

They can crush a ship as easily as I crush this nut. He dropped a walnut on the hardwood floor and brought his heel grinding down on it. "Oh, yes," he said, casually, as if in answer to a question, "I have electricity. We try to be civilized here."

"Civilized? And you shoot down men?"

A trace of anger was in the general's black eyes, but it was there for but a second, and he said, in his most pleasant manner: "Dear me, what a righteous young man you are! I assure you I do not do the thing you suggest. That would be barbarous. I treat these visitors with every consideration. They get plenty of good food and exercize. They get into splendid physical condition. You shall see for yourself to-morrow."

"What do you mean?"

"We'll visit my training school," smiled the general "It's in the cellar. I have about a dozen pupils down there now. They're from the Spanish bark San Lucar that had the bad luck to go on the rocks out there. A very inferior lot, I regret to say. Poor specimens and more accustomed to the deck than to the jungle."

He raised his hand, and Ivan, who served as waiter, brought thick Turkish coffee. Rainsford, with an effort, held his tongue in check.

"It's a game, you see," pursued the general blandly. "I suggest to one of them that we go hunting. I give him a supply of food and an excellent hunting knife. I give him three hours' start. I am to follow, armed only with a pistol of the smallest caliber and range. If my quarry eludes me for three whole days, he wins the game. If I find him"—the general smiled—"he loses."

"Suppose he refuses to be hunted?"

"Oh," said the general, "I give him his option, of course. He need not play that game if he doesn't wish to. If he does not wish to hunt, I turn him over to Ivan. Ivan once had the honor of serving as official knouter to the Great White Czar, and he has his own ideas of sport. Invariably, Mr. Rainsford, invariably they choose the hunt."

"And if they win?"

The smile on the general's face widened. "To date I have not lost," he said.

Then he added, hastily: "I don't wish you to think me a braggart, Mr. Rainsford. Many of them afford only the most elementary sort of problem. Occasionally I strike a tartar. One almost did win. I eventually had to use the dogs."

"The dogs?"

"This way, please. I'll show you."

The general steered Rainsford to a window. The lights from the windows sent a flickering illumination that made grotesque patterns on the courtyard below, and Rainsford could see moving about there a dozen or so huge black shapes; as they turned toward him, their eyes glittered greenly.

"A rather good lot, I think," observed the general. "They are let out at seven every night. If anyone should try to get into my house—or out of it—something extremely regrettable would occur to him." He hummed a snatch of song from the Folies Bergère.

"And now," said the general, "I want to show you my new collection of heads. Will you come with me to the library?"

"I hope," said Rainsford, "that you will excuse me to-night, General Zaroff. I'm really not feeling at all well."

"Ah, indeed?" the general inquired solicitously. "Well, I suppose that's only natural, after your long swim. You need a good, restful night's sleep. To-morrow you'll feel like a new man, I'll wager. Then we'll hunt, eh? I've one rather promising prospect—"

Rainsford was hurrying from the room.

"Sorry you can't go with me to-night," called the general. "I expect rather fair sport—a big, strong black. He looks resourceful— Well, good night, Mr. Rainsford; I hope you have a good night's rest."

The bed was good, and the pajamas of the softest silk, and he was tired in every fiber of his being, but nevertheless Rainsford could not quiet his brain with the opiate of sleep. He lay, eyes wide open. Once he thought he heard stealthy steps in the corridor outside his room. He sought to throw open the door; it would not open. He went to the window and looked out. His room was high up in one of the towers. The lights of the château were out now, and it was dark and silent, but there was a fragment of sallow moon, and by its wan light he could see, dimly, the courtyard; there, weaving in and out in the pattern of shadow, were black, noiseless forms; the hounds heard him at the window and looked up, expectantly, with their green eyes. Rainsford went back to the bed and lay down. By many methods he tried to put himself to sleep. He had achieved a doze when, just as morning began to come, he heard, far off in the jungle, the faint report of a pistol.

General Zaroff did not appear until luncheon. He was dressed faultlessly in the tweeds of a country squire. He was solicitous about the state of Rains-ford's health.

"As for me," sighed the general, "I do not feel so

well. I am worried, Mr. Rainsford. Last night I detected traces of my old complaint."

To Rainsford's questioning glance the general said: "Ennui. Boredom."

Then, taking a second helping of Crêpes Suzette, the general explained: "The hunting was not good last night. The fellow lost his head. He made a straight trail that offered no problems at all. That's the trouble with these sailors; they have dull brains to begin with, and they do not know how to get about in the woods. They do excessively stupid and obvious things. It's most annoying. Will you have another glass of Chablis, Mr. Rainsford?"

"General," said Rainsford firmly, "I wish to leave this island at once."

The general raised his thickets of eyebrows; he seemed hurt. "But, my dear fellow," the general protested, "you've only just come. You've had no hunting—"

"I wish to go to-day," said Rainsford. He saw the dead black eyes of the general on him, studying him. General Zaroff's face suddenly brightened.

He filled Rainsford's glass with venerable Chablis from a dusty bottle.

"To-night," said the general, "we will hunt—you and I."

Rainsford shook his head. "No, general," he said. "I will not hunt."

The general shrugged his shoulders and delicately ate a hothouse grape. "As you wish, my friend," he said. "The choice rests entirely with you. But may I not venture to suggest that you will find my idea of sport more diverting than Ivan's?"

He nodded toward the corner to where the giant

stood, scowling, his thick arms crossed on his hogshead of chest.

"You don't mean—" cried Rainsford.

"My dear fellow," said the general, "have I not told you I always mean what I say about hunting? This is really an inspiration. I drink to a foeman worthy of my steel—at last."

The general raised his glass, but Rainsford sat staring at him.

"You'll find this game worth playing," the general said enthusiastically. "Your brain against mine. Your woodcraft against mine. Your strength and stamina against mine. Outdoor chess! And the stake is not without value, eh?"

"And if I win—" began Rainsford huskily.

"I'll cheerfully acknowledge myself defeated if I do not find you by midnight of the third day," said General Zaroff. "My sloop will place you on the mainland near a town."

The general read what Rainsford was thinking.

"Oh, you can trust me," said the Cossack. "I will give you my word as a gentleman and a sportsman. Of course you, in turn, must agree to say nothing of your visit here."

"I'll agree to nothing of the kind," said Rainsford.

"Oh," said the general, "in that case— But why discuss that now? Three days hence we can discuss it over a bottle of Veuve Cliquot, unless—"

The general sipped his wine.

Then a businesslike air animated him. "Ivan," he said to Rainsford, "will supply you with hunting clothes, food, a knife. I suggest you wear moccasins; they leave a poorer trail. I suggest too that you avoid the big swamp in the southeast corner of the island.

We call it Death Swamp. There's quicksand there. One foolish fellow tried it. The deplorable part of it was that Lazarus followed him. You can imagine my feelings, Mr. Rainsford. I loved Lazarus; he was the finest hound in my pack. Well, I must beg you to excuse me now. I always take a siesta after lunch. You'll hardly have time for a nap, I fear. You'll want to start, no doubt. I shall not follow till dusk. Hunting at night is so much more exciting than by day, don't you think? Au revoir, Mr. Rainsford, au revoir."

General Zaroff, with a deep, courtly bow, strolled from the room.

From another door came Ivan. Under one arm he carried khaki hunting clothes, a haversack of food, a leather sheath containing a long-bladed hunting knife; his right hand rested on a cocked revolver thrust in the crimson sash about his waist. . . .

Rainsford had fought his way through the bush for two hours. "I must keep my nerve. I must keep my nerve," he said through tight teeth.

He had not been entirely clear-headed when the château gates snapped shut behind him. His whole idea at first was to put distance between himself and General Zaroff, and, to this end, he had plunged along, spurred on by the sharp rowels of something very like panic. Now he had got a grip on himself, had stopped, and was taking stock of himself and the situation.

He saw that straight flight was futile; inevitably it would bring him face to face with the sea. He was in a picture with a frame of water, and his operations, clearly, must take place within that frame.

"I'll give him a trail to follow," muttered Rainsford, and he struck off from the rude path he had been fol-

lowing into the trackless wilderness. He executed a
series of intricate loops; he doubled on his trail again
and again, recalling all the lore of the fox hunt, and
all the dodges of the fox. Night found him leg-weary,
with hands and face lashed by the branches, on a
thickly wooded ridge. He knew it would be insane
to blunder on through the dark, even if he had the
strength. His need for rest was imperative and he
thought: "I have played the fox, now I must play
the cat of the fable." A big tree with a thick trunk
and outspread branches was near by, and, taking care
to leave not the slightest mark, he climbed up into the
crotch, and stretching out on one of the broad limbs,
after a fashion, rested. Rest brought him new confidence and almost a feeling of security. Even so zeal-
ous a hunter as General Zaroff could not trace him
there, he told himself; only the devil himself could
follow that complicated trail through the jungle after
dark. But, perhaps, the general was a devil—

An apprehensive night crawled slowly by like a
wounded snake, and sleep did not visit Rainsford,
altho the silence of a dead world was on the jungle.
Toward morning when a dingy gray was varnishing
the sky, the cry of some startled bird focused Rainsford's attention in that direction. Something was
coming through the bush, coming slowly, carefully,
coming by the same winding way Rainsford had come.
He flattened himself down on the limb, and through a
screen of leaves almost as thick as tapestry, he
watched. The thing that was approaching was a man.

It was General Zaroff. He made his way along with
his eyes fixed in utmost concentration on the ground
before him. He paused, almost beneath the tree,
dropped to his knees and studied the ground. Rains-

ford's impulse was to hurl himself down like a panther, but he saw that the general's right hand held something metallic—a small automatic pistol.

The hunter shook his head several times, as if he were puzzled. Then he straightened up and took from his case one of his black cigarets; its pungent incense-like smoke floated up to Rainsford's nostrils.

Rainsford held his breath. The general's eyes had left the ground and were traveling inch by inch up the tree. Rainsford froze there, every muscle tensed for a spring. But he sharp eyes of the hunter stopped before they rea hed the limb where Rainsford lay; a smile spread over his brown face. Very deliberately he blew a smoke ring into the air; then he turned his back on the tree and walked carelessly away, back along the trail he had come. The swish of the underbrush against his hunting boots grew fainter and fainter.

The pent-up air burst hotly from Rainsford's lungs. His first thought made him feel sick and numb. The general could follow a trail through the woods at night; he could follow an extremely difficult trail; he must have uncanny powers; only by the merest chance had the Cossack failed to see his quarry.

Rainsford's second thought was even more terrible. It sent a shudder of cold horror through his whole being. Why had the general smiled? Why had he turned back?

Rainsford did not want to believe what his reason told him was true, but the truth was as evident as the sun that had by now pushed through the morning mists. The general was playing with him! The general was saving him for another day's sport! The Cossack was the cat; he was the mouse. Then it was that Rainsford knew the full meaning of terror.

"I will not lose my nerve. I will not."

He slid down from the tree, and struck off again into the woods. His face was set and he forced the machinery of his mind to function. Three hundred yards from his hiding place he stopped where a huge dead tree leaned precariously on a smaller, living one. Throwing off his sack of food, Rainsford took his knife from its sheath and began to work with all his energy.

The job was finished at last, and he threw himself down behind a fallen log a hundred feet away. He did not have to wait long. The cat was coming again to play with the mouse.

Following the trail with the sureness of a blood-hound, came General Zaroff. Nothing escaped those searching black eyes, no crushed blade of grass, no bent twig, no mark, no matter how faint, in the moss. So intent was the Cossack on his stalking that he was upon the thing Rainsford had made before he saw it. His foot touched the protruding bough that was the trigger. Even as he touched it, the general sensed his danger and leaped back with the agility of an ape. But he was not quite quick enough; the dead tree, delicately adjusted to rest on the cut living one, crashed down and struck the general a glancing blow on the shoulder as it fell; but for his alertness, he must have been smashed beneath it. He staggered, but he did not fall; nor did he drop his revolver. He stood there, rubbing his injured shoulder, and Rainsford, with fear again gripping his heart, heard the general's mocking laugh ring through the jungle.

"Rainsford," called the general, "if you are within

sound of my voice, as I suppose you are, let me congratulate you. Not many men know how to make a Malay man-catcher. Luckily, for me, I too have hunted in Malacca. You are proving interesting, Mr. Rainsford. I am going now to have my wound dressed; it's only a slight one. But I shall be back. I shall be back."

When the general, nursing his bruised shoulder, had gone, Rainsford took up his flight again. It was flight now, a desperate, hopeless flight, that carried him on for some hours. Dusk came, then darkness, and still he pressed on. The ground grew softer under his moccasins; the vegetation grew ranker, denser; insects bit him savagely. Then, as he stepped forward, his foot sank into the ooze. He tried to wrench it back, but the muck sucked viciously at his foot as if it were a giant leech. With a violent effort, he tore his foot loose. He knew where he was now. Death Swamp and its quicksand.

His hands were tight closed as if his nerve were something tangible that some one in the darkness was trying to tear from his grip. The softness of the earth had given him an idea. He stepped back from the quicksand a dozen feet or so and, like some huge prehistoric beaver, he began to dig.

Rainsford had dug himself in in France when a second's delay meant death. That had been a placid pastime compared to his digging now. The pit grew deeper; when it was above his shoulders, he climbed out and from some hard saplings cut stakes and sharpened them to a fine point. These stakes he planted in the bottom of the pit with the points sticking up. With flying fingers he wove a rough carpet of weeds and branches and with it he covered the mouth of the pit. Then, wet with sweat and aching with tiredness, he crouched behind the stump of a lightning-charred tree.

He knew his pursuer was coming; he heard the padding sound of feet on the soft earth, and the night breeze brought him the perfume of the general's cigaret. It seemed to Rainsford that the general was coming with unusual swiftness; he was not feeling his way along, foot by foot. Rainsford, crouching there, could not see the general, nor could he see the pit. He lived a year in a minute. Then he felt an impulse to cry aloud with joy, for he heard the sharp crackle of the breaking branches as the cover of the pit gave way; he heard the sharp scream of pain as the pointed stakes found their mark. He leaped up from his place of concealment. Then he cowered back. Three feet from the pit a man was standing, with an electric torch in his hand.

"You've done well, Rainsford," the voice of the general called. "Your Burmese tiger pit has claimed one of my best dogs. Again you score. I think, Mr. Rainsford, I'll see what you can do against my whole pack. I'm going home for a rest now. Thank you for a most amusing evening."

At daybreak Rainsford, lying near the swamp, was awakened by a sound that made him know that he had new things to learn about fear. It was a distant sound, faint and wavering, but he knew it. It was the baying of a pack of hounds.

Rainsford knew he could do one of two things. He could stay where he was and wait. That was suicide. He could flee. That was postponing the inevitable. For a moment he stood there, thinking. An idea that held a wild chance came to him, and, tightening his belt, he headed away from the swamp.

The baying of the sounds drew nearer, then still nearer, nearer, ever nearer. On a ridge Rainsford climbed a tree. Down a watercourse, not a quarter of a mile away, he could see the bush moving. Straining his eyes, he saw the lean figure of General Zaroff; just ahead of him Rainsford made out another figure whose wide shoulders surged through the tall jungle weeds; it was the giant Ivan, and he seemed pulled forward by some unseen force; Rainsford knew that Ivan must be holding the pack in leash.

They would be on him any minute now. His mind worked frantically. He thought of a native trick he had learned in Uganda. He slid down the tree. He caught hold of a springy young sapling and to it he fastened his hunting knife, with the blade pointing down the trail; with a bit of wild grapevine he tied back the sapling. Then he ran for his life. The hounds raised their voices as they hit the fresh scent. Rainsford knew now how an animal at bay feels.

He had to stop to get his breath. The baying of the hounds stopped abruptly, and Rainsford's heart stopped too. They must have reached the knife.

He shinned excitedly up a tree and looked back. His pursuers had stopped. But the hope that was in Rainsford's brain when he climbed died, for he saw in the shallow valley that General Zaroff was still on his feet. But Ivan was not. The knife, driven by the recoil of the springing tree, had not wholly failed.

Rainsford had hardly tumbled to the ground when the pack took up the cry again.

"Nerve, nerve, nerve!" he panted, as he dashed along. A blue gap showed between the trees dead ahead. Ever nearer drew the hounds. Rainsford forced himself on toward that gap. He reached it. It was the shore of the sea. Across a cove he could see the gloomy gray stone of the château. Twenty feet below him the sea rumbled and hissed. Rainsford hesitated. He heard the hounds. Then he leaped far out into the sea. . . .

When the general and his pack reached the place by the sea, the Cossack stopped. For some minutes he stood regarding the blue-green expanse of water. He shrugged his shoulders. Then he sat down, took a drink of brandy from a silver flask, lit a perfumed cigaret, and hummed a bit from "Madame Butterfly."

General Zaroff had an exceedingly good dinner in his great paneled dining hall that evening. With it he had a bottle of Pol Roger and half a bottle of Chambertin. Two slight annoyances kept him from perfect enjoyment. One was the thought that it would be difficult to replace Ivan; the other was that his quarry had escaped him; of course the American hadn't played the game—so thought the general as he tasted his after-dinner liqueur. In his library he read, to soothe himself, from the works of Marcus Aurelius. At ten he went up to his bedroom. He was deliciously tired, he said to himself, and he locked himself in. There was a little moonlight, so, before turning on his light, he went to the window and looked down at the courtyard. He could see the great hounds, and he called: "Better luck another time," to them. Then he switched on the light.

A man, who had been hiding in the curtains of the bed, was standing there.

"Rainsford!" screamed the general. "How in God's name did you get here?"

"Swam," said Rainsford. "I found it quicker than walking through the jungle."

The general sucked in his breath and smiled. "I congratulate you," he said. "You have won the game."

Rainsford did not smile. "I am still a beast at bay," he said, in a low, hoarse voice. "Get ready, General Zaroff."

The general made one of his deepest bows. "I see," he said. "Splendid! One of us is to furnish a repast for the hounds. The other will sleep in this very excellent bed. On guard, Rainsford."

He had never slept in a better bed, Rainsford decided.

THE LUCK OF ROARING CAMP

By Bret Harte

There was commotion in Roaring Camp. It could not have been a fight, for in 1850 that was not novel enough to have called together the entire settlement. The ditches and claims were not only deserted, but "Tuttle's grocery" had contributed its gamblers, who, it will be remembered, calmly continued their game the day that French Pete and Kanaka Joe shot each other to death over the bar in the front room. The whole camp was collected before a rude cabin on the outer edge of the clearing. Conversation was carried on in a low tone, but the name of a woman was frequently repeated. It was a name familiar enough in the camp, —"Cherokee Sal."

Perhaps the less said of her the better. She was a coarse and, it is to be feared, a very sinful woman. But at that time she was the only woman in Roaring Camp, and was just then lying in sore extremity, when she most needed the ministration of her own sex. Dissolute, abandoned, and irreclaimable, she was yet suffering a martyrdom hard enough to bear even when veiled by sympathizing womanhood, but now terrible in her loneliness. The primal curse had come to her in that original isolation which must have made the punishment of the first transgression so dreadful. It was, perhaps,

(Used by permission of and by arrangement with Houghton Mifflin Co.)

part of the expiation of her sin that, at a moment when
she most lacked her sex's intuitive tenderness and care,
she met only the half-contemptuous faces of her mascu-
line associates. Yet a few of the spectators were, I
think, touched by her sufferings. Sandy Tipton thought
it was "rough on Sal," and, in the contemplation of her
condition, for a moment rose superior to the fact that
he had an ace and two bowers in his sleeve.

It will be seen also that the situation was novel.
Deaths were by no means uncommon in Roaring Camp,
but a birth was a new thing. People had been dismissed the camp effectively, finally, and with no possi-
bility of return; but this was the first time that
anybody had been introduced *ab initio*. Hence the
excitement.

"You go in there, Stumpy," said a prominent citizen
known as "Kentuck," addressing one of the loungers.
"Go in there, and see what you kin do. You've had
experience in them things."

Perhaps there was a fitness in the selection. Stumpy,
in other climes, had been the putative head of two
families; in fact, it was owing to some legal informality
in these proceedings that Roaring Camp—a city of
refuge—was indebted to his company. The crowd approved the choice, and Stumpy was wise enough to
bow to the majority. The door closed on the extempore
surgeon and midwife, and Roaring Camp sat down
outside, smoked its pipe, and awaited the issue.

The assemblage numbered about a hundred men.
One or two of these were actual fugitives from justice,
some were criminal, and all were reckless. Physically
they exhibited no indication of their past lives and
character. The greatest scamp had a Raphael face,
with a profusion of blond hair; Oakhurst, a gambler,

had the melancholy air and intellectual abstraction of a Hamlet; the coolest and most courageous man was scarcely over five feet in height, with a soft voice and an embarrassed, timid manner. The term "roughs" applied to them was a distinction rather than a definition. Perhaps in the minor details of fingers, toes, ears, etc., the camp may have been deficient, but these slight omissions did not detract from their aggregate force. The strongest man had but three fingers on his right hand; the best shot had but one eye.

Such was the physical aspect of the men that were dispersed around the cabin. The camp lay in a triangular valley between two hills and a river. The only outlet was a steep trail over the summit of a hill that faced the cabin, now illuminated by the rising moon. The suffering woman might have seen it from the rude bunk whereon she lay,—seen it winding like a silver thread until it was lost in the stars above.

A fire of withered pine boughs added sociability to the gathering. By degrees the natural levity of Roaring Camp returned. Bets were freely offered and taken regarding the result. Three to five that "Sal would get through with it"; even that the child would survive; side bets as to the sex and complexion of the coming stranger. In the midst of an excited discussion an exclamation came from those nearest the door, and the camp stopped to listen. Above the swaying and moaning of the pines, the swift rush of the river, and the crackling of the fire rose a sharp, querulous cry,— a cry unlike anything heard before in the camp. The pines stopped moaning, the river ceased to rush, and the fire to crackle. It seemed as if Nature had stopped to listen too.

The camp rose to its feet as one man! It was

proposed to explode a barrel of gunpowder; but in consideration of the situation of the mother, better counsels prevailed, and only a few revolvers were discharged; for whether owing to the rude surgery of the camp, or some other reason, Cherokee Sal was sinking fast. Within an hour she had climbed, as it were, that rugged road that led to the stars, and so passed out of Roaring Camp, its sin and shame, forever. I do not think that the announcement disturbed them much, except in speculation as to the fate of the child. "Can he live now?" was asked of Stumpy. The answer was doubtful. The only other being of Cherokee Sal's sex and maternal condition in the settlement was an ass. There was some conjecture as to fitness, but the experiment was tried. It was less problematical than the ancient treatment of Romulus and Remus, and apparently as successful.

When these details were completed, which exhausted another hour, the door was opened, and the anxious crowd of men, who had already formed themselves into a queue, entered in single file. Beside the low bunk or shelf, on which the figure of the mother was starkly outlined below the blankets, stood a pine table. On this a candle-box was placed, and within it, swathed in staring red flannel, lay the last arrival at Roaring Camp. Beside the candle-box was placed a hat. Its use was soon indicated. "Gentlemen," said Stumpy, with a singular mixture of authority and *ex officio* complacency,—"gentlemen will please pass in at the front door, round the table, and out at the back door. Them as wishes to contribute anything toward the orphan will find a hat handy." The first man entered with his hat on; he uncovered, however, as he looked about him, and so unconsciously set an example to the next. In such communities good and bad actions are catching. As the procession filed in comments were audible,—criticisms addressed perhaps rather to Stumpy in the character of showman: "Is that him?" "Mighty small specimen;" "Hasn't more'n got the color;" "Ain't bigger nor a derringer." The contributions were as characteristic: A silver tobacco box; a dubloon; a navy revolver, silver mounted; a gold specimen; a very beautiful embroidered lady's handkerchief (from Oakhurst the gambler); a diamond breastpin; a diamond ring (suggested by the pin, with the remark from the giver that he "saw that pin and went two diamonds better"); a slung-shot; a Bible (contributor not detected); a golden spur; a silver teaspoon (the initials, I regret to say, were not the giver's); a pair of surgeon's shears; a lancet; a Bank of England note for £5; and about $200 in loose gold and silver coin. During these proceedings Stumpy maintained a silence as impassive as the dead on his left, a gravity as inscrutable as that of the newly born on his right. Only one incident occurred to break the monotony of the curious procession. As Kentuck bent over the candle-box half curiously, the child turned, and, in a spasm of pain, caught at his groping finger, and held it fast for a moment. Kentuck looked foolish and embarrassed. Something like a blush tried to assert itself in his weather-beaten cheek. "The d—n little cuss!" he said, as he extricated his finger, with perhaps more tenderness and care than he might have been deemed capable of showing. He held that finger a little apart from its fellows as he went out, and examined it curiously. The examination provoked the same original remark in regard to the child. In fact, he seemed to enjoy repeating it. "He rastled with my finger," he remarked to Tipton, holding up the member, "the d—d little cuss!"

It was four o'clock before the camp sought repose. A light burnt in the cabin where the watchers sat, for Stumpy did not go to bed that night. Nor did Kentuck. He drank quite freely, and related with great gusto his experience, invariably ending with his characteristic condemnation of the newcomer. It seemed to relieve him of any unjust implication of sentiment, and Kentuck had the weaknesses of the nobler sex. When everybody else had gone to bed, he walked down to the river and whistled reflectingly. Then he walked up the gulch past the cabin, still whistling with demonstrative unconcern. At a large redwood-tree he paused and retraced his steps, and again passed the cabin. Halfway down to the river's bank he again paused, and then returned and knocked at the door. It was opened by Stumpy. "How goes it?" said Kentuck, looking past Stumpy toward the candle-box. "All serene!" replied Stumpy. "Anything up?" "Nothing." There was a pause—an embarrassing one—Stumpy still holding the door. Then Kentuck had recourse to his finger, which he held up to Stumpy. "Rastled with it,—the d—d little cuss," he said, and retired.

The next day Cherokee Sal had such rude sepulture as Roaring Camp afforded. After her body had been committed to the hillside, there was a formal meeting of the camp to discuss what should be done with her infant. A resolution to adopt it was unanimous and enthusiastic. But an animated discussion in regard to the manner and feasibility of providing for its wants at once sprang up. It was remarkable that the argument partook of none of those fierce personalities with which discussions were usually conducted at Roaring

Camp. Tipton proposed that they should send the child to Red Dog,—a distance of forty miles,—where female attention could be procured. But the unlucky suggestion met with fierce and unanimous opposition. It was evident that no plan which entailed parting from their new acquisition would for a moment be entertained. "Besides," said Tom Ryder, "them fellows at Red Dog would swap it, and ring in somebody else on us." A disbelief in the honesty of other camps prevailed at Roaring Camp, as in other places.

The introduction of a female nurse in the camp also met with objection. It was argued that no decent woman could be prevailed to accept Roaring Camp as her home, and the speaker urged that "they didn't want any more of the other kind." This unkind allusion to the defunct mother, harsh as it may seem, was the first spasm of propriety,—the first symptom of the camp's regeneration. Stumpy advanced nothing. Perhaps he felt a certain delicacy in interfering with the selection of a possible successor in office. But when questioned, he averred stoutly that he and "Jinny"—the mammal before alluded to—could manage to rear the child. There was something original, independent, and heroic about the plan that pleased the camp. Stumpy was retained. Certain articles were sent for to Sacramento. "Mind," said the treasurer, as he pressed a bag of gold-dust into the expressman's hand, "the best that can be got,—lace, you know, and filigree-work and frills,—d—n the cost!"

Strange to say, the child thrived. Perhaps the invigorating climate of the mountain camp was compensation for maternal deficiencies. Nature took the foundling to her broader breast. In that rare atmosphere of the Sierra foothills,—that air pungent with balsamic odor, that ethereal cordial at once bracing and exhilarating,—he may have found food and nourishment, or a subtle chemistry that transmuted ass's milk to lime and phosphorus. Stumpy inclined to the belief that it was the latter and good nursing. "Me and that ass," he would say, "has been father and mother to him! Don't you," he would add, apostrophizing the helpless bundle before him, "never go back on us."

By the time he was a month old the necessity of giving him a name became apparent. He had generally been known as "The Kid," "Stumpy's Boy," "The Coyote," (an allusion to his vocal powers), and even by Kentuck's endearing diminutive of "The d—d little cuss." But these were felt to be vague and unsatisfactory, and were at last dismissed under another influence. Gamblers and adventurers are generally superstitious, and Oakhurst one day declared that the baby had brought "the luck" to Roaring Camp. It was certain that of late they had been successful. "Luck" was the name agreed upon, with the prefix of Tommy for greater convenience. No allusion was made to the mother, and the father was unknown. "It's better," said the philosophical Oakhurst, "to take a fresh deal all around. Call him Luck, and start him fair." A day was accordingly set apart for the christening. What was meant by this ceremony the reader may imagine who has already gathered some idea of the reckless irreverence of Roaring Camp. The master of ceremonies was one "Boston," a noted wag, and the occasion seemed to promise the greatest facetiousness. This ingenious satirist had spent two days in preparing a burlesque of the Church service, with pointed local allusions. The choir was properly trained, and Sandy Tipton was to stand godfather. But after the procession had marched to the grove with music and banners, and the child had been deposited before a mock altar, Stumpy stepped before the expectant crowd. "It ain't my style to spoil fun, boys," said the little man, stoutly eying the faces around him, "but it strikes me that this thing ain't exactly on the squar. It's playing it pretty low down on this yer baby to ring in fun on him that he ain't goin' to understand. And ef there's goin' to be any godfathers round, I'd like to see who's got any better rights than me." A silence followed Stumpy's speech. To the credit of all humorists be it said that the first man to acknowledge its justice was the satirist thus stopped of his fun. "But," said Stumpy, quickly following up his advantage, "we're here for a christening, and we'll have it. I proclaim you Thomas Luck, according to the laws of the United States and the State of California, so help me God." It was the first time that the name of the Diety had been otherwise uttered than profanely in the camp. The form of christening was perhaps even more ludicrous than the satirist had conceived; but strangely enough, nobody saw it and nobody laughed. "Tommy" was christened as seriously as he would have been under a Christian roof, and cried and was comforted in as orthodox fashion.

And so the work of regeneration began in Roaring Camp. Almost imperceptibly a change came over the settlement. The cabin assigned to "Tommy Luck"—or "The Luck," as he was more frequently called—first showed signs of improvement. It was kept scrupulously clean and whitewashed. Then it was boarded, clothed, and papered. The rosewood cradle, packed eighty miles by mule, had, in Stumpy's way of putting it, "sorter killed the rest of the furniture." So the rehabilitation

of the cabin became a necessity. The men who were
in the habit of lounging in at Stumpy's to see "how
'The Luck' got on" seemed to appreciate the change,
and in self-defense the rival establishment of "Tuttle's
grocery" bestirred itself and imported a carpet and
mirrors. The reflections of the latter on the appearance
of Roaring Camp tended to produce stricter habits of
personal cleanliness. Again Stumpy imposed a kind of
quarantine upon those who aspired to the honor and
privilege of holding The Luck. It was a cruel mortifi-
cation to Kentuck—who, in the carelessness of a large
nature and the habits of frontier life, had begun to
regard all garments as a second cuticle, which, like a
snake's, only sloughed off through decay—to be de-
barred this privilege from certain prudential reasons.
Yet such was the subtle influence of innovation that
he thereafter appeared regularly every afternoon in a
clean shirt and face still shining from his ablutions.
Nor were moral and social sanitary laws neglected.
"Tommy," who was supposed to spend his whole existence in a persistent attempt to repose, must not be
disturbed by noise. The shouting and yelling, which
had gained the camp its infelicitous title, were not
permitted within hearing distance of Stumpy's. The
men conversed in whispers or smoked with Indian
gravity. Profanity was tacitly given up in these sacred
precincts, and throughout the camp a popular form of
expletive, known as "D—n the luck!" and "Curse the
luck!" was abandoned, as having a new personal bearing. Vocal music was not interdicted, being supposed
to have a soothing, tranquilizing quality; and one song,
sung by "Man-o'-War Jack," an English sailor from
her Majesty's Australian colonies, was quite popular
as a lullaby. It was a lugubrious recital of the exploits

of "the Arethusa, Seventy-four," in a muffled minor, ending with a prolonged dying fall at the burden of each verse, "On b-oo-o-ard of the Arethusa." It was a fine sight to see Jack holding The Luck, rocking from side to side as if with the motion of a ship, and crooning forth this naval ditty. Either through the peculiar rocking of Jack or the length of his song,—it contained ninety stanzas, and was continued with conscientious deliberation to the bitter end,—the lullaby generally had the desired effect. At such times the men would lie at full length under the trees in the soft summer twilight, smoking their pipes and drinking in the melodious utterances. An indistinct idea that this was pastoral happiness pervaded the camp. "This 'ere kind o' think," said the Cockney Simmons, meditatively reclining on his elbow, "is 'evingly." It reminded him of Greenwich.

On the long summer days The Luck was usually carried to the gulch from whence the golden store of Roaring Camp was taken. There, on a blanket spread over pine boughs, he would lie while the men were working in the ditches below. Latterly there was a rude attempt to decorate this bower with flowers and sweet-smelling shrubs, and generally some one would bring him a cluster of wild honeysuckles, azaleas, or the painted blossoms of Las Mariposas. The men had suddenly awakened to the fact that there were beauty and significance in these trifles, which they had so long trodden carelessly beneath their feet. A flake of glittering mica, a fragment of variegated quartz, a bright pebble from the bed of the creek, became beautiful to eyes thus cleared and strengthened, and were invariably put aside for The Luck. It was wonderful how many treasures the woods and hillsides yielded that "would do for Tommy." Surrounded by playthings such as never child out of fairyland had before, it is to be hoped that Tommy was content. He appeared to be serenely happy, albeit there was an infantine gravity about him, a contemplative light in his round gray eyes, that sometimes worried Stumpy. He was always tractable and quiet, and it is recorded that once, having crept beyond his "corral,"—a hedge of tessellated pine boughs, which surrounded his bed,—he dropped over the bank on his head in the soft earth, and remained with his mottled legs in the air in that position for at least five minutes with unflinching gravity. He was extricated without a murmur. I hesitate to record the many other instances of his sagacity, which rest, unfortunately, upon the statements of prejudiced friends. Some of them were not without a tinge of superstition. "I crep' up the bank just now," said Kentuck one day, in a breathless state of excitement, "and dern my skin if he wasn't a-talking to a jaybird as was a-sittin' on his lap. There they was, just as free and sociable as anything you please, a-jawin' at each other just like two cherrybums." Howbeit, whether creeping over the pine boughs or lying lazily on his back blinking at the leaves above him, to him the birds sang, the squirrels chattered, and the flowers bloomed. Nature was his nurse and playfellow. For him she would let slip between the leaves golden shafts of sunlight that fell just within his grasp; she would send wandering breezes to visit him with the balm of bay and resinous gum; to him the tall redwoods nodded familiarly and sleepily, the bumblebees buzzed, and the rooks cawed a slumbrous accompaniment.

Such was the golden summer of Roaring Camp.

They were "flush times," and the luck was with them. The claims had yielded enormously. The camp was jealous of its privileges and looked suspiciously on strangers. No encouragement was given to immigration, and, to make their seclusion more perfect, the land on either side of the mountain wall that surrounded the camp they duly preempted. This, and a reputation for singular proficiency with the revolver, kept the reserve of Roaring Camp inviolate. The expressman—their only connecting link with the surrounding world—sometimes told wonderful stories of the camp. He would say, "They've a street up there in 'Roaring' that would lay over any street in Red Dog. They've got vines and flowers round their houses, and they wash themselves twice a day. But they're mighty rough on strangers, and they worship an Ingin baby."

With the prosperity of the camp came a desire for further improvement. It was proposed to build a hotel in the following spring, and to invite one or two decent families to reside there for the sake of The Luck, who might perhaps profit by female companionship. The sacrifice that this concession to the sex cost these men, who were fiercely skeptical in regard to its general virtue and usefulness, can only be accounted for by their affection for Tommy. A few still held out. But the resolve could not be carried into effect for three months, and the minority meekly yielded in the hope that something might turn up to prevent it. And it did.

The winter of 1851 will long be remembered in the foothills. The snow lay deep on the Sierras, and every mountain creek became a river, and every river a lake. Each gorge and gulch was transformed into a tumultuous watercourse that descended the hillsides, tearing down giant trees and scattering its drift and débris along the plain. Red Dog had been twice under water, and Roaring Camp had been forewarned. "Water put the gold into them gulches," said Stumpy. "It's been here once and will be here again!" And that night the North Fork suddenly leaped over its banks and swept up the triangular valley of Roaring Camp.

In the confusion of rushing water, crashing trees, and crackling timber, and the darkness which seemed to flow with the water and blot out the fair valley, but little could be done to collect the scattered camp. When the morning broke, the cabin of Stumpy, nearest the river-bank, was gone. Higher up the gulch they found the body of its unlucky owner; but the pride, the hope, the joy, The Luck, of Roaring Camp had disappeared. They were returning with sad hearts when a shout from the bank recalled them.

It was a relief-boat from down the river. They had picked up, they said, a man and an infant, nearly exhausted, about two miles below. Did anybody know them, and did they belong here?

It needed but a glance to show them Kentuck lying there, cruelly crushed and bruised, but still holding The Luck of Roaring Camp in his arms. As they bent over the strangely assorted pair, they saw that the child was cold and pulseless. "He is dead," said one. Kentuck opened his eyes. "Dead?" he repeated feebly. "Yes, my man, and you are dying too." A smile lit the eyes of the expiring Kentuck. "Dying!" he repeated; "he's a-taking me with him. Tell the boys I've got The Luck with me now;" and the strong man, clinging to the frail babe as a drowning man is said to cling to a straw, drifted away into the shadowy river that flows forever to the unknown sea.

THE RUN OF THE YELLOW MAIL

By Frank H. Spearman

There wasn't another engineer on the division who dared talk to Doubleday the way Jimmie Bradshaw did.

But Jimmie had a grievance, and every time he thought about it, it made him nervous.

Ninety-six years. It seemed a good while to wait; yet in the regular course of events on the mountain division there appeared no earlier prospect of Jimmie's getting a passenger run.

"Got your rights, ain't you?" said Doubleday, when Jimmie complained.

"I have and I haven't," grumbled Jimmie, winking hard; "there's younger men than I am on the fast runs."

"They got in on the strike; you've been told that a hundred times. We can't get up another strike just to fix you out on a fast run. Hang on to your freight. There's better men than you in Ireland up to their belt in the bog, Jimmie."

"It's a pity they didn't leave you there, Doubleday."

"You'd have been a good while hunting for a freight run if they had."

Then Jimmie would get mad and shake his finger and talk fast: "Just the same, I'll have a fast run here when you're dead."

"Maybe; but I'll be alive a good while yet, my son," the master mechanic would laugh. Then Jimmie would walk off very warm, and when he got into private with himself he would wink furiously and say friction things about Doubleday which needn't now be printed, because it is different. However, the talk always ended that way, and Jimmie Bradshaw knew it always would end that way.

The trouble was, no one on the division would take Jimmie seriously, and he felt that the ambition of his life would never be fulfilled; that he would go plugging to gray hairs and the grave on an old freight train; and that even when he got to the right side of the Jordan there would still be something like half a century between him and a fast run. It was funny to hear him complaining about it, for everything, even his troubles, came funny to him, and in talking he had an odd way of stuttering with his eyes, which were red. In fact, Jimmie was nearly all red; hair, face, hands— they said his teeth were freckled.

When the first rumors about the proposed Yellow Mail reached the mountains Jimmie was running a new ten-wheeler; breaking her in on a freight "for some fellow without a lick o' sense to use on a limited passenger run," as Jimmie observed bitterly. The rumors about the mail came at first like stray mallards —opening signs of winter—and as the season advanced flew thicker and faster. Washington never was very progressive in the matter of improving the transcontinental service, but they once put in a postmaster-general down there, by mistake, who wouldn't take the old song. When the bureau fellows that put their brains up in curl papers told him it couldn't be done he smiled softly, but he sent for the managers of the crack lines across the continent, without suspecting how it bore incidentally on Jimmie Bradshaw's grievance against his master mechanic.

The postmaster-general called the managers of the big lines, and they had a dinner at Chamberlain's, and *they* told him the same thing. "It has been tried," they said in the old, tired way; "really it can't be done."

"California has been getting the worst of it for years on the mail service," persisted the postmaster-general moderately. "But Californians ought to have the best of it. We don't think anything about putting New York mail in Chicago in twenty hours. It ought to be simple to cut half a day across the continent and give San Francisco her mail a day earlier. Where's the fall-down?" he asked, like one refusing no for an answer.

The general managers looked at our representative sympathetically, and coughed cigar smoke his way to hide him.

"West of the Missouri," murmured a Pennsylvania swell, who pulled indifferently at a fifty-cent cigar. Everybody at the table took a drink on the *exposé*, except the general manager, who sat at that time for the Rocky Mountains.

The West End representative was unhappily accustomed to facing the finger of scorn on such occasions. It had become with our managers a tradition. There was never a conference of continental lines in which we were not scoffed at as the weak link in the chain of everything—mail, passenger, specials, what not—the trouble was invariably laid at our door.

But this time there was a new man sitting for the line at the Chamberlain dinner: a youngish man with a face that set like cement when the West End was trod upon.

The postmaster-general was inclined, from the reputation we had, to look on our chap as a man looks at a dog without a pedigree, or at a dray horse in a bunch of standard breeds. But something in the mouth of the West End man gave him pause; since the Rough Riders, it has been a bit different about verdicts on things Western. The postmaster-general suppressed a rising sarcasm with a sip of Chartreuse, for the dinner was ripening, and waited; nor did he mistake— the West Ender *was* about to speak.

"Why west of the Missouri?" he asked, with a lift of the face that was not altogether candid. The Pennsylvania man shrugged his brows; to explain might have seemed indelicate.

"If it is put through, how much of it do you propose to take yourself?" inquired our man, looking evenly at the Alleghany official.

"Sixty-five miles, including stops from New York post-office to Canal Street," replied the Pennsylvania man, and his words flowed with irritating smoothness and ease.

"What do you take?" continued the man with the jaw, turning to the Burlington representative, who was struggling, belated, with an artichoke.

"*About* seventy from Canal to Tenth and Mason. Say, seventy," repeated the "Q" manager, with the lordliness of a man who has smiles to throw at almost anybody, and knows it.

"Then suppose we say sixty-five from Tenth and Mason to Ogden," suggested the West Ender. There was a well-bred stare the table round, a lifting of glasses to mask expressions that might give pain. Sixty-five miles an *hour?* Through the *Rockies?*

But the postmaster-general struck the table quickly and heavily; he didn't want to let it get away. "Why, hang it, Mr. Bucks," he exclaimed with emphasis; "if you will say sixty, the business is done. We don't ask you to do the Rockies in the time these fellows take to cut the Alleghanies. Do sixty, and I will put mail in 'Frisco a day earlier every week in the year."

"Nothing on the West End to keep you from doing it," said General Manager Bucks. He had been put up then only about six months. "But—"

Every one looked at the young manager. The Pennsylvania man looked with confidence, for he instantly suspected there must be a string to such a proposition, or that the new representative was "talking through his hat."

"But what?" asked the Cabinet member, uncomfortably apprehensive.

"But we are not putting on a sixty-five mile schedule just because we love our country, you understand, nor to lighten an already glorious reputation. Oh, no," smiled Bucks faintly, "we are doing it for 'the stuff.' You put up the money; we put up the speed. Not sixty miles; sixty-five—from the Missouri to the Sierras. No; no more wine. Yes, thank you, I will take a cigar."

The trade was on from that minute. Bucks said no more then; he was a good listener. But next day— when it came to talking money—he talked more money into the West End treasury for one year's running than was ever talked before on a mail contract for the best three years' work we ever did.

When they asked him how much time he wanted to

get ready, and told him to take plenty, three months' were stipulated. The contracts were drawn, and they were signed by our people without hesitation because they knew Bucks. But while the preparations for the fast schedule were being made, the Government weakened on signing. Nothing ever got through a Washington department without hitch, and they said our road had so often failed on like proposition that they wanted a test. There was a deal of wrangling, then a test run was agreed upon by all the roads concerned. If it proved successful—if the mail was put to the Golden Gate on the second of the schedule—public opinion and the interests in the Philippines, it was concluded, would justify the heavy premium asked for the service.

In this way the dickering and the figuring became, in a measure, public, and keyed up everybody interested to a high pitch. We said nothing for publication, but under Bucks' energy sawed wood for three whole months. Indeed, three months goes as a day getting a system into shape for an extraordinary schedule. Success meant with us prestige; but failure meant obloquy for the road and for our division chief who had been so lately called to handle it.

The real strain, it was clear, would come on his old— the mountain—division; and to carry out the point rested on the motive power of the mountain division; hence, concretely, on Doubleday, master mechanic of the hill country.

In thirty days Neighbor, superintendent of the motive power, called for reports from the division master mechanics on the preparations for the Yellow Mail run, and they reported progress. In sixty days he called again. The subordinates reported well except

Doubleday. Doubleday said merely "Not ready"; he was busy tinkering with his engines. There was a third call in eighty days, and on the eighty-fifth a peremptory call. Everybody said ready except Doubleday. When Neighbor remonstrated sharply, he would say only that he would be ready in time. That was the most he would promise, though it was generally understood that if he failed to deliver the goods he would have to make way for somebody who could.

The plains division of the system was marked up for seventy miles an hour, and, if the truth were told, a little better; but, with all the help they could give us, it still left sixty for the mountains to take care of, and the Yellow Mail proposition was conceded to be the toughest affair the motive power at Medicine Bend ever faced. However, forty-eight hours before the mail left the New York post-office Doubleday wired to Neighbor, "Ready"; Neighbor to Bucks, "Ready"; and Bucks to Washington, "Ready"—and we were ready from end to end.

Then the orders began to shoot through the mountains. The test run was of especial importance, because the signing of the contract was believed to depend on the run of it. Once signed, accidents and delays might be explained; for the test run there must be no delays. Despatches were given the 11, which meant Bucks; no lay-outs, no slows for the Yellow Mail. Road masters were notified: no track work in front of the Yellow Mail. Bridge gangs were warned, yard masters instructed, section bosses cautioned, track walkers spurred—the system was polished like a barkeeper's diamond, and swept like a parlor car for the test flight of the Yellow Mail.

Doubleday. working like a boiler washer, spent all

ɑay Thursday and all Thursday night in the round-house. He had personally gone over the engines that were to take the racket in the mountains. Ten-wheel-ers they were, the 1012 and the 1014, with fifty-six-inch drivers and cylinders big enough to sit up and eat breakfast in. Spick and span both of them, just long enough out of the shops to run smoothly to the work; and on Friday Oliver Sollers, who, when he opened a throttle, blew miles over the tender like feathers, took the 1012, groomed as you'd groom a Wilkes mare, down to Piedmont for the run up to the Bend.

Now Oliver Sollers was a runner in a thousand, and steady as a clock; but he had a fireman who couldn't stand prosperity, Steve Horigan, a cousin of Johnnie's. The glory was too great for Steve, and he spent Fri-day night in Gallagher's place celebrating, telling the boys what the 1012 would do to the Yellow Mail. Not a thing, Steve claimed after five drinks, but pull the stamps clean off the letters the minute they struck the foothills. But when Steve showed up at five A. M. to superintend the movement, he was seasick. The instant Sollers set eyes on him he objected to taking him out. Mr. Sollers was not looking for any un-necessary chances on one of Bucks' personal matters, and for the general manager the Yellow Mail test had become exceedingly personal. Practically everybody East and West had said it would fail; Bucks said no.

Neighbor himself was on the Piedmont platform that morning, watching things. The McCloud despatchers had promised the train to our division on time, and her smoke was due with the rise of the sun. The big superintendent of motive power, watching anxiously for her arrival, and planning anxiously for her out going, glared at the bunged fireman in front of him, and, when Sollers protested, Neighbor turned on the swollen Steve with sorely bitter words. Steve swore mightily he was fit and could do the trick—but what's the word of a railroad man that drinks. Neighbor spoke wicked words, and while they poured on the guilty Steve's crop there was a shout down the platform. In the east the sun was breaking over the sandhills, and below it a haze of black thickened the horizon. It was McTerza with the 808 and the Yellow Mail. Neighbor looked at his watch; she was, if anything, a minute to the good, and before the car tinks could hustle across the yard, a streak of gold cut the sea of purple alfalfa in the lower valley, and the narrows began to smoke with the dust of the race for the platform.

When McTerza blocked the big drivers at the west end of the depot, every eye was on the new equipment. Three standard railway mail cars, done in varnished buttercup, strung out behind the sizzling engine, and they looked pretty as cowslips. While Neighbor vaguely meditated on their beauty and on his boozing fireman, Jimmie Bradshaw, just in from a night run down from the Bend, walked across the yard. He had just seen Steve Horigan making a "sneak" for the bath-house, and from the yard gossip Jimmie had guessed the rest.

"What are you looking for, Neighbor?" asked Jimmie Bradshaw.

"A man to fire for Sollers—up. Do you want it?" Neighbor threw it at him across and carelessly, not having any idea Jimmie was looking for trouble. But Jimmie surprised him; Jimmie did want it.

"Sure, I want it. Put me on. Tired? No. I'm

fresh as rainwater. Put me on, Neighbor; I'll never get fast any other way. Doubleday wouldn't give me a fast run in a hundred years. Neighbor," exclaimed Jimmie, greatly wrought, "put me on, and I'll plant sunflowers on your grave."

There wasn't much time to look around; the 1012 was being coupled on to the mail for the hardest run on the line.

"Get in there, you blamed idiot," roared Neighbor presently at Jimmie. "Get in and fire her; and if you don't give Sollers 210 pounds every inch of the way I'll set you back wiping."

Jimmie winked furiously at the proposition while it was being hurled at him, but he lost no time climbing in. The 1012 was drumming then at her gage with better than 200 pounds. Adam Shafer, conductor for the run, ran backward and forward a minute examining the air. At the final word from his brakeman he lifted two fingers at Sollers; Oliver opened a notch, and Jimmie Bradshaw stuck his head out of the gangway. Slowly, but with swiftly rising speed, the yellow string began to move out through the long lines of freight cars that blocked the spurs; and those who watched that morning from the Piedmont platform thought a smoother equipment than Bucks' mail train never drew out of the mountain yards.

Jimmie Bradshaw jumped at the work in front of him. He had never in his life lifted a pick in as swell a cab as that. The hind end of the 1012 was as big as a private car; Jimmie had never seen so much play for a shovel in his life, and he knew the trick of his business better than most men even in West End cabs—the trick of holding the high pressure every minute, of feeling the drafts before they left the throttle; and as Oliver let the engine out very, very fast, Jimmie Bradshaw sprinkled the grate bars craftily and blinked at the shivering pointer, as much as to say, "It's you and me now for the Yellow Mail, and nobody else on earth."

There was a long reach of smooth track in front of the foothills. It was there the big start had to be made, and in two minutes the bark of the big machine had deepened to a chest tone full as thunder. It was all fun for an hour, for two hours. It was that long before the ambitious fireman realized what the new speed meant: the sickening slew, the lurch on lurch so fast that the engine never righted, the shortened breath along the tangent, the giddy roll to the elevation and the sudden shock of the curve, the roar of the flight on the ear, and, above it all, the booming purr of the maddened steel. The canoe in the heart of the rapids, the bridge of a liner at sea, the gun in the heat of the fight, take something of this—the cab of the mail takes it all.

When they struck the foothills, Sollers and Jimmie Bradshaw looked at their watches and looked at each other, but like men who had turned their backs on every mountain record. There was a stop for water— speed drinks so hard—an oil round, an anxious touch on the journals; then the Yellow Mail drew reeling into the hills. Oliver eased her just a bit for the heavier curves, but for all that the train writhed frantically as it cut the segments, and the men thought, in spite of themselves, of the mountain curves ahead. The worst of the run lay ahead of the pilot, because the art in mountain running is not alone or so much in getting up hill; it is in getting down hill. But by the way the Yellow Mail got that day up hill and down, it seemed as if Steve Horigan's dream would be realized and that the 1012 actually would pull the stamps off the letters. Before they knew it they were through the gateway, out into the desert country, up along the crested buttes, and then, sudden as eternity the wheel-base of the 1012 struck a tight curve, a pent-down rail sprang out like a knitting-needle, and the Yellow Mail shot staggering off the track into a gray borrow-pit.

There was a crunching of truck and frame, a crashing splinter of varnished cars, a scream from the wounded engine, a cloud of gray ash in the burning sun, and a ruin of human effort in the ditch. In the twinkle of an eye the mail train lay spilled on the alkali; for a minute it looked desperately bad for the general manager's test.

It was hardly more than a minute, tho, then like ants from out a trampled hill men began crawling from the yellow wreck. There was more—there was groaning and worse, yet little for so frightful a shock. And first on his feet, with no more than scratches, and quickest back under the cab after his engineer, was Jimmie Bradshaw, the fireman.

Sollers, barely conscious, lay wedged between the tank and the footboard. Jimmie, all by himself, eased him away from the boiler. The conductor stood with a broken arm directing his brakeman how to chop a crew out of the head mail car, and the hind crews were getting out themselves. There was a quick calling back and forth, and the cry, "Nobody killed!" But the engineer and conductor were put out of action. There was, in fact, but one West End man unhurt; yet that was enough—for it was Jimmie Bradshaw.

The first wreck of the fast mail—there had been

worse since—took place just east of Crockett's siding. A west-bound freight lay at that moment on the passing track waiting for the mail. Jimmie Bradshaw cast up the possibilities of the situation the minute he righted himself.

Before the freight crew had reached the wreck, Jimmie was hustling ahead to tell them what he wanted. The freight conductor demurred; and when they discussed it with the freight engineer, Kingsley, he objected. "My engine won't never stand it; it'll pound her to pieces," he argued. "I reckon the safest thing to do is to get orders."

"Get orders!" stormed Jimmie Bradshaw, pointing at the wreck. "Get orders! Are you running an engine on this line and don't know the orders for those mail bags? The orders is to move 'em! That's orders enough. Move 'em! Uncouple three of those empty box-cars and hustle 'em back. By the Great United States! any man that interferes with the moving of this mail will get his time—that's what he'll get. That's Doubleday, and don't you forget it. The thing is to move the mail—not stand here chewing about it!"

"Bucks wants the stuff hustled," put in the freight conductor, weakening before Jimmie's eloquence. "Everybody knows that."

"Uncouple there!" cried Jimmie, climbing into the Mogul cab. "I'll pull the bags, Kingsley; you needn't take any chances. Come back there, every mother's son of you, and help on the transfer."

He carried his points with a gale. He was conductor and engineer and general manager all in one. He backed the boxes to the curve below the spill, and set every man at work piling the mail from the wrecked train to the freight cars. The wounded cared for the wounded, and the dead might have buried the dead; Jimmie moved the mail. Only one thing turned his hair gray; the transfer was so slow, it looked as if it would defeat his plan. As he stood fermenting, a stray party of Sioux bucks on a vagrant hunt rose out of the desert passes, and halted to survey the confusion. It was Jimmie Bradshaw's opportunity. He had the blanket men in council in a trice. They talked for one minute, in two he had them regularly sworn in and carrying second-class. The registered stuff was jealously guarded by those of the mail clerks who could still hobble—and who, head for head, leg for leg, and arm for arm, can stand the wrecking that a mail clerk can stand? The mail crews took the registered matter; the freight crews and Jimmie, dripping sweat and anxiety, handled the letter bags; but second and third class were temporarily hustled for the Great White Father by his irreverent children of the Rockies.

Before the disabled men could credit their senses the business was done, themselves made as comfortable as possible, and with the promise of speedy aid back to the injured, the Yellow Mail, somewhat disfigured, was again heading westward in the box-cars. This time Jimmie Bradshaw, like a dog with a bone, had the throttle. Jimmie Bradshaw for once in his life had the coveted fast run, and till he sighted Fort Rucker he never for a minute let up.

Meantime there was a desperate crowd round the despatcher at Medicine Bend. It was an hour and twenty minutes after Ponca Station reported the Yellow Mail out, before Fort Rucker, eighteen miles farther west, reported the box-cars and Jimmie Bradshaw in, and followed with a wreck report from the

Crockett siding. When that end of it began to tumble into the Wickiup office Doubleday's face went very hard—fate was against him, the contract was gone glimmering, he didn't feel at all sure his own head and the roadmaster's wouldn't follow it. Then the Rucker operator began again to talk about Jimmie Bradshaw, and "Who's Bradshaw?" asked somebody; and Rucker went on excitedly with the story of the Mogul and of three box-cars, and of a war party of Sioux squatting on the brake-wheels; it came so mixed that Medicine Bend thought everybody at Rucker Station had gone mad.

While they fumed, Jimmie Bradshaw was speeding the mail through the mountains. He had Kingsley's fireman, big as an ox and full of his own enthusiasm. In no time they were flying across the flats of the Spider Water, threading the curves of the Peace River, and hitting the rails of the Painted Desert, with the Mogul sprinting like a Texas steer, and the box-cars leaping like yearlings at the points. It was no case of scientific running, no case of favoring the roadbed, of easing the strain on the equipment; it was simply a case of galloping to a Broadway fire with a Silsby rotary on a 4—11 call. Up hill and down, curve and tangent, it was all one. There was speed made on the plains with that mail, and there was speed made in the foothills with the fancy equipment, but never the speed that Jimmie Bradshaw made when he ran the mail through the gorges in three box-cars; and frightened operators and paralyzed station-agents all the way up the line watched the fearful and wonderful train jump the switches with Bradshaw's red head sticking out of the cab window.

Medicine Bend couldn't get the straight of it over

the wires. There was an electric storm in the mountains, and the wires went bad in the midst of the confusion. They knew there was a wreck, and supposed there was mail in the ditch, and, with Doubleday frantic, the despatchers were trying to get the track to run a train down to Crockett's. But Jimmie Bradshaw had asked at Rucker for rights to the Bend, and in an unguarded moment they had been given; after that it was all off. Nobody could get action on Jimmie Bradshaw to head him off. He took the rights, and stayed not for stake and stopped not for stone. In thirty minutes the operating department was ready to kill him, but he was making such time it was concluded better to humor the lunatic than to try to hold him up anywhere for a parley. When this was decided Jimmie and his war party were already reported past Bad Axe, fifteen miles below the Bend, with every truck on the box-cars smoking.

The Bad Axe run to the Bend was never done in less than fourteen minutes until Bradshaw that day brought up the mail. Between those two points the line is modeled on the curves of a ram's horn, but Jimmie with the Mogul found every twist on the right of way in eleven minutes; that particular record is good yet. Indeed, before Doubleday, then in a frenzied condition, got his cohorts fairly on the platform to look for Jimmie, the hollow scream of the big freight engine echoed through the mountains. Shouts from below brought the operators to the upper windows; down the Bend they saw a monster locomotive flying from a trailing horn of smoke. As the stubby string of freight cars slewed quartering into the lower yard, the startled officials saw them from the Wickiup windows wrapped in a stream of flame. Every journal was afire, and the blaze from the boxes, rolling into the steam from the stack, curled hotly around a bevy of Sioux Indians, who clung sternly to the foot-boards and brake-wheels on top of the box-cars. It was a ride for the red men that is told around the council fires yet. But they do not always add in their traditions that they were hanging on, not only for life, but also for a butt of plug tobacco promised for their timely help at Crockett siding.

By the time Jimmie slowed up his amazing equipment the fire brigade was on the run from the roundhouse. The Sioux warriors climbed hastily down the fire escapes, a force of bruised and bareheaded mail clerks shoved back the box-car doors, the car tinks tackled the conflagration, and Jimmie Bradshaw, dropping from the cab with the swing of a man who has done it, waited at the gangway for the questions to come to him, and for a minute they came hot.

"What the blazes do you mean by bringing in an engine in that condition?" yelled Doubleday, pointing to the blown machine.

"I thought you wanted the mail," winked Jimmie.

"How the devil are we to get the mail with you blocking the track for two hours?" demanded Calahan insanely.

"Why, the mail's here—in these box-cars," responded Jimmie Bradshaw, pointing to his bobtail train. "Now don't look daffy like that; every sack is right here. I thought the best way to get the mail here was to bring it. Hm! We're forty minutes late, ain't we?"

Doubleday waited to hear no more. Orders flew like curlews from the superintendent and the master mechanic. They saw there was a life for it yet. A string of new mail cars was backed down beside the train before the fire brigade had done with the trucks. The relieving mail crews waiting at the Bend took hold like cats at a pudding, and a dozen extra men helped them sling the pouches. The 1014, blowing porpoise-wise, was backed up just as Benedict Morgan's train pulled down for Crockett's siding, and the Yellow Mail, rehabilitated, rejuvenated, and exultant, started up the gorge for Bear Dance, only fifty-three minutes late, with Hawksworth in the cab.

"And if you can't make that up, Frank, you're no good on earth," sputtered Doubleday at the engineer he had put in for that special endeavor. And Frank Hawksworth did make it up, and the Yellow Mail went on and off the West End on the test, and into the Sierras for the coast, *on time*.

"There's a butt of plug tobacco and transportation to Crockett's coming to these bucks, Mr. Doubleday," winked Jimmie Bradshaw uncertainly, for with the wearing off of the strain came the idea to Jimmie that he might have to pay for it himself. "I promised them that," he added, "for helping with the transfer. If it hadn't been for the blankets we wouldn't have got off for another hour. They chew Tomahawk—rough and ready preferred—Mr. Doubleday. Hm!"

Doubleday was looking off into the mountains.

"You've been on a freight run some time, Jimmie," said he tentatively after a while.

The Indian detachment was crowding in pretty close on the red-headed engineer. He blushed. "If you'll take care of my tobacco contract, Doubleday, we'll call the other matter square. I'm not looking for a fast run as much as I was."

"If we get the mail contract," resumed Doubleday

reflectively, "and it won't be your fault if we don't—hm!—we may need you on one of the runs. Looks to me like you ought to have one."

Jimmie shook his head. "I don't want one—don't mind me; just fix these gentlemen out with some tobacco before they scalp me, will you?"

The Indians got their leaf, and Bucks got his contract, and Jimmie Bradshaw got the pick of the runs on the Yellow Mail, and ever since he's been kicking to get back on a freight. But they don't call him Bradshaw any more. No man in the mountains can pace him on a dare-devil run. And when the head brave of the hunting party received the butt of tobacco on behalf of his company, he looked at Doubleday with dignity, pointed to the sandy engineer, and spoke freckled words in the Sioux.

That's the way it came about. Bradshaw holds the belt for the run from Bad Axe to Medicine Bend; but he never goes by the name of Bradshaw any more. West of McCloyd, everywhere up and down the mountains, they give him the name that the Sioux gave him that day—Jimmie the Wind.

THE DUMMY-CHUCKER

By Arthur Somers Roche

There were many women on East Fourteenth Street. With the seeing eye of the artist, the dummy-chucker looked them over and rejected them. Kindly-seeming, generously fat, the cheap movie houses disgorged them. A dozen alien tongues smote the air, and every one of them hinted of far lands of poverty, of journeys made and hardships undergone. No better field for beggary in all Manhattan's bounteous acreage.

But the dummy-chucker shook his head and shuffled ever westward. These were good souls, but—they thought in cents. Worse than that, they translated their financial thoughts into the pitiful coinage of their birthplaces. And in the pocket of the dummy-chucker rested a silver dollar.

A gaunt man, who towered high, and whose tongue held the cadences of the wide spaces, had slipped this dollar into the receptive hand of the dummy-chucker. True, it was almost a fortnight ago, and the man might ave gone back to his Western home—but Broadway uad yielded him up to the dummy-chucker. Broadway might yield up such another.

At Union Square, the dummy-chucker turned north. Past the Flatiron Building he shuffled, until, at length, the Tenderloin unfolded itself before him. These were the happy hunting-grounds!

Of course—and he glanced behind him quickly—there were more fly cops on Broadway than on the lower East Side. One of them had dug his bony fingers between the shabby collar of the dummy-chucker's coat and the lank hair that hung down his neck. He had yanked the dummy-chucker to his feet. He had dragged his victim to a patrol-box; he had taken him to a police station, whence he had been conveyed to Jefferson Market Court, where a judge had sentenced him to a sojourn on Blackwell's Island.

That had been ten days ago. This very day, the municipal ferry had landed the dummy-chucker, with others of his slinking kind, upon Manhattan's shores again. Not for a long time would the memory of the Island menu be effaced from the dummy-chucker's palate, the locked doors be banished from his mental vision.

A man might be arrested on Broadway, but he might also get the money. Timorously, the dummy-chucker weighed the two possibilities. He felt the dollar in his pocket. At a street in the Forties, he turned westward. Beyond Eighth Avenue there was a place where the shadow of prohibition was only a shadow.

Prices had gone up, but, as Finisterre Joe's bartender informed him, there was more kick in a glass of the stuff that cost sixty cents to-day than there had been in a barrel of the old juice. And, for a good customer, Finisterre Joe's bartender would shade the price a trifle. The dummy-chucker received two portions of the crudely blended poison that passed for whisky in exchange for his round silver dollar. It was with less of a shuffle and more of a stride that he retraced his steps toward Broadway.

Slightly north of Times Square, he surveyed his field of action. Across the street, a vaudeville house was discharging its mirth-surfeited audience. Half a block north, laughing groups testified that the comedy they had just left had been as funny as its press-agent claimed. The dummy-chucker shook his head. He moved south, his feet taking on that shuffle which they had lost temporarily.

"She Loved and Lost"—that was the name of the picture being run this week at the Concorde. Outside was billed a huge picture of the star, a lady who received more money for making people weep than most actors obtain for making them laugh. The dummy-chucker eyed the picture approvingly. He took his stand before the main entrance. This was the place! If he tried to do business with a flock of people that had just seen Charlie Chaplin, he'd fail. He knew! Fat women who'd left the twins at home with the neighbor's cook in order that they might have a good cry at the Concorde—these were his mutton-heads.

He reeled slightly as several flappers passed—just for practise. Ten days on Blackwell's Island hadn't spoiled his form. They drew away from him; yet, from their manners, he knew that they did not suspect him of being drunk. Well, hurrah for prohibition, after all! Drunkenness was the last thing people suspected of a hard-working man nowadays. He slipped his hand in his pocket. They were coming now—the fat women with the babies at home, their handkerchiefs still at their eyes. His hand slipped to his mouth. His jaws moved savagely. One thing was certain: out of to-day's stake he'd buy some decent-tasting soap. This awful stuff that he'd borrowed from the Island——

The stoutest woman paused; she screamed faintly as

the dummy-chucker staggered, pitched forward, and fell at her short-vamped feet. Excitedly she grasped her neighbor's arm.

"He's gotta fit!"

The neighbor bent over the prostrate dummy-chucker.

"Ep'lepsy," she announced. "Look at the foam on his lips."

"Aw, the poor man!"

"Him so strong-looking, too!"

"Ain't it the truth? These husky-looking men some-times are the sickliest."

The dummy-chucker stirred. He sat up feebly. With his sleeve, he wiped away the foam. Dazedly he spoke.

"If I had a bite to eat——"

He looked upward at the first stout woman. Well and wisely had he chosen his scene. Movie tickets cost fractions of a dollar. There is always some stray silver in the bead bag of a movie patron. Into the dummy-chucker's outstretched palm fell pennies, nickels, dimes, quarters. There was present to-day no big-hearted Westerner with silver dollars, but here was comparative wealth. Already the dummy-chucker saw himself again at Finisterre Joe's, this time to purchase no bottled courage but to buy decantered ease.

"T'ank, ladies," he murmured. "If I can get a bite to eat and rest up——"

"'Rest up!'" The shrill jeer of a newsboy broke in upon his pathetic speech. "Rest up again on the Island! That's the kind of a rest up you'll get, y' big tramp."

"Can't you see the man's sick?" The stoutest one turned indignantly upon the newsboy. But the scoffer held his ground.

" 'Sick?' Sure he's sick! Eatin' soap makes anyone sick. Youse dames is easy. He's chuckin' a dummy."

" 'A dummy'?"

The dummy-chucker sat a bit straighter.

"Sure, ma'am. That's his game. He t'rows phony fits. He eats a bit of soap and makes his mouth foam. Last week, he got pinched right near here——"

But the dummy-chucker heard no more. He rolled sidewise just as the cry: "Police!" burst from the woman's lips. He reached the curb, rose, burst through the gathering crowd, and rounded a corner at full speed.

He was half-way to Eighth Avenue, and burning lungs had slowed him to a jog-trot, when a motor-car pulled up alongside the curb. It kept gentle pace with the fugitive. A shrewd-featured young man leaned from its fashionably sloped wheel.

"Better hop aboard," he suggested. "That policeman is fat, but he has speed."

The dummy-chucker glanced over his shoulder. Looming high as the Woolworth Building, fear overcoming the dwarfing tendency of distance, came a policeman. The dummy-chucker leaped to the motor's running-board. He climbed into the vacant front seat.

"Thanks, feller," he grunted. "A li'l speed, please."

The young man chuckled. He rounded the corner into Eighth Avenue and darted north among the trucks.

At Columbus Circle, the dummy-chucker spoke.

"Thanks again, friend," he said. "I'll be steppin' off here."

His rescuer glanced at him.

"Want to earn a hundred dollars?"

"Quitcher kiddin'," said the dummy-chucker.

"No, no; this is serious," said the young man.

The dummy-chucker leaned luxuriously back in his seat.

"Take me *anywhere*, friend," he said.

Half-way round the huge circle at Fifty-ninth Street, the young man guided the car. Then he shot into the park. They curved eastward. They came out on Fifth Avenue, somewhere in the Seventies. They shot eastward another half-block, and then the car stopped in front of an apartment-house. The young man pressed the button on the steering-wheel. In response to the short blast of the electric horn, a uniformed man appeared. The young man alighted. The dummy-chucker followed suit.

"Take the car around to the garage, Andrews," said the young man. He nodded to the dummy-chucker. In a daze, the mendicant followed his rescuer. He entered a gorgeously mirrored and gilded hall. He stepped into an elevator chauffeured by a West Indian of the haughtiest blood. The dummy-chucker was suddenly conscious of his tattered garb, his ill-fitting, run-down shoes. He stepped, when they alighted from the lift, as gingerly as though he trod on tacks.

A servant in livery, as had been the waiting chauffeur downstairs, opened a door. If he was surprised at his master's choice of guest, he was too well trained to show it. He did not rebel even when ordered to serve sandwiches and liquor to the dummy-chucker.

"You seem hungry," commented the young man.

The dummy-chucker reached for another sandwich with his left hand while he poured himself a drink of genuine Scotch with his right.

"*And* thirsty," he grunted.

"Go to it," observed his host genially.

The dummy-chucker went to it for a good

minutes. Then he leaned back in the heavily up-holstered chair which the man servant had drawn up for him. He stared round him.

"Smoke?" asked his host.

The dummy-chucker nodded. He selected a slim panetela and pinched it daintily between the nails of his thumb and forefinger. His host watched the operation with interest.

"Why?" he asked.

"Better than cuttin' the end off," explained the dummy-chucker. "It's a good smoke," he added, puffing.

"You know tobacco," said his host. "Where did you learn?"

"Oh, we all have our ups and downs," replied the dummy-chucker. "But don't get nervous. I ain't goin' to tell you that I was a millionaire's son, educated at Harvard. I'm a bum."

"Doesn't seem to bother you," said his host.

"It don't," asserted the dummy-chucker. "Except when the police butt into my game. I just got off Blackwell's Island this morning."

"And almost went back this afternoon."

The dummy-chucker nodded.

"Almost," he said. His eyes wandered around the room. "*Some* dump!" he stated. Then his manner became business-like. "You mentioned a hundred dollars—what for?"

The young man shrugged.

"Not hard work. You merely have to look like a gentleman, and act like——"

"Like a bum?" asked the dummy-chucker.

"Well, something like that."

The dummy-chucker passed his hand across his stubby chin.

"Shoot!" he said. "Anything short of murder—*anything*, friend."

His host leaned eagerly forward.

"There's a girl——" he began.

The dummy-chucker nodded.

"There always is," he interrupted. "I forgot to mention that I bar kidnaping, too."

"It's barred," said the young man. He hitched his chair a trifle nearer his guest. "She's beautiful. She's young."

"And the money? The coin? The good red gold?"

"I have enough for two. I don't care about her money."

"Neither do I," said the dummy-chucker; "so long as I get my hundred. Shoot!"

"About a year ago," resumed the host, "she accepted, after a long courtship, a young man by the name of—oh, let's call him Jones."

The dummy-chucker inhaled happily.

"Call him any darned thing you like," he said cheerily.

"Jones was a drunkard," said the host.

"And she married him?" The dummy-chucker's eyebrows lifted slightly.

"No. She told him that if he'd quit drinking she'd marry him. She stipulated that he go without drink for one year."

The dummy-chucker reached for a fresh cigar. He lighted it and leaned back farther in the comfortable chair.

"Jones," continued the young man, "had tried to quit before. He knew himself pretty well. He knew that, even with war-time prohibition just round the corner, he couldn't keep away from liquor. Not while he stayed in New York. But a classmate of his had been appointed head of an expedition that was to conduct exploration work in Brazil. He asked his classmate for a place in the party. You see, he figured that in the wilds of Brazil there wouldn't be any chance for drunkenness."

"A game guy," commented the dummy-chucker. "Well, what happened?"

"He died of jungle-fever two months ago," was the answer. "The news just reached Rio Janeiro yesterday."

The dummy-chucker lifted his glass of Scotch.

"To a regular feller," he said, and drank. He set his glass down gently. "And the girl? I suppose she's all shot to pieces?"

"She doesn't know," said the host quietly.

The dummy-chucker's eyebrows lifted again.

"I begin to get you," he said. "I'm the messenger from Brazil who breaks the sad news to her, eh?"

The young man shook his head.

"The news isn't to be broken to her—not yet. You see—well, I was Jones' closest friend. He left his will with me, his personal effects, and all that. So I'm the one that received the wire of his death. In a month or so, of course, it will be published in the newspapers —when letters have come from the explorers. But, just now, I'm the only one that knows it."

"Except me," said the dummy-chucker.

The young man smiled dryly.

"Except you. And you won't tell. Ever wear evening clothes?"

The dummy-chucker stiffened. Then he laughed sardonically.

"Oh, yes; when I was at Princeton. What's the idea?"

His host studied him carefully.

"Well, with a shave, and a hair-cut, and a manicure, and the proper clothing, and the right setting—well, if a person had only a quick glance—that person might think you were Jones."

The dummy-chucker carefully brushed the ashes from his cigar upon a tray.

"I guess I'm pretty stupid to-night. I still don't see it."

"You will," asserted his host. "You see, she's a girl who's seen a great deal of the evil of drink. She has a horror of it. If she thought that Jones had broken his pledge to her, she'd throw him over."

"'Throw him over?' But he's *dead!*" said the dummy-chucker.

"She doesn't know that," retorted his host.

"Why don't you tell her?"

"Because I want to marry her."

"Well, I should think the quickest way to get her would be to tell her about Jones——"

"You don't happen to know the girl," interrupted the other. "She's a girl of remarkable conscience. If I should tell her that Jones died in Brazil, she'd enshrine him in her memory. He'd be a hero who had died upon the battle-field. More than that—he'd be a hero who had died upon the battle-field in a war to which she had sent him. His death would be upon her soul. Her only expiation would be to be faithful to him forever."

"I won't argue about it," said the dummy-chucker.

"I don't know her. Only—I guess your whisky has got me. I don't see it at all."

His host leaned eagerly forward now.

"She's going to the opera to-night with her parents. But, before she goes, she's going to dine with me at the Park Square. Suppose that, while she's there, Jones should come in. Suppose that he should come in reeling, noisy, *drunk!* She'd marry me to-morrow."

"I'll take your word for it," said the dummy-chucker. "Only, when she's learned that Jones had died two months ago in Brazil——"

"She'll be married to me then," responded the other fiercely. "What I get, I can hold. If she were Jones' wife, I'd tell her of his death. I'd know that, sooner or later, I'd win her. But if she learns now that he died while struggling to make himself worthy of her, she'll never give to another man what she withheld from him."

"I see," said the dummy-chucker slowly. "And you want me to——"

"There'll be a table by the door in the main dining-room engaged in Jones' name. You'll walk in there at a quarter to eight. You'll wear Jones' dinner clothes. I have them here. You'll wear the studs that he wore, his cuff-links. More than that, you'll set down upon the table, with a flourish, his monogrammed flask. You'll be drunk, noisy, disgraceful——"

"How long will I be all that—in the hotel?" asked the dummy-chucker dryly.

"That's exactly the point," said the other. "You'll last about thirty seconds. The girl and I will be on the far side of the room. I'll take care that she sees you enter. Then, when you've been quietly ejected, I'll go over to the *mâitre d'hôtel* to make inquiries. I'll bring back to the girl the flask which you will have left upon the table. If she has any doubt that you are Jones, the flask will dispel it."

"And then?" asked the dummy-chucker.

"Why, then," responded his host, "I propose to her. You see, I think it was pity that made her accept Jones in the beginning. I think that she cares for me."

"And you really think that I look enough like Jones to put this over?"

"In the shaded light of the dining-room, in Jones' clothes—well, I'm risking a hundred dollars on it. Will you do it?"

The dummy-chucker grinned.

"Didn't I say I'd do *anything,* barring murder? Where are the clothes?"

One hour and a half later, the dummy-chucker stared at himself in the long mirror in his host's dressing-room. He had bathed, not as Blackwell's Island prisoners bathe, but in a luxurious tub that had a head-rest, in scented water, soft as the touch of a baby's fingers. Then his host's man servant had cut his hair, had shaved him, had massaged him until color crept into the pale cheeks. The sheerest of knee-length linen underwear touched a body that knew only rough cotton. Silk socks, heavy, gleaming, snugly encased his ankles. Upon his feet were correctly dull pumps. That the trousers were a wee bit short mattered little. In these dancing-days, trousers should not be too long. And the fit of the coat over his shoulders—he carried them in a fashion unwontedly straight as he gazed at his reflection—balanced the trousers' lack of length. The soft shirt-bosom gave freely, comfortably as he breathed. Its plaited whiteness enthralled him. He turned anxiously to his host:

"Will I do?" he asked.

"Better than I'd hoped," said the other. "You look like a gentleman."

The dummy-chucker laughed gaily.

"I feel like one," he declared.

"You understand what you are to do?" demanded the host.

"It ain't a hard part to act," replied the dummy-chucker.

"And you *can* act," said the other. "The way you fooled those women in front of the Concorde proved that you——"

"Sh-sh!" exclaimed the dummy-chucker reproach-fully. "Please don't remind me of what I was before I became a gentleman."

His host laughed.

"You're all right." He looked at his watch. "I'll have to leave now. I'll send the car back after you. Don't be afraid of trouble with the hotel people. I'll explain that I know you, and fix matters up all right. Just take the table at the right hand side as you enter——"

"Oh, I've got it all right," said the dummy-chucker. "Better slip me something on account. I may have to pay something——"

"You get nothing now," was the stern answer. "One hundred dollars when I get back here. And," he added, "if it should occur to you at the hotel that you might pawn these studs, or the flask, or the clothing for more than a hundred, let me remind you that my chauffeur will be watching one entrance, my valet another, and my chef another."

The dummy-chucker returned his gaze scornfully.

"Do I look," he asked, "like the sort of man who'd
steal?"

His host shook his head.

"You certainly don't," he admitted.

The dummy-chucker turned back to the mirror. He
was still entranced with his own reflection, twenty
minutes later, when the valet told him that the car was
waiting. He looked like a millionaire. He stole another
glance at himself after he had slipped easily into the
fur-lined overcoat that the valet held for him, after he
had set somewhat rakishly upon his head the soft
black-felt hat that was the latest accompaniment to the
dinner coat.

Down-stairs, he spoke to Andrews, the chauffeur.

"Drive across the Fifty-ninth Street bridge first."

The chauffeur stared at him.

"Who you givin' orders to?" he demanded.

The dummy-chucker stepped closer to the man.

"You heard my order?"

His hands, busily engaged in buttoning his gloves, did
not clench. His voice was not raised. And Andrews
must have outweighed him by thirty pounds. Yet the
chauffeur stepped back and touched his hat.

"Yes, sir," he muttered.

The dummy-chucker smiled.

"The lower classes," he said to himself, "know rank
and position when they see it."

His smile became a grin as he sank back in the
limousine that was his host's evening conveyance. It
became almost complacent as the car slid down Park
Avenue. And when, at length, it had reached the center
of the great bridge that spans the East River, he
knocked upon the glass. The chauffeur obediently

stopped the car. The dummy-chucker's grin was absolutely complacent now.

Down below, there gleamed lights, the lights of
ferries, of sound steamers, and—of Blackwell's Island.
This morning, he had left there, a lying mendicant.
To-night, he was a gentleman. He knocked again upon
the glass. Then, observing the speaking-tube, he said
through it languidly.

"The Park Square, Andrews."

An obsequious doorman threw open the limousine
door as the car stopped before the great hotel. He
handed the dummy-chucker a ticket.

"Number of your car, sir," he said obsequiously.

"Ah, yes, of course," said the dummy-chucker. He
felt in his pocket. Part of the silver that the soft-
hearted women of the movies had bestowed upon him
this afternoon found repository in the doorman's hand.

A uniformed boy whirled the revolving door that the
dummy-chucker might pass into the hotel.

"The coat-room? Dining here, sir? Past the news-
stand, sir, to your left. Thank you, sir." The boy's
bow was as profound as though the quarter in his palm
had been placed there by a duke.

The girl who received his coat and hat smiled as
pleasantly and impersonally upon the dummy-chucker
as she did upon the whiskered, fine-looking old gentleman who handed her his coat at the same time. She
called the dummy-chucker's attention to the fact that
his tie was a trifle loose.

The dummy-chucker walked to the big mirror that
stands in the corner made by the corridor that parallels
Fifty-ninth Street and the corridor that separates the
tea-room from the dining-room. His clumsy fingers

found difficulty with the tie. The fine-looking old gentleman, adjusting his own tie, stepped closer.

"Beg pardon, sir. May I assist you?"

The dummy-chucker smiled a grateful assent. The old gentleman fumbled a moment with the tie.

"I think that's better," he said. He bowed as one man of the world might to another, and turned away.

Under his breath, the dummy-chucker swore gently.

"You'd think, the way he helped me, that I belonged to the Four Hundred."

He glanced down the corridor. In the tea-room were sitting groups who awaited late arrivals. Beautiful women, correctly garbed, distinguished-looking men. Their laughter sounded pleasantly above the subdued strains of the orchestra. Many of them looked at the dummy-chucker. Their eyes rested upon him for that well-bred moment that denotes acceptance.

"One of themselves," said the dummy-chucker to himself.

Well, why not? Once again he looked at himself in the mirror. There might be handsomer men present in this hotel, but—was there any one who wore his clothes better? He turned and walked down the corridor.

The *maître d'hôtel* stepped forward inquiringly as the dummy-chucker hesitated in the doorway.

"A table, sir?"

"You have one reserved for me. This right-hand one by the door."

"Ah, yes, of course, sir. This way, sir."

He turned toward the table. Over the heads of intervening diners, the dummy-chucker saw his host. The shaded lights upon the table at which the young man sat revealed, not too clearly yet well enough, the features of a girl.

"A lady!" said the dummy-chucker, under his breath.
"The real thing!"

As he stood there, the girl raised her head. She did
not look toward the dummy-chucker, could not see him.
But he could see the proud line of her throat, the glory
of her golden hair. And opposite her he could see the
features of his host, could note how illy that shrewd
nose and slit of a mouth consorted with the gentle face
of the girl. And then, as the *maître d'hôtel* beckoned,
he remembered that he had left the flask, the monogrammed flask, in his overcoat pocket.

"Just a moment," he said.

He turned and walked back toward the corner where
was his coat. In the distance, he saw some one, approaching him, noted the free stride, the carriage of
the head, the set of the shoulders. And then, suddenly,
he saw that the "some one" was himself. The mirror
was guilty of the illusion.

Once again he stood before it, admiring himself. He
summoned the face of the girl who was sitting in the
dining-room before his mental vision. And then he
turned abruptly to the check-girl.

"I've changed my mind," he said. "My coat, please."

He was lounging before the open fire when three-
quarters of an hour later his host was admitted to the
luxurious apartment. Savagely the young man pulled
off his coat and approached the dummy-chucker.

"I hardly expected to find you here," he said.

The dummy-chucker shrugged.

"You said the doors were watched. I couldn't make
an easy getaway. So I rode back here in your car.

And when I got here, your man made me wait, so—here we are," he finished easily.

" 'Here we are!' Yes! But when you were there— I saw you at the entrance to the dining-room—for God's sake, why didn't you do what you'd agreed to do?"

The dummy-chucker turned languidly in his chair. He eyed his host curiously.

"Listen, feller," he said: "I told you that I drew the line at murder, didn't I?"

" 'Murder?' What do you mean? What murder was involved?"

The dummy-chucker idly blew a smoke ring.

"Murder of faith in a woman's heart," he said slowly. "Look at me! Do I look the sort who'd play your dirty game?"

The young man stood over him.

"Bannon," he called. The valet entered the room. "Take the clothes off this—this bum!" snapped the host. "Give him his rags."

He clenched his fists, but the dummy-chucker merely shrugged. The young man drew back while his guest followed the valet into another room.

Ten minutes later, the host seized the dummy-chucker by the tattered sleeve of his grimy jacket. He drew him before the mirror.

"Take a look at yourself, you—bum!" he snapped. "Do you look, now, like the sort of man who'd refuse to earn an easy hundred?"

The dummy-chucker stared at himself. Gone was the debonair gentleman of a quarter of an hour ago. Instead, there leered back at him a pasty-faced, under-fed vagrant, dressed in the tatters of unambitious, satisfied poverty.

"Bannon," called the host, "throw him out!"

For a moment, the dummy-chucker's shoulders squared, as they had been squared when the dinner jacket draped them. Then they sagged. He offered no resistance when Bannon seized his collar. And Bannon, the valet, was a smaller man than himself.

He cringed when the colored elevator-man sneered at him. He dodged when little Bannon, in the mirrored vestibule, raised a threatening hand. And he shuffled as he turned toward Central Park.

But as he neared Columbus Circle, his gait quickened. At Finisterre Joe's he'd get a drink. He tumbled in his pockets. Curse the luck! He'd given every cent of his afternoon earnings to doormen and pages and coat-room girls!

His pace slackened again as he turned down Broadway. His feet were dragging as he reached the Concorde moving-picture theater. His hand, sunk deep in his torn pocket, touched something. It was a tiny piece of soap.

As the audience filed sadly out from the teary, gripping drama of "She Loved and Lost," the dummy-chucker's hand went from his pocket to his lips. He reeled, staggered, fell. His jaws moved savagely. Foam appeared upon his lips. A fat woman shrank away from him, then leaned forward in quick sympathy.

"He's gotta fit!" she cried.

"Ep'lepsy," said her companion pityingly.

A FIGHT WITH A CANNON

By Victor Hugo

La Vieuville was suddenly cut short by a cry of despair, and at the same time a noise was heard wholly unlike any other sound. The cry and sounds came from within the vessel.

The captain and lieutenant rushed toward the gun-deck, but could not get down. All the gunners were pouring up in dismay.

Something terrible had just happened.

One of the carronades of the battery, a twenty-four pounder, had broken loose.

This is the most dangerous accident that can possibly take place on shipboard. Nothing more terrible can happen to a sloop of war in open sea and under full sail.

A cannon that breaks its moorings suddenly becomes some strange, supernatural beast. It is a machine transformed into a monster. That short mass on wheels moves like a billiard-ball, rolls with the rolling of the ship, plunges with the pitching, goes, comes, stops, seems to meditate, starts on its course again, shoots like an arrow from one end of the vessel to the other, whirls around, slips away, dodges, rears, bangs, crashes, kills, exterminates. It is a battering ram capriciously assaulting a wall. Add to this the fact that the ram is of metal, the wall of wood.

It is matter set free; one might say, this eternal slave

was avenging itself; it seems as if the total depravity concealed in what we call inanimate things has escaped, and burst forth all of a sudden; it appears to lose patience, and to take a strange mysterious revenge; nothing more relentless than this wrath of the inanimate. This enraged lump leaps like a panther, it has the clumsiness of an elephant, the nimbleness of a mouse, the obstinacy of an ox, the uncertainty of the billows, the zigzag of the lightning, the deafness of the grave. It weighs ten thousand pounds, and it rebounds like a child's ball. It spins and then abruptly darts off at right angles.

And what is to be done? How put an end to it? A tempest ceases, a cyclone passes over, a wind dies down, a broken mast can be replaced, a leak can be stopped, a fire extinguished, but what will become of this enormous brute of bronze. How can it be captured? You can reason with a bulldog, astonish a bull, fascinate a boa, frighten a tiger, tame a lion; but you have no resource against this monster, a loose cannon. You can not kill it, it is dead; and at the same time it lives. It lives with a sinister life which comes to it from the infinite. The deck beneath it gives it full swing. It is moved by the ship, which is moved by the sea, which is moved by the wind. This destroyer is a toy. The ship, the waves, the winds, all play with it, hence its frightful animation. What is to be done with this apparatus? How fetter this stupendous engine of destruction? How anticipate its comings and goings, its returns, its stops, its shocks? Any one of its blows on the side of the ship may stave it in. How foretell its frightful meanderings? It is dealing with a projectile, which alters its mind, which seems to have ideas, and changes its direction every instant. How check

the course of what must be avoided? The horrible
cannon struggles, advances, backs, strikes right, strikes
left, retreats, passes by, disconcerts expectation, grinds
up obstacles, crushes men like flies. All the terror of
the situation is in the fluctuations of the flooring. How
fight an inclined plane subject to caprices? The ship
has, so to speak, in its belly, an imprisoned thunder-
storm, striving to escape; something like a thunderbolt
rumbling above an earthquake.

In an instant the whole crew was on foot. It was the
fault of the gun captain, who had neglected to fasten
the screw-nut of the mooring-chain, and had insecurely
clogged the four wheels of the gun carriage; this gave
play to the sole and the framework, separated the two
platforms, and the breeching. The tackle had given
way, so that the cannon was no longer firm on its
carriage. The stationary breeching, which prevents recoil, was not in use at this time. A heavy sea struck
the port, the carronade, insecurely fastened, had recoiled
and broken its chain, and began its terrible course over
the deck.

To form an idea of this strange sliding, let one
imagine a drop of water running over a glass.

At the moment when the fastenings gave way, the
gunners were in the battery, some in groups, others
scattered about, busied with the customary work among
sailors getting ready for a signal for action. The carronade, hurled forward by the pitching of the vessel.
made a gap in this crowd of men and crushed four at
the first blow; then sliding back and shot out again as
the ship rolled, it cut in two a fifth unfortunate, and
knocked a piece of the battery against the larboard side
with such force as to unship it. This caused the cry
of distress just heard. All the men rushed to the com-

panion-way. The gun-deck was vacated in a twinkling.

The enormous gun was left alone. It was given up to itself. It was its own master and master of the ship. It could do what it pleased. This whole crew, accustomed to laugh in time of battle, now trembled. To describe the terror is impossible.

Captain Boisberthelot and Lieutenant la Vieuville, altho both dauntless men, stopped at the head of the companion-way and, dumb, pale, and hesitating, looked down on the deck below. Some one elbowed past and went down.

It was their passenger, the peasant, the man of whom they had just been speaking a moment before.

Reaching the foot of the companion-way, he stopped.

The cannon was rushing back and forth on the deck. One might have supposed it to be the living chariot of the Apocalypse. The marine lantern swinging overhead added a dizzy shifting of light and shade to the picture. The form of the cannon disappeared in the violence of its course, and it looked now black in the light, now mysteriously white in the darkness.

It went on in its destructive work. It had already shattered four other guns and made two gaps in the side of the ship, fortunately above the water-line, but where the water would come in, in case of heavy weather. It rushed frantically against the framework; the strong timbers withstood the shock; the curved shape of the wood gave them great power of resistance; but they creaked beneath the blows of this huge club, beating on all sides at once, with a strange sort of ubiquity. The percussions of a grain of shot shaken in a bottle are not swifter or more senseless. The four wheels passed back and forth over the dead men, cutting them, carving them, slashing them, till the five corpses were a score of stumps rolling across the deck; the heads of the dead men seemed to cry out; streams of blood curled over the deck with the rolling of the vessel; the planks, damaged in several places, began to gape open. The whole ship was filled with the horrid noise and confusion.

The captain promptly recovered his presence of mind and ordered everything that could check and impede the cannon's mad course to be thrown through the hatchway down on the gun-deck—mattresses, hammocks, spare sails, rolls of cordage, bags belonging to the crew, and bales of counterfeit assignats, of which the corvet carried a large quantity—a characteristic piece of English villainy regarded as legitimate warfare.

But what could these rags do? As nobody dared to go below to dispose of them properly, they were reduced to lint in a few minutes.

There was just sea enough to make the accident as bad as possible. A tempest would have been desirable, for it might have upset the cannon, and with its four wheels once in the air there would be some hope of getting it under control. Meanwhile, the havoc increased.

There were splits and fractures in the masts, which are set into the framework of the keel and rise above the decks of ships like great, round pillars. The convulsive blows of the cannon had cracked the mizzenmast, and had cut into the mainmast.

The battery was being ruined. Ten pieces out of thirty were disabled; the breaches in the side of the vessel were increasing, and the corvet was beginning to leak.

The old passenger having gone down to the gun-deck, stood like a man of stone at the foot of the steps. He cast a stern glance over this scene of devastation. He did not move. It semed impossible to take a step forward. Every movement of the loose carronade threatened the ship's destruction. A few moments more and shipwreck would be inevitable.

They must perish or put a speedy end to the disaster; some course must be decided on; but what? What an opponent was this carronade! Something must be done to stop this terrible madness—to capture this lightning—to overthrow this thunderbolt.

Boisberthelot said to La Vieuville:

"Do you believe in God, chevalier?"

La Vieuville replied:

"Yes—no. Sometimes."

"During a tempest?"

"Yes, and in moments like this."

"God alone can save us from this," said Boisberthelot.

Everybody was silent, letting the carronade continue its horrible din.

Outside, the waves beating against the ship responded with their blows to the shocks of the cannon. It was like two hammers alternating.

Suddenly, in the midst of this inaccessible ring, where the escaped cannon was leaping, a man was seen to appear, with an iron bar in his hand. He was the author of the catastrophe, the captain of the gun, guilty of criminal carelessness, and the cause of the accident, the master of the carronade. Having done the mischief, he was anxious to repair it. He had seized the iron bar in one hand, a tiller-rope with a slip-noose in the other, and jumped down the hatchway to the gun-deck.

Then began an awful sight; a Titanic scene: the contest between gun and gunner; the battle of matter and intelligence; the duel between man and the inanimate.

The man stationed himself in a corner, and, with bar and rope in his two hands, he leaned against one of the riders, braced himself on his legs, which seemed two steel posts, and livid, calm, tragic, as if rooted to the deck, he waited.

He waited for the cannon to pass by him.

The gunner knew his gun, and it seemed to him as if the gun ought to know him. He had lived long with it. How many times he had thrust his hand into its mouth! It was his own familiar monster. He began to speak to it as if it were his dog.

"Come!" he said. Perhaps he loved it.

He seemed to wish it to come to him.

But to come to him was to come upon him. And then he would be lost. How could he avoid being crushed? That was the question. All looked on in terror.

Not a breast breathed freely, unless perhaps that of the old man, who was alone in the battery with the two contestants, a stern witness.

He might be crushed himself by the cannon. He did not stir.

Beneath them the sea blindly directed the contest.

At the moment when the gunner, accepting this frightful hand-to-hand conflict, challenged the cannon, some chance rocking of the sea caused the carronade to remain for an instant motionless and as if stupefied. "Come, now!" said the man.

It seemed to listen.

Suddenly it leaped toward him. The man dodged the blow.

The battle began. Battle unprecedented. Frailty

struggling against the invulnerable. The gladiator of
flesh attacking the beast of brass. On one side, brute
force; on the other, a human soul.

All this was taking place in semi-darkness. It was
like the shadowy vision of a miracle.

A soul—strange to say, one would have thought the
cannon also had a soul; but a soul full of hatred and
rage. This sightless thing seemed to have eyes. The
monster appeared to lie in wait for the man. One
would have at least believed that there was craft in this
mass. It also chose its time. It was a strange, gigantic
insect of metal, having or seeming to have the will of
a demon. For a moment this colossal locust would
beat against the low ceiling overhead, then it would
come down on its four wheels like a tiger on its four
paws, and begin to run at the man. He, supple, nimble,
expert, writhed away like an adder from all these
lightning movements. He avoided a collision, but the
blows which he parried fell against the vessel, and continued their work of destruction.

An end of broken chain was left hanging to the
carronade. This chain had in some strange way become twisted about the screw of the cascabel. One end
of the chain was fastened to the gun-carriage. The
other, left loose, whirled desperately about the cannon,
making all its blows more dangerous.

The screw held it in a firm grip, adding a thong to a
battering-ram, making a terrible whirlwind around the
cannon, an iron lash in a brazen hand. This chain complicated the contest.

However, the man went on fighting. Occasionally, it
was the man who attacked the cannon; he would creep
along the side of the vessel, bar and rope in hand; and
the cannon, as if it understood, and as though suspect-

ing some snare, would flee away. The man, bent on victory, pursued it.

Such things can not long continue. The cannon seemed to say to itself, all of a sudden, "Come, now! Make an end of it!" and it stopped. One felt that the crisis was at hand. The cannon, as if in suspense, seemed to have, or really had—for to all it was a living being—a ferocious malice prepense. It made a sudden, quick dash at the gunner. The gunner sprang out of the way, let it pass by, and cried out to it with a laugh, "Try it again!" The cannon, as if enraged, smashed a carronade on the port side; then, again seized by the invisible sling which controlled it, it was hurled to the starboard side at the man, who made his escape. Three carronades gave way under the blows of the cannon; then, as if blind and not knowing what more to do, it turned its back on the man, rolled from stern to bow, injured the stern and made a breach in the planking of the prow. The man took refuge at the foot of the steps, not far from the old man who was looking on. The gunner held his iron bar in rest. The cannon seemed to notice it, and without taking the trouble to turn around, slid back on the man, swift as the blow of an axe. The man, driven against the side of the ship, was lost. The whole crew cried out with horror.

But the old passenger, till this moment motionless, darted forth more quickly than any of this wildly swift rapidity. He seized a package of counterfeit assignats, and, at the risk of being crushed, succeeded in throwing it between the wheels of the carronade. This decisive and perilous movement could not have been made with more exactness and precision by a man trained in all the exercises described in Durosel's "Manual of Gun Practise at Sea."

The package had the effect of a clog. A pebble may stop a log, the branch of a tree turn aside an avalanche. The carronade stumbled. The gunner, taking advantage of this critical opportunity, plunged his iron bar between the spokes of one of the hind wheels. The cannon stopped. It leaned forward. The man, using the bar as a lever, held it in equilibrium. The heavy mass was overthrown, with the crash of a falling bell, and the man, rushing with all his might, dripping with perspiration, passed the slipnoose around the bronze neck of the subdued monster.

It was ended. The man had conquered. The ant had control over the mastedon; the pygmy had taken the thunderbolt prisoner.

The mariners and sailors clapped their hands.

The whole crew rushed forward with cables and chains, and in an instant the cannon was secured.

The gunner saluted the passenger.

"Sir," he said, "you have saved my life."

The old man had resumed his impassive attitude, and made no reply.

The man had conquered, but the cannon might be said to have conquered as well. Immediate shipwreck had been avoided, but the corvet was not saved. The damage to the vessel seemed beyond repair. There were five breaches in her sides, one, very large, in the bow; twenty of the thirty carronades lay useless in their frames. The one which had just been captured and chained again was disabled; the screw of the cascabel was sprung, and consequently leveling the gun made impossible. The battery was reduced to nine pieces. The ship was leaking. It was necessary to repair the damages at once, and to work the pumps.

The gun-deck, now that one could look over it, was frightful to behold. The inside of an infuriated elephant's cage would not be more completely demolished.

However great might be the necessity of escaping observation, the necessity of immediate safety was still more imperative to the corvet. They had been obliged to light up the deck with lanterns hung here and there on the sides.

However, all the while this tragic play was going on, the crew were absorbed by a question of life and death, and they were wholly ignorant of what was taking place outside the vessel. The fog had grown thicker; the weather had changed; the wind had worked its pleasure with the ship; they were out of their course, with Jersey and Guernsey close at hand, further to the south than they ought to have been, and in the midst of a heavy sea. Great billows kissed the gaping wounds of the vessel—kisses full of danger. The rocking of the sea threatened destruction. The breeze had become a gale. A squall, a tempest, perhaps, was brewing. It was impossible to see four waves ahead.

While the crew were hastily repairing the damages to the gun-deck, stopping the leaks, and putting in place the guns which had been uninjured in the disaster, the old passenger had gone on deck again.

He stood with his back against the mainmast.

He had not noticed a proceeding which had taken place on the vessel. The Chevalier de la Vieuville had drawn up the marines in line on both sides of the mainmast, and at the sound of the boatswain's whistle the sailors formed in line, standing on the yards.

The Count de Boisberthelot approached the passenger.

Behind the captain walked a man, haggard, out of

breath, his dress disordered, but still with a look of satisfaction on his face.

It was the gunner who had just shown himself so skilful in subduing monsters, and who had gained the mastery over the cannon.

The count gave the military salute to the old man in peasant's dress, and said to him:

"General, there is the man."

The gunner remained standing, with downcast eyes, in military attitude.

The Count de Boisberthelot continued:

"General, in consideration of what this man has done, do you not think there is something due him from his commander?"

"I think so," said the old man.

"Please give your orders," replied Boisberthelot.

"It is for you to give them, you are the captain."

"But you are the general," replied Boisberthelot.

The old man looked at the gunner.

"Come forward," he said.

The gunner approached.

The old man turned toward the Count de Boisberthelot, took off the cross of Saint-Louis from the captain's coat and fastened it on the gunner's jacket.

"Hurrah!" cried the sailors.

The mariners presented arms.

And the old passenger, pointing to the dazzled gunner, added:

"Now, have this man shot."

Dismay succeeded the cheering.

Then in the midst of the death-like stillness, the old man raised his voice and said:

"Carelessness has compromised this vessel. At this very hour it is perhaps lost. To be at sea is to be in front of the enemy. A ship making a voyage is an army waging war. The tempest is concealed, but it is at hand. The whole sea is an ambuscade. Death is the penalty of any misdemeanor committed in the face of the enemy. No fault is reparable. Courage should be rewarded, and negligence punished."

These words fell one after another, slowly, solemnly, in a sort of inexorable meter, like the blows of an ax upon an oak.

And the man, looking at the soldiers, added:

"Let it be done."

The man on whose jacket hung the shining cross of Saint-Louis bowed his head.

At a signal from Count de Boisberthelot, two sailors went below and came back bringing the hammock-shroud; the chaplain, who since they sailed had been at prayer in the officers' quarters, accompanied the two sailors; a sergeant detached twelve marines from the line and arranged them in two files, six by six; the gunner, without uttering a word, placed himself between the two files. The chaplain, crucifix in hand, advanced and stood beside him. "March," said the sergeant. The platoon marched with slow steps to the bow of the vessel. The two sailors, carrying the shroud, followed. A gloomy silence fell over the vessel. A hurricane howled in the distance.

A few moments later, a light flashed, a report sounded through the darkness, then all was still, and the sound of a body falling into the sea was heard.

The old passenger, still leaning against the mainmast, had crossed his arms, and was buried in thought.

Boisberthelot pointed to him with the forefinger of his left hand, and said to La Vieuville in a low voice:

"La Vendée has a head."